IMMORTALITY?

Or something like it? Yes—in the safe, technologized world of 2071—where nice people take their anti-death serum and believe what they see on television.

A MESSAGE FROM BEYOND THE GRAVE?

Yes—in a place where souls are still unconquered—and secrets that could destroy a civilization are hidden in a woman's womb.

A WAR TO THE DEATH?

Yes—between two cultures that can never live side by side. Archaic Knowledge against Science. Hope against inexorable destruction!

THE
TRAVELING
SOUL

HUGH C. RAE

AVON
PUBLISHERS OF BARD, CAMELOT AND DISCUS BOOKS

TRAVELING SOUL is an original publication of Avon Books. This work has never before appeared in book form.

Cover illustration by Jose Cruz/Sketch Pad Studios.

AVON BOOKS
A division of
The Hearst Corporation
959 Eighth Avenue
New York, New York 10019

First Avon Printing, February, 1978

AVON TRADEMARK REG. U.S. PAT. OFF. AND IN
OTHER COUNTRIES, MARCA REGISTRADA,
HECHO EN U.S.A.

Printed in the U.S.A.

THE
TRAVELING
SOUL

-: VECTOR :-

MORELLO STEPPED TO THE EDGE of morning. He leaned on the platform rail and stared out over the black barge to contemplate the rising sun. The reservoir was ribbed with hot dawn colors. In slanting light the rig's alloy super-structure towered like a sculpture spun from molten gold. Wavelets gently rocked the high flotation deck, fanning back from three fugitive wildfowl, the only type that seemed to thrive in this particular region. Species' ratings were immaterial to Morello. He confined the chore of the naming of life's sundry parts to his professional stints, saving the rest of the day to dream of rare lost beauties, dead now as unicorns, embalmed only in poets' imagery and on miles of videotape.

The birds swung through the dazzling azimuth, circled back over the rig, and headed west into the wastes of Poza Rica. As they passed across the cooler sky they were trans-formed again into dull, stubby objects feathered in plain-jane brown. Now and then Narvaez plugged a brace to exchange for booze, or bullets for his Colt Replicas. They made good eating, those ordinary, innominate ducks. Morello liked them spit-roasted, served with sweet potatoes and lima beans. Thinking of food helped him shuck off sleep. Yawning, he stretched, hands grasping for the sun.

Naked to the waist, Morello's body showed big, tawny, and coarse. Nankeen trews clipped over a belly plated with hard muscle. A drooping chestnut mustache accented the sensual fullness of his mouth and a large nose which, snif-fing like a hound dog's, was easily wooed from transcen-dental matters by the aroma of fresh coffee seeping from the broken windows of the shack. He abandoned his casual

9

morning ritual, his imaginative transmutation of that belt of bland gray-green jungle into a tarzan land where a man could be truly free, shot, once for all, of the need to waste the morning hours spinning wordplays to keep the urban masses content.

But he needed credit: that was the long and the short of it. Blunt, his partner back home, claimed that however much of a rebel he thought himself to be, he, Eugene Morello, could calculate credit ratings down to the last dollar-decimal with the speed of a ZIGTRAC major. Poor Blunt never could understand that a man was a compound of many elements, inherited as well as conditioned, that the dominance of one talent did not preclude the silent operation of another. Morello tried not to think of Blunt: it tended to spoil his enjoyment of the morning.

He felt very alive today, virile, creative, and full of juice. He drew in a deep breath of clean-tasting air, without the taint of sulfur and long-stored ores that marred the atmosphere when the wind was from the west. Holding it in his lungs like a swimmer, he went on back into the shack to storm his daily chore before he was tempted to squander energy on personal pursuits.

The Mexican girl was by the stove. She looked good by the stove. The heat brought a modest blush to her cheeks. She had opened a couple of buttons on her blouse so that he could see the tops of her breasts peeking at him, tantalizingly. She was full of promise and—just—ripe enough for plucking. Jesus, he would work well today, burn off vitality the way furnace supervisors over in the Poza Rica plant used to ignite excess gases on top of the pencil-thin vents that, rusted and wind-hollowed now, still poked above the trees.

Quietly the girl poured him coffee, handed him the tin cup and a can of milk substitute. He lagged the syrup into the black liquid and, with the cup in one hand and a tortilla in the other, walked resolutely into the back room and kicked the door shut with his heel. He wasn't mad, not even surly, just asserting his authority by displaying a little of that artistic temperament to which his status still entitled him.

The Interlink Portable stood on a folding table. The plyboard sagged under the weight of the device. He was out on the bow of the rig now. Both open windows looked out onto the lake and distant trees. He still had no notion as to why a marine oil-drilling rig had been erected here on the reservoir of a small industrial town. Maybe some half-cocked company director had bought geological reports to the area, the way eccentric panhandlers once, long ago, had been suckered into purchasing maps of El Dorado.

The history of his temporary quarters didn't interest Morello. Here, he was out of Narvaez's way for a while, deliberately lost again, as safe as he could ever hope to be —which was to say that he was as safe as a tightrope walker on a slack wire in a high wind over the chasm of Grand Canyon. He doubted if the agents would run him to earth in this hideaway.

From the east window he could make out old Papan crouched in the stern of the barge, like a female chimpanzee without a mate to pick fleas from her pelt. Though she had tagged along with him—or he with her—for eight, nine seasons now, her presence still disturbed him. He had seen some of the tricks she could do, the kind of rabbits she could pull out of the hat when it suited her or when he came on heavy and commanded them of her. It was not the tricks he had witnessed that troubled him but the unplumbed depths of her sorcery, techniques of magic and strands of forgotten lore that, eventually, he would have to cajole from her to fulfill the purpose that had dispatched him into the hinterland of Central America.

Papan, the hatchet-featured Aztec pureblood, twisted her neck and stared at him disapprovingly. She did that often in the mornings, silently accusing him of idleness, shaming him into working. Talent, like a Park Avenue poodle, had to be exercised, otherwise it would grow fat and constipated. But it wasn't even talent now, that was the problem: it was only craft, reiterative, facile, and sentimental. Effortlessly, he churned out the contract fodder, droned it onto tape, beamed it all the way to New York, where Blunt was waiting to pick out the fattest titbits to digest and crap forth, suitably papped, to enhance the name of Florian's Studios and satisfy the public.

Morello stuffed his mouth with tortilla and washed it down with coffee. He turned his back on Papan, though her penetrating gaze still stuck in his shoulder blades like a dart.

Cramming in the rest of the breakfast cake, he hugged the Interlink and drew it bodily back from the fading

11

influences of October sunlight. He drank more coffee, rolled and lit a natural tobacco cigarette, then checked the strength of the portable minibatteries which he had charged a month ago at a Joe Dealer factory up north: his Gypsy ticket allowed him that privilege. The batteries were strong enough to last the whole winter season, but Morello was a thorough professional and this ritual was anything but casual.

Finishing coffee, he wiped his hands on his trews and activated the Interlink's transceiving keys and video-verbal recording units. It would be six, eight hours before Blunt took up the quota. That was the virtue—the only goddamn virtue—of the Florian contraption. It kept Blunt and him a thousand miles apart. Blunt would have shriveled in this backwoods climate. Blunt was a New York orchid, an artificial bloom, a prissy old maid-type Bachelor. It would take time to change him, lots of time. The waiting, and the wandering, would have driven poor Blunt out of his square skull in a week.

Agents provocateur didn't grow on trees. They had to be cultivated. Morello thanked his stars that he was one of the lucky ones. By now the city would have stifled him, or he would have shown his flag carelessly and fallen victim to a Bureau accident. It might happen yet. The disadvantage in keeping himself cut off from New York was that he now had no way of knowing how the situation had altered or what devious manipulations to reel him in were on hand. Eventually they might even realize how dangerous he really was.

Grinding out the cigarette, Morello was ready at last to begin his morning's work. There was no sound at all from the kitchen. He glanced from the east window. Papan had gone. The lake was like glass, a jade mirror, now that the sun had cleared the trees and distant mountains.

Morello scratched his chest. He was uncommonly restless today. He felt hemmed in by Mexico as once he had felt hemmed in by New York. An instinct told him that he should pack and go, slip off to the north again to another of his sundry bolt-holes. He sat quite still before the Interlink's screen, seeing in the beveled edges of the glass his own miniature reflections like an album of faded postage stamps, the kind his granddaddy had collected with such enthusiasm eighty years back.

Sensitively, Morello examined and identified the sensation: not restlessness—threat. Jesus, he felt *threatened*. Panic spluttered in him. He resisted the temptation to leap from the wooden chair and hurl himself out into the shack in search of reassurance. Papan would comfort him. The girl would comfort him. He gripped the chair's edges tightly with his fists. Paranoid tension did not lessen. In the humid silence he could hear his heart beating like Papan's skin drum.

The deck rocked a little, wavelets slopping on the alloy collars, shifting the portraits in the Interlink screen. Morello clenched his fists and struggled to relax. Sweat dripped from his mustache, riveleted down his naked spine to soak into the waistband of the trews. His back was to the door. He did not turn around. With sudden ferocious determination he yielded to obsessive anxiety and punched the transmission key of the Interlink. If this portended what he suspected, then the least he could do was begin to go out in style.

"Blunt," he said, urgently. "Alexander, listen . . ."

Maybe it was too late even for that.

A sly grin stole over Morello's sweating face; his brown eyes gleamed wickedly. The automatic distribution drums hummed, drawing in every sound, recording it, and, simultaneously, winging it away like an acoustical missile to lodge in the mated system in Blunt's apartment liner in Brooklyn Heights, New York: safe there, stored there for Blunt and for posterity.

Leaning forward, Morello spoke.

A moment later the connection was broken forever.

–: PART ONE :–

The Madness of Alexander Blunt

FRIEND, STAY BACK
BE SAFE AND STEADY
HERE AT HOME.
YOUR MIND AND BODY
ARE ALIKE UNFIT TO TRUST.
BUT WHEN WE ARE COJOINED
AGAIN, AS ONCE BEFORE,
THEN I WILL BE YOUR GUIDE
AND WE WILL NAVIGATE
THE CHEERFUL REACHES
OF THE STARS AND ALL
THE OPTIMISTIC EVERGLADES
THAT MAN IS HEIR TO,
SEEKING NEW FRIENDSHIP
IN THAT SWEET HEARTSFOLD
WHICH, IN OUR DIRE CONTENT,
REMAINS UNRECOGNIZED.

Eugene Morello

: 1 :

NEW YORK! NEW YORK! It's a wonderful town!

True or false?

True of course: never been truer. Once New York had merely been great. Now, in Alexander Blunt's humble opinion, it was magnificent.

All through the wars of civil insurrection it had fed on its cosmopolitan energy, had survived and prospered, preserving its grand old traditions intact. The Bronx was still up, the Battery still down; the city's gridwork of streets and avenues, galleries, studios and sonic halls, parks, pantheons, plazas, apartment blocks, lidos and marbled promenades firmly fixed in history, rendered immutable by the native New Yorker's respect for the treasures of his town.

On the walls of the Florian complex in Upper Manhattan hung graphs of the city rising generation by generation back two centuries and more. Often, as he waited for tapes to be programmed, Alexander Blunt would pore over the artifacts that Florian had collected to record the triumphs of urban civilization. It was the only kind of civilization that Alexander knew, though in his boyhood New York had been a battlefield and in danger of becoming the stinkhole of the Western world. The hardships and horrors of the last quarter of the twentieth century were long gone, however, and the birth pangs of the great social movements now seemed like children's games.

Even the most notorious landmarks had acquired a patina of robust innocence. Only a few blocks from the Appledore, Alexander's supper club, the Hartmann Gang had fermented the verbal revolution. Alexander had been

17

weaned on Hartmann's comix adventures in the yellowpress to which his father, a hard-nosed traditionalist, had subscribed.

Dowd Hartmann had been the seed bull of the cultural revival. Robert Lambard, Hartmann's principal disciple, had become the first national hero promoted by the Florian Studio, host of a weekly Marchat Show, an in-depth exposé which commanded prime time on All-City wave bands season after season, until Lambard was lasered to death by a genetic throwback on the steps of the Pentecost Memorial Studio. Alexander had never been so shocked by any national event. Even now, sixty years on, he could hardly watch clips of Lambard Marchats on the educational wave band without suffering pangs of romantic disillusionment.

It was a debate over the value of the Hartmann/Lambard contribution to the cultural revival that escalated into the quarrel that almost ruined Alexander's career. The argument was fired by Eugene Morello, Alexander's partner. Though Alexander was the mildest of men, the discussions rapidly became violent, setting the tone for a stormy personal relationship.

Only Florian's ingenuity enabled the partnership to weather 112 seasons unscathed. Florian had first brought Blunt and Morello together console by console in the old Ogham Building in Queens, had first detected the vital creative arc between them, had nursed it to maturity, had promoted the team into the Laureate Class which brought them all the fame, status, and credit that any sane New Yorker could want. Trouble was that Eugene Morello was an eccentric. Difficult, recalcitrant, almost criminally unethical. Morello rubbed Alexander quite the wrong way; so much so that Alexander had had to subject himself to four dreary months of bioanalysis to stave off the urge to grab Morello's throat and grind his hyoid bone to powder.

Alexander's reaction provoked Eugene into scornful retaliation and only Florian's intervention saved the partnership. He whisked Gene away. One bright September morning Alexander entered the office to find that Morello's equipment had vanished, and Morello with it. Relief flooded over Alexander, though he knew that Gene would still be around someplace: Florian contracts were inviolable.

Enigmatically, Florian explained that Morello had

elected to ship off west, into the bleak and dangerous hinterlands. The professional partnership, however, would continue to function thanks to a neat little device that Florian's workshops had designed to combat the crisis.

The Riss-Interlink Transceiver was a development of a standard intercity tee-vee phone mated to video-verbal printout units, bristling with all the aids to which Florian stars were accustomed. The sleek chocolate-brown machine was wheeled into Alexander's liner in Wendekin Towers on the Brooklyn Heights in the early summer of 2051. It was agreed that the partners would not communicate "live": they would be fenced off behind tape drums in a necessary no-man's-land of space and time. The Interlink was installed on the deck overlooking the river and Alexander worked to the pleasant accompaniment of the booming of hippos and the blowing of whales, the sounds drifting up from the aquatarium north of the old Sutler Dock.

Creative flow was quickly reestablished. Within a month the Interlink more than recouped its cost to Florian. The Blunt-Morello partnership moved into its most fruitful phase. Honors and awards, acknowledged by Alexander alone, were heaped on the team. Gene chose to steer clear of New York, to reveal to his partner nothing of his location or his life-style. He never used the video, never came on "live."

For a year or two Alexander worried that Gene might even be failing to register his annual Montagu Boosters, the shots that kept the citizens of America, whatever their status, healthy and long-lived. In the hinterlands ROT factions lurked. Alexander had never met a Right of Termination heretic face to face, of course, but he was familiar with their methods from material distributed by the Bureau of Ethics. Gene was the same age as Alexander, still a decade short of century one, not yet into his prime. Provided he kept up with his Serum, Morello could look forward to another century of active professional life. After a time, Alexander became convinced that Gene was not going morally to seed. Morello had too much talent to crave unnatural termination. Besides, no morbid influences ever showed in his work: his scenarios were as vivid, logical, and conventional as ever.

Two decades slipped past. Alexander stayed snug in his

19

beloved New York. Supplied with a Gypsy concession and floating credit, Gene Morello wandered the American landscape. Through the mediumship of the Riss-Interlink, the pair composed a body of literary work that gained them All-City recognition. In meeting the demands of their art, Alexander Blunt and Eugene Morello were closer than brothers. In everything else, however, they were poles apart.

The system worked perfectly for ninety-eight seasons, then, on the night of October 5, 2071, it blew apart.

And Alexander's long nightmare began.

The sun dipped low behind the Kleinshorn Palisades, mellowing the river with russet light. Leaves of beech and sycamore drifted into Berger Avenue on the breeze that whispered up from the bay, and a faint chill in the air suggested that fall might be at hand.

Alexander was wearing his favorite working rig, a copy of a twentieth-century admiral's uniform. He had supped a dish of peppermint tea on the terrace adjoining the deck, preparing himself for the moment when he must commune with Morello. In the beginning he had preceded his stint with a few polite conversational remarks; Gene's lack of response had rapidly scotched the pleasantry. Now Alexander would dig directly into the core of the assignment, dismembering Gene's inflexionless prose, tapering sentences, shaving nuances, separating the wheat, lexigraphically, from the chaff. He would pull a clean print for Publications, then address himself to streamlining a spoken text for CR Redistribution, who had commissioned the piece for their "After Hours" program, a nightly hour of comfort for those in the last phase of life.

Behind the Interlink was a panel to which Miss Abbott, Alexander's minder, had slotted the visuals that would rhythmically dissolve through the word patterns. For ease of mating a prism displayed the visuals again to the left of Alexander's front field of vision.

At five after six, NY-ST, Alexander shucked off his braided coat and leatherine cap and draped them neatly on the davenport. He closed the slides and checked the temperature gauge: it had compensated upward by four degrees, a sure sign that winter was on the wing. On the crescent worktop Alexander laid out his key cards, his *Manual of Symbiotic Phrases*, a quelle of chilled liebfraumilch, and a carton of Menthols. He fitted a Menthol into an amber holder and fired it from his wristband. Contentedly, he seated himself in the swayback before the Interlink and expertly activated the systems.

The screen glowed faintly green, and the hiss of the feedout speaker told him that, as usual, Morello had transrecorded his material in advance. Alexander waited for the first dynamic line: Gene made it a point of pride to open well.

Nothing happened.

Alexander waited. Nothing happened. He leaned forward and checked the row of dabkeys, all of which glowed the proper shade of red.

"Come on, Morello," murmured Alexander.

Defiantly the screen remained blank.

The Riss-Interlink had never given trouble before. Inbuilt correctional devices were tuned to trigger self-diagnoses directly to the Florian repairshops. Alexander ran back tape, cut and accurately picked up the chirp which marked the end of the previous day's quota. The blank lasted only a split second.

Clearly Gene had powered the Interlink as usual, yet seconds accumulated into minutes without a solitary word, printed or spoken, slithering from the coils. Elapsed time was digitally recorded: 1.40 min: 1.41 min: 1.42 min: 1.43 . . . Menthol smoke spiraled toward the ceiling as Alexander clenched his teeth. Impatiently he reached for the communications phone inset into the chair's headrest.

At that moment a single letter skidded onto the screen.

Another letter followed.

And another.

Alexander's hand dropped like a lead pigeon.

No dry Morello commentary embellished the alphabet letters that flicked across the screen in sharp interim pica.

Bewildered, Alexander mouthed them noiselessly as they built into an alien word. Preset for terminal hold, the visual clicked off, holding its message; the tape ran sibilant, silent, and empty.

Alexander lunged back against the chair's padding, eyes bulging. The Menthol holder clattered to the worktop.

No error: no instant wipe.

Even as the meaning of the message registered in Alexander's brain, the crump of a gunshot balled from the

21

speaker. In his heart Alexander knew that Eugene Morello had taken back his life.

The screen read:

ADÍOS, MOTHERFUCKER.

Alexander screamed aloud.

: 2 :

"DEAR BOY!" said Florian. "How are you?"

Florian had changed into a suit of umber worsted. His mourning vest was beaded with black silk cord and draped with a filigree gold chain to which were attached appropriate propitiatory trinkets. His starched shirt gleamed like snow, cuffs projecting six inches onto the mounds of his plump pink palms. Pinky-white hair was groomed across his scalp and gold-rimmed pince-nez, worn for decoration, were clipped to the flesh of his nose. Not for the first time, Alexander was reminded of avuncular gentlemen in the prized paintings in the Rockwell Museum of Modern Art. Florian's soft pink underlip quivered emotionally as he hugged Alexander.

"Have you recovered?" he asked solicitously.

Alexander nodded numbly.

Medication, administered by a nurse from Florian's medical center, had honed the jagged edges of shock. Alexander felt calmer now, lucid enough to project the scene pictorially in his mind's eye: two highly respectable gentlemen emotionally embracing on news of the death of a fellow Bachelor—a touching portrait duet by Minnisberg or April Schnell.

They were quite alone in the suite. In all his years in the organization Alexander had never been admitted to the upper sanctum before. It was a large, luxuriously old-fashioned apartment, all soft leather and Colonial wood. The maroon morocco bindings of Florian's collection of master tapes which lined the walls made the atmosphere womblike and secure. Crystal decanters on a silver tray, slender-stemmed glasses like Roman lachrymae, a grand-

23

daughter clock, the graceful wings of the statuette that symbolized Florian's elevation to the status of Freeman of New York, all glistened in beautifully discreet lighting.

With an effort, Alexander got control of himself.

Only thirty-four minutes had elapsed since the sound of the fatal gunshot recorded Morello's final message. Only moments after Alexander's scream had filtered into the Interlink's sensors, Florian's emergency crew had swarmed into the liner. Alexander had been hustled down to the underground eco-unit, through an exit ramp and into a waiting limousine, a long black Cadillac Replica, one of forty leased only to Freemen. Then there was another shuffling trot across the bridge of the docking area into an executive elevator which whisked him up to the eighty-third floor of the Florian Building. He was taken directly to a retiring room where a Harvard suit was laid out, together with the crushed black-dyed carnation that he, as a Laureate, must wear in his lapel to signify the transition of a loved one.

The problem was, he hadn't loved Gene Morello.

Hairsplitting: it was formality. In any case, he could not rendezvous with Florian in a disheveled state. Shock, waning rapidly, was replaced by selfish speculation on what would become of him now.

"Now!" Florian wore the wisp of a smile. "Now, you *are* all right, Alex, aren't you?"

More positively, Alexander nodded again.

"I assume that the monitor check just lucked out enough to pick up the gunshot," he said.

"Quite!" said Florian. "I'm glad you weren't isolated."

"Confirmation?"

"It came through five minutes ago," said Florian. "Eugene is dead: no hope of revival or medical engineering."

"How . . . how did he . . . ?"

"A mercury slug through the palate."

"Who reported it: the Bureau of Ethics?"

"Fortunately not."

"But . . ."

"Such a gypsy, poor Gene." Florian decanted Burgundy, stained his lip with it, then, hospitably, offered the glass to Alexander. "Here today and gone tomorrow. A hideous, but not inappropriate demise in Gene's case."

"Is Right of Termination infiltration suspected?"

24

Florian frowned. "Emphatically *not*."

"He took his own life, didn't he?"

"That isn't necessarily designated as an Act of Termination."

"All right; Spiritual Cessation," said Alexander. "Call it what you like, it's the same misdemeanor, isn't it?"

"You're upset."

"Of course I'm upset. I can't believe that Eugene Morello would willingly relinquish his unspent talents."

"He was always inclined toward cynicism," said Florian. "However, his motives—poor fellow—are of little consequence. Consider the living, if I may paraphrase Gene's loveliest poem."

"Will any stigma attach itself to me?" said Alexander.

"Stigma: what sort of stigma?"

"Morello's death was patently anti-Ethical. I've been his partner for thirty-odd years."

"As far as the nation is concerned," Florian spoke with care. "Eugene Morello is not . . . ah, defunct."

"You mean . . . ?"

"I mean he will meet with an accident soon. But not just yet."

"You intend to cover up the fact of his death?"

"Naturally!" said Florian. "But only because I have your interests at heart, Alexander."

"And Florian's?"

"I don't deny it. It's incumbent upon me to protect *all* innocent parties. You and I know what sort of fellow Gene was, but the public can't be expected to change their image of him overnight. To *kill* himself: it's too radical, too sophisticated for them to absorb. Laureates just don't *do* that sort of thing."

"What sort of an 'accident' will he meet with?"

Florian shrugged. "A functional defect in a primitive ecosystem, an explosion: something along those lines."

"Where?"

"Where?" repeated Florian.

"Come now, sir," said Alexander, rather sharply. "I'm not naive enough to imagine that Gene *lived* in my Riss-Interlink."

"Ah, you mean the location?" said Florian. "Out west."

"Where?"

"Bellerophon."

Alexander looked blank. Though his profession demanded a working knowledge of colorful geographical jargon, he was abysmally ignorant of how one part of the continent related to another. He left all that stuff to employees of Frankenheimer's, the import-export group whose building stood adjacent to Florian's along the walkway north of Manhattan Central. No doubt Florian was right in his assessment of public reaction. The Freemen of New York were always right; that was how they got elected Freemen. He could not recall a single instance when a Freeman of the Illustrious City had been wrong, not in four decades. Ergo: Florian's decision was correct and, under the circumstances, proper.

Gene Morello's eccentric ways had, finally, caught up with him. What were needed now were measures extreme enough to protect the innocent from harm. Innocents like himself. His sense of relief increased, washing away the peculiar mistrust that had troubled him since the sudden, swift descent of Florian's crew. He supped the Burgundy thirstily, allowing it only a moment on his tongue to transfer its bouquet to his taste buds. He managed a smile.

"What shall I do now, Florian?"

"Go home. Take a quarter's sabbatical. You're entitled."

"And my—our—assignments?"

"I'll reallocate where I can," said Florian. "In the meantime, you will rest. You will not, of course, divulge the fact of Eugene's death to anyone. In due course, say a month, we'll put out a release on it, at which time you may be involved in some modest memorial ceremonies."

Alexander finished the wine. He put the glass on the silver salver. He could feel the liquid sifting into the fibers of his psyche, soothing muscles and nerves, cooling his inflamed imagination.

Arm about his shoulder, Florian steered Alexander gradually toward the elevator tube. "In the meantime, I'll find you another partner."

"Another partner?" Alexander was surprised.

"You're the best wordsmith in the business." Florian patted his collarbone. "Leave it to Florian. I'll find someone *better* than Morello, someone more your type. How does that appeal?"

"Sounds just fine, sir. Thank you."

"Don't thank me," said Florian, guiding the young man into the tube. "At times like this the family must stick together."

26

Alexander nodded at the profundity of the remark and, as the elevator door closed softly, raised his hand in a gesture of farewell.

They allowed him to walk. No impediment was put on his movements. Already he had the feeling that the whole unfortunate incident was over and poor Gene Morello emotionally laid to rest. He would be marginally involved in some small mourning displays, a discreet propitiation ceremony or two, and that would be an end of it, the end of their collaboration. Strangely, he felt no grief, no uncertainty, only a kind of selfish triumph. For all his dominance, Gene had run out the loser. He, Alexander Blunt, had survived.

As he walked through the crisp October night, under the warm sun-lanterns of the city's archways, he felt content. He could have followed the route blindfolded. Via Broadway and Brooklyn Bridge, he would be home in a couple of hours or so. He considered taking a late supper at the Appledore but medication had robbed him of appetite. Besides, there would be acquaintances in the supper rooms and he did not lie convincingly. The taste of the city was like wine in his mouth, like Florian's Burgundy. The street was quiet. Only a handful of pedestrians strolled the precincts. He headed for Brooklyn Bridge. He could have crossed the river at Manhattan, but tonight a stroll over Brooklyn Bridge seemed more appropriate.

From Brooklyn Bridge, many years ago, he had watched the whales come up from the sea, great gleaming, eager pods rushing inland along the river's freshening course. No longer did the water lie thick and brown as turtle soup. It had the tang of the open sea, the sea's ever-shifting spectrum of greens and blues.

The whole population of New York had turned out to watch the whales' arrival, to gasp and cheer as the huge sea mammals passed under the shadow of the Brooklyn span. A quarter of a million souls, the full city register, lined the banks. The event was beamed across the civilized world. Alexander, a round-eyed college boy of forty, then, had been startled by the devastating effect of the public spectacle upon him. Deep levels of creativity were touched. In the course of that breathtaking afternoon he discovered his true voice and wrote an epic poem. *Whale Song* was the piece that had brought him to Florian's attention and won him a contract of employment as soon as he left Columbia.

As he ambled across the high walkway of the bridge, he recalled Morello's attack on *Whale Song*. His partner had praised it by damning all the rest of his work by comparison, an attack that had bruised his professional pride. He had played over the tape of *Whale Song* many times in a vain attempt to understand Morello's argument. *Whale Song* was still on the lists. The crew of the first—and last—deep-space mission ship, *Double Kay,* had selected it for inclusion in their library. Even that honor had drawn sarcasm from Morello, who predicted that *Double Kay* would vanish into the void between the stars and that all the great ambitious plans for seeding the universe would fade with it and be forgotten.

For once, Morello had been proved correct. *Double Kay* had drifted out of contact and had failed to respond to repeated radio probes. Two hundred and ten souls were, as the SSPC put it, still missing. Space was subsequently closed, the SSPC disbanded.

Sprinkled with light, the river ran full and salty. Alexander lingered a while on the bridge's central platform. Leaning on the rail, he stared wistfully out to the horizon. It was dotted with the riding lights of the supply ships that would berth at dawn at the Flannigan piers. Little boats beating against the storm—only there was no storm, and the boats were hardly little.

Pushing himself away, he headed home toward the Heights.

The quivering started in his legs. Low in his calves, ankles, it caught hold, like nascent fever. He had never had fever, but he had read of it and had tried, unsuccessfully, to imagine the sensation. Now it was there, emotional, not physical, more like a spasm than a sickness, an irresistible twitching in his sinews. When he fought it, it pressured his muscles and reached nervous tendrils into his buttocks to thrust him forward.

He began to run, fast at first, then, when he found relief from the terrifying phenomenon, slowing to a lope. It was sixty years since last he had broken sweat or moved at a pace above briskness. Now he was running, jogging in rhythm to the rebellious pulse in his torso. He could not help himself. Bachelors of the Laureate Class just did not run, but Alexander slowed to an acceptable pedestrian

28

pacc only when a Bureau of Ethics cab swished around the corner of Washington Street and Wickersham and cruised suspiciously past him. For the rest of the route, he ignored the startled glances of the citizens and prayed that nobody would be outraged enough to summon intervention. Running ruffled the easy flow of foot traffic on the streets and promenades. After a couple of miles, though, Alexander no longer wrestled with social considerations; he ran like hell for Wendekin Towers, raced across the hushed foyer of his apartment block, and entered the elevator tube. Breaking in at the door of the liner, he sprinted the breadth of the room and hurled himself into the swaychair on the deck.

The Riss-Interlink glowed, sinister and surly.

Alexander's breath rasped painfully in his throat. His hands shook as they clasped the knobs of the chair. His mouth was arid, yet he hadn't the will power to reach for the lukewarm liebfraumilch. The Interlink printed:

WHAT KEPT YOU, LAD?
DID THEY GIVE YOU THE BIG SHAKEDOWN?
DEAD?
RIGHT: DEAD.
EUGENE MORELLO, LATE OF THE WESTERN WORLD.
DEFUNCT.
TERMINATED.
HOLED THROUGH THE SOFT PALATE.
BRAIN JELLIED AGAINST THE ROOF.
NEW HEAD, IN FLAMINEAUX PLASTIC, FOUND FOR THE FUNERARY RIGHTS.
GREAT GENE MORELLO LAID OUT ON THE MARBLE, WAITING TO DIE AGAIN.

Alexander read without fear. He felt weightless, as if *he* were the disembodied voice that activated the device. No printed copy slithered from the slot on the flank of the Interlink. The tape coils were motionless. Only the screen recorded the message from a dead man laid out for burial a thousand, maybe ten thousand miles away.

DID YOU EVER TASTE A MERCURY BULLET?
ULTIMATE EPICUREAN THRILL, BELIEVE ME.
I HAD NO CHOICE, LAD.
I AM GONE TO JOIN THE BONES OF ALL THE WHALES

THAT DIED TO PRESERVE THE PURITY OF PEACE IN
OUR TIME.
I AM ONE WITH THE DEER AND THE JAGUAR, THE
LLAMA, THE AUK, THE JACKRABBIT, OKAPI, AND
DESERT FOX.
I AM DEAD.
SHIT. AM I DEAD.

Critical displeasure stirred in Alexander. He tapped a dab-
key. It was cold and inoperative. He had no convenient
tools to edit Morello's mutterings.

Instead, Alexander lit a Menthol, finally poured a snort
of liebfraumilch and quenched his thirst.

ITCH FOR ME, ALEXANDER.
IS THAT ALL I ASK?
THE HELL IT IS.
THEY PUT THE BALL AGAINST MY EAR AND LET ME
HEAR THE SLUG.
THEY GAVE ME THAT LAST EXPERIENCE.
I COULD HAVE DONE WITHOUT THE
SOUND OF MY ENCROACHING DEATH.
I OPENED MY MOUTH LIKE A FOOL.
I TASTED THE BULLET.
IT TASTED UNCOMMONLY LIKE DEATH.

The picture was perfectly clear. Morello was laboring
his points again.

Casually Alexander poured another glass of wine. He
could not quite figure out his lack of natural response. He
should have been terrified, retreated in a state of shock to
the sanctuary of a Florian Medication Center. Instead he
sat motionless in the swaychair and watched Morello's
voice print out treasonable accusations.

DO YOU WANT TO KNOW WHO DID IT?

"Come to the point, Eugene."

ASK ME, JUST ASK ME WHO DID IT?

Alexander sighed: "All right Gene. Who did it?"

FLORIAN.

"That's hardly original."

FLORIAN. DO YOU READ ME?

"Oh, I read you, Eugene."

Alexander was amused. Eugene was dead and he was alive. Words tapped out on an Interlink had no power to hurt him. He could control them.

That spasm of the limbs? The running fit? He could probably control that too if he really exerted himself.

Phantoms.

I WANT REVENGE, ALEXANDER.

"On whom?"

ON FLORIAN.

"Nonsense, Eugene."

Alexander put the Menthol to his lips and drew a deep, corporeal lungful of smoke. He blew it at the screen.

"Drivel," he said.

YOU MAY BE NEXT, LAD.

Alexander snorted derisively. Even after death, Eugene was about as subtle as a Wittgenstein epigram.

YOU DON'T BELIEVE ME?

"Frankly, Eugene, no."

LOOK BEHIND YOU.

Alexander swiveled in the chair, then lunged to his feet.

A girl was standing in the doorway of the bunkroom. She was tall and broad-shouldered with high breasts under a pale cream tunic. Her blond hair was cue-cut, her features pert, her eyes blue.

"Who are you?" Alexander demanded.

"Miss Abbott."

"But . . . ?"

"Your minder."

"You're supposed to be a Daily."

31

"I've been reappointed Permanent."

"But . . . ?"

"Mr. Florian ordered it."

"But . . . "

"What were you doing just now, Mr. Blunt?"

"I . . . I . . . nothing."

Smiling, Miss Abbott approached. She looked past him at the Interlink.

A flood of guilt engulfed over Alexander. His senses reeled. He gripped the chair for support and let his gaze fall once more upon the screen.

The screen was blank.

Dead: like Gene.

Smiling, Miss Abbott stooped.

"I'm sorry about this," she said.

She held up the severed stretch-cable by which the device had been attached to its power plug.

"Rectification, you understand," she said. "Mr. Florian's personal instructions."

"Yes," Alexander croaked. "I understand."

The girl let the half-length of cable drop. Like a slender black serpent it wriggled back into the side wall of the Interlink.

"Now, Mr. Blunt," she said, "may I fetch your supper?"

"Yes," Alexander said. "Bourbon."

"I beg your pardon?"

"Bourbon," Alexander said, in a tone that no minder, however authoritarian, dared refuse.

: 3 :

IT WASN'T THE BOURBON. He knew it wasn't the bourbon. And it wasn't a delayed effect of Gene Morello's death that abruptly demolished him. The stability of his life had been undermined by inner erosion. The collapse of his mental faculties manifested itself, for openers, in conversations with the big, dead, chocolate-shelled Riss-Interlink which crouched in wait upon the mahogany deck. He had no choice. He was compelled to approach it, commune with it as if it were some god symbol in need of regular verbal propitiations.

The whole traumatic experience might be comprehensible, Alexander told himself, if I had cared for Morello. But I did not. I do not care for him now. Come to think of it, if it turns out that Florian *was* somehow responsible for Eugene's death I would be almost inclined to congratulate my employer on a good job well done.

Because he was ashamed of his madness, Alexander took pains to avoid offending Miss Abbott. Not only did he not wish to offend her, he just didn't want her to find out that he was talking to himself in the guise of a machine. That, of course, was what was happening. Gene Morello's ghost, the wandering cerebral energy of the fellow, had nothing whatever to do with it. Alexander understood the situation. At least he was man enough to face the truth squarely. He, not some astral guerrilla, was operating the unpowered Interlink. All the rubbish it spouted forth came from *his* mind, *his* imagination. Proof of that fact was established by the repetitious nature of the so-called Morello messages. By the fourth session, philosophy had dwindled to a few remnants of former argument between the partners.

33

The rest of the dialogue was a diatribe of petty accusations, just the sort of thing that a crass popular bard might dream up to furnish suspense in lieu of inspiration.

The game was played on two fronts. Not only did Alexander spar with the machine, he also sparred with Miss Abbott, who, he feared, strongly suspected that her client was going off his head.

Back of Miss Abbott was Florian. Florian's authority over his life had never been more apparent. Indeed, though Alexander had never quite thought of it before, Florian could, if he so wished, destroy him as easily as a hank of tape fed into a recirculator was broken down to its molecules. *The Parable of the Tape* was one of the Bureau of Ethics' more telling instructional movies: Alexander and Eugene had written the embellishments. Florian could shred and reduce him to nothing at the drop of a hat. Not that Florian *would*, of course. Florian was too old-fashioned an employer for that. But Florian was also a Freeman of New York, a commercial shaman. He had a duty to his public, his staff, and to the other thirty-nine Fathers of the noble city. Loyalty to a long-serving employee did not match up against duties of that caliber.

Alexander wrestled with the problem. He lay on his back on the argon bed, nursing a pint of best Leatherstocking hooch—which Miss Abbott seemed able to supply ad lib in spite of its scarcity—and brooded. When he wasn't brooding he was slinking about the liner trying to discover where Miss Abbott was hiding so that he could lob himself into the swayback, pick at the scabs of his own irrationality, and converse with the bubbles of schismatic lunacy that showed as words upon the printed screen.

For eight days Alexander did not leave the liner. He did not have tapes to program. He did not have the desire to visit the Appledore, a haven that seemed to belong to a different period in his life. He did not dare walk the streets in case the twitching demon again took possession of his limbs and whipped him back to Wendekin Towers or, more likely, straight into a B. of E. interrogation chapel.

Bioanalysis might solve his problem. On the other hand Gene had always claimed that every goddamn bioanalyst in the goddamn city was a frontman for the Freemen's Club. It was certainly true that one required a professional notary's scroll before one could begin a course of treatment in bioanalysis, and that professional notaries were also employees of the Freemen. Florian carried four in the Contracts Department alone.

By the eighth day of his self-regulated madness Alexander was playing the role of drunken writer to the hilt. He did so without conscious thought, sampling his personality to the full. He chose a shaggy simulated-wool sweater and baggy corduroys, let his beard grow, his hair grow, his cuticles and nails become ragged. He spilled gravy on his beard and laced his sweater with bourbon. He took to stubbing out his Menthols on the leatherine sole of his Hausa sandals. He even practiced leering at Miss Abbott. But that was too much for him, and he quit after a couple of unsuccessful grimaces.

During Blunt's Blasted Heath Phase Miss Abbott continued about her duties, few though they were, as if Alexander were just the gentleman he had always been.

She was Florian trained. That made all the difference. Even when she caught him muttering and mumbling to the Interlink, she avoided any outward display of astonishment or contempt. She did not reprimand him, and denied him nothing. She fulfilled his orders for Leatherstocking, sweet Maybelle Scarlet, and crushed Susquehanna Hemp to roll into needle-thin Menthols in clips of old broadtape. Whoever he was, whoever he was in process of becoming, during those first eight days, Miss Abbott treated him as a decent, normal Florian Laureate.

It was after the Day of the Booster that their relationship changed and the situation absorbed its creator.

Close to noon on October 14 Alexander opened his eyes. He did not remember that it was the Day of the Booster, that special day of the year on which he had to present himself at his Montagu Center, in the basement of the Florian Building, and bare his arm for an air-nozzle injection of partial immortality. He opened his eyes, and promptly closed them again.

The black beam on the white ceiling over the argon bed's circular nook seemed much, much lower. Small brown insects were tunneling out of the wood. That in itself was ridiculous; the wood was Endural, guaranteed against everything, including holocaust, for five centuries. A battalion of tiny brown monsters, each soldier equipped with tungsten-tipped teeth, was devouring the roof of his liner.

Alexander swore a couple of times. Schoolboyish obscenities were all he could think of, except for the nasty Freudian phrase that Morello had handed him on a plate and which was far too ugly for any wordsmith even under the stress of tempermental deformity.

"Golly!" he exclaimed, eyes shut tightly. "Omigosh!"

Miss Abbott said, softly, "Booster Day, Mr. Blunt."

"Where are you?"

"Open your eyes, Mr. Blunt."

Alexander opened his eyes.

"It's a hangover, Mr. Blunt."

"Is . . . is *this* a hangover?"

"Bacon and eggs, Mr. Blunt?"

Alexander levered up on his left elbow. He groaned loudly. He had fallen asleep hugging an empty plastic of Leatherstocking, which Miss Abbott had apparently removed. He still wore the sweater and cords. His feet were naked. He itched all over and his mouth was full of gritty prawn-tasting slime.

"Bacon, eggs, and coffee, Mr. Blunt." She held the tray on the flat of one palm. She looked very tall and straight in the jet pantsuit. "We must refresh you for presentation at the Florian Station, you know."

"You're too good to me, Miss Abbott."

"Sit up now."

Alexander held on to his skull and climbed painfully into a sitting position. He supposed that this acute discomfort was classifiable as pain. Clearly Miss Abbott had never experienced pain in her life. Her empathical training had been thorough and far-reaching, though. She looked properly sympathetic.

The aroma of grilled bacon and coffee wafted down to him.

Alexander sucked his cheeks and made a few disgusting sounds, like a hog in a wallow.

Booster Day! As a lad he had celebrated his Booster Day with enthusiasm. His mother had baked a flan inscribed with his name and Eternity Number and had put upon it one of the angelica shapes that you could buy in the stores, an air-hypo enclosed in a heart. He had lighted a bead on the family plaque which his father had connected the previous night while he had been asleep, and he had opened the small gifts that the family had brought for him.

He always liked Aunt Tina's gifts best and saved those parcels for last.

"What's wrong, Mr. Blunt?"

"Nothing," he said. "How old are you, Miss Abbott?"

"I have been with Florian's for thirty seasons, Mr. Blunt."

"You won't remember Booster Day celebrations, then?"

"We didn't celebrate in our establishment."

Squinting, Alexander studied the girl more closely. He had forgotten that he was no longer quite the youngest generation of employees in the city. Miss Abbott must be one of the new breed, the convent-trained orphans of the Freemen's Favorite Charity. Life in an FFC convent was, as the name implied, conventional in the extreme. Some critics said it was so Spartan that the girls and boys were not as content as they should be under a civic regime.

"Any of that Leatherstocking left?"

"No, Mr. Blunt."

"Get me some, will you?"

"We'll see, Mr. Blunt."

Alexander inched himself up the wall. The memory of family times had restored him a shade. He could even contemplate the adventure of walking down to the Florian Station with some anticipation. Miss Abbott would have been taught to understand that emotion. He cracked a smile, as courteous as he could manage, and indicated that the girl should put his breakfast on the trolley.

This she did.

She was very lithe, he noticed absently.

Booster Day! Golly, didn't they come round fast.

"My Booster Day uniform is in the red closet," he said. "Shall I wear my fez or my crimson Pernel?"

"I'll lay out both, Mr. Blunt."

In the end he chose the fez. He charged off his stubble and stray locks of hair, used the home manicure in the bathroom, showered, and changed into his handsome suit. He surveyed himself in the mirror. On the surface at any rate, the old Alexander had reappeared. Happily, the old Alexander would soon blossom again within the skin.

Going into the living area, he stepped on to the deck and speculatively confronted the Riss-Interlink. It gave no sign of recognizing him. It remained lifeless and implacable. Maybe Morello had at last been buried, physically, psychologically, and in Alexander's schizothymic neural system.

At the door of the liner Miss Abbott wished him farewell. Alexander took to the streets for a pleasant stroll up to the Florian Building.

The shot would surely revive him. There was a slight tendency for the spirit to flag in the dog days of an Eternal year. The booster would reenergize him, sluice the last traces of madness from body and brain. Morello would no longer find an abode in his intelligence. In celebration, he would eat supper at the Appledore, chat with his friends, hear the word that had got out on Eugene, if any. He would return to Wendekin Towers for a light snack and a dewdrop of Madeira. He would pass the evening listening to his favorite piece of music, Zerbst's moving *Lament for the Double Kay*. In a couple of days or so, he would be ready to tackle a poem for one of the sentimental morning shows. It would do him good to get back to work. He must mention that to Florian. Without doubt, Florian would have been informed of his moodiness. But Florian, understanding and forgiving Florian, had a habit of leaving people to work out their own destinies.

At five-thirty-five, NY-ST, Alexander checked into the Montagu Center at the Florian Station and gave his name, status, and code to the programmer on duty. Though there were fifteen or twenty other people in the antechamber, Alexander was taken into surgery immediately. By five-forty-two, he was out on the street again, a shot of life-giving Montagu fluid chunking through his veins.

At seven-fifty-four, he left the Appledore, having polished off a delicious supper and discussed solipsistic adverbs with Randolph Marks, who hadn't heard a word about Morello. He set off home. The "leg-demon" did not trouble him. He reached Wendekin Towers at a quarter of ten and at twelve minutes to the hour saw his first naked lady.

There was nothing unusual in a full-grown, almost mid-aged gentleman being ignorant of first-hand experience of the opposite sex. Naturally, Alexander and all his gallant, well-reared brethren were conversant with the Facts of Life insofar as those facts affected the breeding classes and denizens of the animal kingdom. They were also aware that the Facts of Life, like any other set of facts, were best utilized by experts. Girls were inculcated with similar modesty. Indeed, it was part of the feminine code that the body should remain covered at all times. The old nursery jingle still had a grain of truth in it—*From nape to knee, no one shall see. The secret beneath is the secret of me.*

Mystery was its own reward. Voyeurism was sublimated, exhibitionism converted into sound capital investment. Alexander believed that the men and women of the twenty-first century were much more honest about such matters than their forebears, who had reputedly practiced all sorts of unpleasant, tortuous contortions to slake their disappointment at the limitations of sexual congress.

So, at the age of almost a century, Alexander had never gotten to see a naked lady: nor had he ever really *wanted to see* a naked lady. Having seen a naked lady, he did not feel privileged or improved—only a little disgusted by his unexpected responses.

The lady in question was Miss Abbott. He called her a lady, though minders were invariably girls. Miss Abbott was more girlish than some, more womanly than others. The manner in which Alexander Blunt stumbled upon Venus Unadorned was simplicity itself. He had opened the door of the minder's quarters, though even that action would not have been considered quite proper. The door catch, of course, was silent. He was in search of Miss Abbott from no more prurient a motive than to ascertain where the devil she was. An eight-day habit brought Alexander to grief.

Miss Abbott was lying on her circular air-filled bed. The bed was covered by a single green sheet, like close-cropped grass. Miss Abbott's head was to the door. Her feet were propped, apart, on the curve of the low headboard. She wore a scarlet quilted mask across her eyes. Her pert little nose pointed up from the arch of the mask and two slim black velvet ribbons secured it to her head above her ears. Her hair was a smooth cap of pure spun platinum. The nest between her thighs, though, was coarser, like lightly toasted wheat. The spots of the solar regenerator were trained upon her body, giving it that golden glow that Forrester's Appurtenances claimed was a surefire aid to contentment. It seemed like it, Alexander thought. Miss Abbott's pose—wide, wide open and utterly relaxed—might, in a former era, have proved a perfect advertising logo, a boon to the ailing Forrester campaign. Miss Abbott's arms were raised, head resting on her wrists. Her breasts were tossed forward. When she breathed her rib cage arched and thrust out the pink oval nipples. Her belly was smooth and deep, her diaphragm in motion with the rhythm of breathing. Her legs were aesthetically very pleasing in shape. She wriggled her toes a little, making the long muscles ripple under her fair skin. She was smiling to herself. Contentedly.

Until yesterday, even under the duress of a snootful of hooch, Alexander Blunt would have fled in horror. Yesterday: not today.

Alexander's throat thickened. His nerves quivered and trembled. He suffered an increase in blood flow to a set of capillaries that had never been flushed before and a sense of weight that, within seconds, amounted to tumescence. His hand was still on the door, one foot on the threshold. His eyes were drawn by the beams of the cross lights, to their exact point of merger. The wheaten zone which cloaked the girl's pubic bone spread densely, downward. He was looking at her upside down, from the sort of foreshortened angle that Wain Pyrrah's elegant nude studies favored, only in Pyrrah's graphics there was none of that rough, real stuff at the focal core.

Alexander tried to swallow. His tongue was cleft to the roof of his mouth. His eyes were bugging out. He could feel them straining against the sockets, the meshwork of nerves and cords that bound them to his brain stretching like a thousand rubber bands. If he had been wearing his Hausa sandals, not mid-heel Smartboy boots, he might even have crept in for a closer inspection. The really astounding thing was that the visual imprint on his brain cells stirred a need to induce tactile satisfaction. He longed to press his forefingers onto those pink nipples. He longed to dip his hands into the wheatfield, to discover what special secrets nature had hidden there. Alexander gagged.

Miss Abbott stirred, arching her back so that she rested the weight of her body on her heels and the crown of her head. With one finger she snapped up a corner of the scarlet mask and surveyed Alexander—presumably also upside down—with dispassion.

"Can I fetch you something, Mr. Blunt?"

"No, I . . . no, I . . . no."

"Leatherstocking?"

"No."

The door whisked shut, blotting out the sight of the wheatfield, the ovals, and the smile.

Sweating, Alexander leaned against the door panel. A short corridor lead into the liner's living area, the rectilinear shape framing the chocolate-colored Interlink. Never before, after a booster, had he felt this way. In fact, the recent batch of boosters was guaranteed to cause no detrimental side effects. For all that he trusted the propaganda, Alexander was convinced that it was the afternoon's shot that had underscored his reactions with a wild, unruly flourish. Sexual desire was worse than the compulsion of the leg-demon, worse than the drudgery of shaking off a hangover, worse even than the twofold effect of knowing that when he conversed with Morello's voiceprint he was in reality only talking to himself.

A scream gurgled in his throat. But remembering what had happened last time he had expressed his agonies in acoustical terms, he subdued it to a low, mammalian growl. Bent over, Alexander crawled for comfort and relief to the big, dead device on the mahogany deck.

Morello—a term for Alexander's own hyperactive cerebral releasers—had obligingly printed out advice. It was, however, unthinkable advice couched in terms of unpardonable crudity. Alexander hardly knew what the words meant: cryptograms, archaic vulgarisms for involved reproductive acts, breeding-cell secrets requiring a low kind of expertise and a practical, as opposed to a theoretic, knowledge of biogenetics.

Alexander leaned on the swaychair and gawped at the phrases his rioting libido had vacuumed up from some forgotten source and stored in the sump of his memory. To think evil was bad enough: to think to act evil was heinous.

Did Florian's investigators have the liner staked? Were they able to monitor not only what he said aloud but what he thought, what he felt, all the irrational experiences which, if recorded, would dossier up to a case of Potential anti-Ethical Behavior? His status and his talent would not protect him from a major inquisition. A man of Florian's community standing dared not become involved in any reprieve attempt. In Alexander's limited knowledge of law there had been few open cases of prosecution for assault on the privacy of a minder. The dearth of precedents may have been due to the fact that status hands seldom got to meet their minders, a profession groomed to be as invisible as the south wind. Minders did what machines could not. They were not scaled to be companions, except in instances where the status hand was aged, or undergoing some minor emotional trauma. Now that he thought of it, Alexander realized that Florian had misjudged the seriousness of his grief trauma. There had been no need at all to engage a permanent, live-in minder. After all, with the Interlink blasting out two-way psychotherapy in highly original style, Florian had the perfect keyhole to his employee's shifting mental states.

With a throbbing groin, Alexander wriggled against the chairback and fought to control himself.

The screen read:

PENETRATION.

Was that an injunction connected with poor Miss Abbott, or a warning that Florian had installed microelectrical tentacles in the liner? Guile, cunning, and a keen, edgy kind of anger replaced sexual frustration. Slitting his eyes, Alexander scanned walls and window bay but, naturally, detected no trace of hypno-ducts or bee-eye visual tracers: Florian's scrutineers were the best in the field.

The screen printed:

CAUTION IS NOT ENOUGH.

"What is, then?" muttered Alexander.

YOU DON'T BELIEVE THAT IT IS ME, DO YOU?

"I know it isn't you, Gene. But that's really immaterial at this point in time."

DO YOU THINK THAT YOU HAVE DEVELOPED A SEVERE CASE OF POHL'S DUALITY DISEASE?

"I'm no clinician. I don't know what the hell's wrong with me."

YOU, LAD, ARE BEING GOT AT.

"By whom?"

FLORIAN.

"Why do you persist in attacking Florian?"

HE KILLED ME.

"I just don't accept that, Morello."

WHY DO YOU CALL ME MORELLO IF YOU DO NOT BELIEVE I EXIST?

"Because I won't criticize Florian."

THEN I MUST EXIST.

"I . . . No, of course you don't exist. You're dead."

YOU THEN MUST CRITICIZE FLORIAN.

"Are we being monitored?"

NO ANSWER TO THAT.

"Are you—whatever you are—responsible for what's happening to me, for my . . . my madness?"

SANITY HAS MANY GUISES.

"Answer me, Eugene. What must I do?"

RIDE IT OUT.

"Ride what out, goddamn it!"

NO ANSWER TO THAT.

"You were killed by the ROT faction, Morello."

NO ROT FACTION.

"Naturally, even now, you won't admit it."

NO ROT FACTION.

"Everybody knows you were anti-Ethical."

NO ROT FACTION.

"Your stupid denials don't help *me*, Morello. What must I do?"

RUN.

Alexander spun the swayback and kicked the Interlink with his heel. That only hurt him and did no damage to the Interlink's hard shell. The word remained:

RUN.

He thumped the dome with his fists. Abruptly the injunction vanished and the screen cooled to gray.

The violent gestures relieved much of the pressure in his groin. Alexander nudged the swayback into its usual position, straightened his cravat, and glanced behind him. Miss Abbott's door was firmly closed. He steepled his fingers and touched them to his brow. Was he going mad from the inside out, or was some force, some Morello-inspired power, really trying to ruin him? Maybe it was all part of a ROT conspiracy to bring down Florian's teams, a conspiracy that, with a little more perseverance, would soon render him professionally impotent. The notion that he was being attacked by a nominal agency, presumably through the mediumship of a radiophonic device or charging process, brought Alexander to earth with a comfortable thump, by restoring his status and social importance. No, there must be no more bourbon, Maybelle. Scarlet, or hemp Menthols: no more prying into his minder's privacy. Tomorrow he would request an appointment with Florian. Person to person. In fact, he would do it now. Pulling the phone from the chair cushion, he coded Florian's personal staff office, which was manned round the clock, spoke with Miss Seita, and was granted an audience with Florian at eight P.M. the following evening. Tomorrow he would confess everything to Florian, absolutely everything. He would request that Miss Abbott be restored to standard duties, that the corpse of the Interlink

44

be removed, that he be allocated a console in the Florian Building and given a full work load—wi h or without a new partner—to help take his mind off the weird events of the past ten days. Work would cure him.

Alexander opened the doors to the terrace and stepped out. During the period of his madness he had hardly noticed the encroachment of winter weather. Tonight the air was decidedly cold. He could almost taste snow. The massy sycamores whispered in Berger Street. The whales in the aquatarium breached languidly and dolphins called in piping falsetto voices. The streets were deserted, supper rooms and movie pits closed for the curfew. The lamps of a cruising B. of E. cab winked fleetingly far across the river.

Alexander sighed and, soon after, went to bed.

The dream was unpleasant only in its effect. In shallow sleep he was aware of a massive, uncomfortable pleasure which made him writhe gently upon the argon bed. The dream itself was uncomplicated. Alexander Blunt dreamed of Miss Abbott. He dreamed of her as a person upon whom he could pour all the creative warmth that had been reserved for his work and once, long, long ago, fleetingly expended upon a pod of whales which roiled in from the sea.

In the dream Miss Abbott was attired in a decorous white gown and lace veil. Her slender hands nursed a bouquet of white carnations. Alexander's longing was indefinable: not the urge to dominate, rather an inexplicable need to share, to know and be known by his minder. A ridiculously heretical dream, in fact. Then Alexander realized he had been awake for several minutes and that the vision of Miss Abbott in an antique wedding dress remained intact, like an old photograph of his mother, lying so far back in his childhood that it might have been the imperfectly shared memory of a stranger. Sixty years, more, maybe, since there had been a marriage ceremony, a primitive celebration of the tying of a blood knot to bind two souls together. Ethically, it was all wrong to lock up your life. Each man was his own, each woman her own. No personal relationship could endure a life span of two centuries. Only the City and the institutions of the Fathers were large enough to accommodate the sense of belonging that the human psyche required for its well-being. Yet Alexander thought, swooningly, of his mother, of the faded snapshot in the album in the bottom drawer of the chest in the bedroom back home in the past, thought of the wistful smile upon her face and how the veil blew in the wind, lifting away from her mouth. How long ago? One hundred years and more. The wedding chapel on the East Side had long since crumbled to dust.

Alexander sat up.

A moonglow strip lit the bedroom. He could see a corner of the room from the bed nook. It was like peeping into a set in the Memorial Studios, only there was no bustle of preparation, no sparks, grips, or cosmeticians.

There was only Miss Abbott.

If she had been now as she had been before under the solar beams, the effect would have been too strong. His conformity would have rejected her. But there was enough wistfulness in him to react to the outfit which covered, yet revealed Miss Abbott's young body.

A French lace brassiere cupped her breasts. The ovals showed above the scalloped edge. Matching lace briefs allowed only a glimpse of nude flesh, golden fair, and a gusset of opaque white silk hid the most private zone of all. Above the supple swell of her hips, Miss Abbott had fastened a belt of frilly lace from which stocking attachments stretched to dainty clips which in turn kept taut her pecan-colored hose. Pinned to her hair was a white satin pillbox from which a series of translucent veils wafted in the draft from a heating vent. Upon her feet were high-block white shoes and clasped around her left thigh, just below the stocking top, was a crimped pale-blue garter. In her fist snuggled a miniature bouquet of red and white rosebuds entwined with fern-ribbon.

As Alexander hoisted himself in bed, Miss Abbott pivoted into profile and placed her left foot upon a white wicker stool. She inclined her upper torso, looked directly at him, golden body gracefully poised, and pursed her lips.

Alexander's reaction was no longer one of horror. New York and its ethical restrictions drifted away like a Flannigan supply ship in the night. His movements were unhurried as he stepped from the bed to the mouth of the alcove and leaned against the inner arch.

"Good evening, Miss Abbott."

"Good evening, Mr. Blunt."

"May I escort you?"

"Why, yes, thank you, Mr. Blunt."

With unsuspected suavity and tenderness, Alexander Blunt scooped Miss Abbott into his arms. He felt incredibly, overwhelmingly strong as he carried her into the alcove and laid her upon the bed.

Even under the stimulus of the aphrodisiac that had been substituted for his booster shot, Alexander was enough of a gentleman to be gentle with the shy young maiden. Patiently, carefully he peeled off the laces and satin parts and made her nude, except for her white pillbox hat, veil, and shoes. Softly he arranged her smooth, pliant limbs, then with the lordly authority of a stallion he mounted her and tilled the wheatfield until the girl's response demanded response in return.

Four times Miss Abbott keened in ecstasy, thrashed, arched, and sank, quivering, beneath him. Four times Alexander moved from gargantuan selfishness into murmuring tenderness, and back again. He no longer cared about the Bureau, the Freemen, Florian, or Eugene Morello's ghost.

At four o'clock in the morning, NY-ST, Alexander Blunt finally slumped into sleep, his arm draped lovingly over the breasts of the sleeping bride.

It was after dawn, long after dawn. Whales breached and snorted solemnly, the sounds loud in the wet air. Tainted with a breath of snow from the north, rain teemed in from the Atlantic. In his heated pool in the Hudson, a melancholy hippo boomed, atavistically dreaming of Africa. Berger Avenue was full of beech leaves piled like paper trash in gutters and curbs. Suction trucks from the Foker Institute of Public Works were still prowling Broadway. It would be noon before the first of the mobile compost tanks nosed its trunk into Berger Avenue and the neighborhood of Wendekin Towers.

It was probably the whales that woke him. The liner was warm, dimly lighted by the moonglow, and he might have slept the clock around undisturbed.

Alexander's hand rested lightly on Miss Abbott's breast. He spread his fingers, awake but not prepared to move. Morally he didn't feel so bad, though his reflexes were sluggish and his body pressed with dull, bruiselike pains. The pains were part of the good memory of the night. He rotated his hand, stroking the girl's breast lovingly. At that time, he was without desire.

Her flesh was a little cold.

Alexander's hand stole across the girl's flanks. Momentarily, he expected her to stir, turn in toward him, put her arms about him, and hug him. From the pocket of nostalgia that had remained buttoned for so long, he recalled now, how on Sunday mornings he would find his mother and father in that sort of embrace, as he scrambled into bed beside them to share their security.

Sticky fluid wet his fingertips. Involuntarily his exploring hand recoiled, then, with more urgency, swept across the girl's stomach.

Crying out, Alexander shot to his feet. He swung from the bed onto the square yard of floor between the bottom of the argon mattress and the alcove wall.

Miss Abbott was spread-eagled on her back, bridal hat raffishly cocked over one dead eye. A shoe dangled from its strap. Across her belly a spoor of crimson fingerprints marked his trail. Blood leaked from four puckered wounds in Miss Abbott's youthful torso. Blood filled her navel and saturated the granular pad of hair below her pubic bone. Between her thighs, in a depression on the argon mattress, a great wet atlas of blood had formed.

For all his sheltered upbringing, Alexander Blunt immediately acknowledged that his minder was dead.

Somehow he had killed her.

Weeping silently, Alexander backed down the corridor into the living room. He might have continued backing away until he toppled over the terrace rail and plunged to the promenade below. But, as he was halfway across the living area, shuffling inexorably toward the window bay, a loud shout impinged on his shock. Whipping around, he gaped at the upper deck.

The Riss-Interlink spoke once more.

: 4 :

ACCORDING TO contemporary educationalists, the history of modern New York dated from the founding of the Freemen's Club in 2021. Since then there had been only three acknowledged murders in the city. News of outer urban killings occasionally drifted in, but extremist behavior was only to be expected from the underprivileged minions who lived in the hinterlands. The Right of Termination faction had conducted several assassinations, one of them actually in New York. Their outlandish cupidity for power somehow exempted the Death Wishers from consideration in Alexander's legalistic debate with himself.

The three recorded murders had been media presented without emphasis, though details had gotten out to a privileged few. In each case the murderer had proved to be a genetic throwback. Now, in 2071, the last traces of irrational ancestry had been bred right out. In theory such murders would not happen. Each of the killings had stemmed from a disagreement between the parties on interpretation of a Bureau of Ethics' edict, but—like Alexander's own heated arguments with Eugene—had involved certain deep-seated differences in historical principle. The murders had been almost accidental. In fact one of the victims was later revived, though not until some hours after his attacker had been declared guilty of Life-Theft and sentenced to death. Execution was finally commuted to Annulment of Status. That was serious enough, for the fellow had been a Senior Leading Executive for Fullerton Landways and did not take well to hosing out and scraping fish barrels in a primitive New Brunswick shantytown for the rest of his natural life.

There would be no such humane punishment for Alexander Blunt. He would be arraigned, charged, defended, accused, condemned, and executed by summary process of the Bureau's own Justice Division. Under the circumstances, the trial would not cost the Fathers much. It would be over in five or six hours. As employer of both victim and offender, Florian would be obliged to appear. As a Freeman, he would give his evidence out of camera. Obviously, he would not be called upon to deliver the mandatory Claim for Clemency which would have pertained had he employed only the offender.

After being found guilty of Life-Theft, to say nothing of other charges which might be filed against him, Alexander would be transported by barge to the All-City Penal Institute on Nantucket Island. There, in the laboratory wing, he would be injected with a curare derivative guaranteed to kill him instantly. As it was not considered decent to use the body of an executed man for medical purposes, his cadaver would be encased in lead-base, conveyed by A.C.P.I. lighter to a point over the Buzzard's Bay ore fault, and discharged.

There would be no ceremony, no black carnations or trinkets. His former acquaintances in the Appledore would talk of him, if they dared talk of him at all, in hushed voices. None of them would even begin to wonder if the ecstasy he had enjoyed with Miss Abbott had been worth the sacrifice of a century of contented, creative fulfillment.

Whatever effect the gradual introduction of certain subversive pharmacological substances had on Alexander's medial cortex, the cumulative cellular confusion was rendered void by the organism's own misunderstood defenses. The submolecular laboratory of the human animal could, in conditions of excessive stress, whip up enough biochemical cream to soothe anything and, as it happened, did not take kindly to being deluged with urgent synaptic transmissions which, when decoded, printed out as: *Jesus! They're going to do for the lot of us.*

With the aid of a little Leatherstocking to assist the neuronal protein synthesis, Alexander got control of his reason with remarkable rapidity. Maybe his stocks of RNA had nothing to do with it. Maybe he had just grown used to ducking. Whatever, Alexander did not chew the rug, beat his temples on the chocolate-brown shell, or lob himself into Berger Avenue after the manner of a Wall Street broker in the big crash of 1982. Instead he slipped neatly into the role of fugitive. He did not panic, did not rush madly out of Wendekin Towers, did not skip unprepared into the hostile regions beyond the boundaries of New York. Realizing that the city would soon be too hot to hold him and that he would be obliged to seek sanctuary elsewhere, he figured that he must adopt a disguise so perfect that the Freemen's Club Associates wouldn't recognize him if he leaped naked from a keg of their best Madeira singing snatches of *Alice Ambrose* in pidgin German.

Sobered by bourbon, Alexander seated himself in front of the Riss-Interlink and commanded it to talk. Though there were no visuals now, the device was no longer dumb.

In a sonorous metallic tone, the mobile Transceiver boomed:

BELLEROPHON.

"Now, where is that, please?"

BELLEROPHON.

"Come on: all I know is that Bellerophon is out west."

BELLEROPHON.

"How do I get there?"

BELLEROPHON.

Alexander craned forward in the swaychair. Plastic pint and Menthol clutched in his hand, he jutted a forefinger threateningly at the screen.

"Listen, you, I've had just about all the compost I intend to take. You know goddamn well I didn't kill Miss Abbott. I'm being . . . sold up the river, railroaded, framed. Nobody makes a monkey out of me. Particularly an inert cluster of microwires and cord-cables."

BELLEROPHON.

"Repetition went out with Pepsi-Cola," Alexander said.

51

Anger welled up through layers of guilt. He could play the vigilante, in Miss Abbott's honor, just as well as he could act out the role of criminal. He did not feel hunted, desperate. Mainly, he was irritated at being locked out of his own personality, probably for keeps, and being treated like an acoustical testing box by a hunk of advanced electronics.

He stabbed his finger again.

"Now, where the hell is this Bellerophon, and why should I accept your advice and go there?"

BELLEROPHON.

The voice, fading, deepened.

BELLEROPHON.

Alexander slugged from the pint and, dragging on his Menthol, got up and thumped the Interlink a couple of times.

BEL . . .
LER . . .
OOOOOOOOOO . . . PHINNNNNNN.

Now he knew it was dead. He hadn't just insulted the goddamn contraption. He had silenced it completely. So he was stuck with himself, robbed of the consolation of an alter ego with whom to debate escape strategy.

Still standing, he drained the pint and tossed the empty over his shoulder. With the Menthol in his mouth, he flung open the windows and stepped out onto the terrace.

Rain beat into him, plastering the night-suit to his flesh. He looked down at his body, at the curlicues of hair under the silky material, at muscles that had been sculptured to look manly without ever being used for manly purposes. How had it been back before the days of the hollow men, in the infant years of the Golden Age when nobody walked if they could ride and four wheels grew on everybody's ass? Invisible muscles had atrophied, not the adductors and gracilis, flexors and extensors that controlled the limbs, but that other kind of muscle that every man, according to legend, was supposed to have within him, its fibers as tough as esparto grass and as profuse as kelp. How was it that he, product of the twenty-first-century system, scion of Creative Reason, as four-square as a quartet of Jumel Street lawyers, found the jargon of his boyhood so easy to pump to the surface? He could hardly have been more than twenty when that violent phase had been quashed. But the role was *so* comfortable, the thinking process so light within that he might have been born and raised to it.

At that moment, on the terrace of Wendekin Towers in New York City's beautiful Brooklyn Heights, Alexander Blunt gave himself up to the teeming cold noon rain, and the realization that he had never, ever really been himself. This might be the beginning for Alexander Blunt, birth of the real man who had been rooted in the real boy who had early been deprived, by sudden overwhelming social revolutions, of light and air and the navigational beams of the fantastical sun. Civic schematization had equipped him to deal out dreams that were nothing but the appeasement of man's crazy urge to protect the added body-time that the authorities had gained for him.

Dreaming again, on his own account, Alexander seemed to see Morello's bearded countenance afloat in the gray streaming air, and Gene's vindictive grin.

Bellerophon.

Whether it was Gene's advice or not, Bellerophon was all he had, that and the comfort of his crooked role.

Whoever, whatever had equipped him to plough the wheatfield, had obviously failed to take account of its effect on his *cojones*.

Alexander spat over the terrace rail, flicked away the Menthol butt, and hurried back inside.

After dusk Alexander Blunt hit the street. He wore a brown leather bullhipper, selected for its waterproof qualities and because it was common enough to attract no attention, Ferox Standard Smartboys, and a pair of Flaxknit Huron pants which he had bartered for once when he was younger. A tan leather Pernel crowned his head. A Menthol was stuck in the corner of his mouth. In various pouches and pockets he carried his status cards, Laureate medallion, gloves, five pocket handkerchiefs, a spare wristband, four boxes of Menthols, a pair of manicure clippers, and a fruit knife carefully wrapped in tissue—not the weapon that had killed Miss Abbott.

In the five hours and twelve minutes that elapsed between the revelation of his true self and departure from the apartment that had been his home for thirty years, Alex had not been idle. First off, he had gone through all the deductive procedures necessary to establish that he could not have risen in the night and, in a fit of obsessive guilt, have done for the girl.

Whoever had murdered Miss Abbott had been fiendishly quiet about it. But they had not been quite smart enough to plant the weapon in a proper place. The lethal knife—a tape-splicer's skewer—had been tossed into a corner of the bedroom. Tiny whorls of blood on the cream wall indicated that the knife had been flung from the doorway, not from the bed area. Kneeling, Alex had studied this evidence very carefully. He did not touch the weapon. It not only had blood on the blade but there were obvious prints on the handle. Any duplicator, however, was sensitive enough to mock up Alex's prints from a take. Strangely, there was no blood at all upon his sleeping-suit, except for a smudge on the left sleeve. Of course, the liner would be knee-deep in microanalyzable evidence, enough to pack a dossier in no time flat. The invisible stuff usually convicted contract felons under Bureau of Ethics Statute Regulations. Even the least severe of civil cases, Potentials, leaned heavily on details that were generally irrefutable to anyone not in possession of a million bucks' worth of laboratory equipment.

None of that mattered.

Alex knew that he had not killed Miss Abbott. He was satisfied.

The case, however, was so watertight that a Bureau Freshman could have presented it successfully without straining his imagination. The crux of the indictment charge would be that Alexander Blunt, Bachelor of the Laureate Class, had had knowledge of the private parts of an appointed minder and, for reasons not revealed by bioanalysis, had conducted upon the said minder experiments reserved for Select Cell Breeders: thus he had caused the said minder's death by unchecked hemorrhage, in a compound felony of mercifully rare instance. He would be classed as the last in a line of "last" genetic throwbacks, and dropped like bait into Buzzard's Bay.

Alex had not tampered with much of the evidence. He had cleaned Miss Abbott's cadaver with an astringent cosmetic tonic and laid the girl out, just as she was, on a fresh rose-red sheet. He had adjusted the pillbox hat and had drawn the veil discreetly over her staring eyes. He had restrapped the white shoe and put her legs modestly together. But somehow the ligaments insisted in drawing the wretched creature's knees apart and, in the end, impatient with her in death as he had not been in life, Alex simply slammed the bedroom door.

As dusk fell Alex Blunt mingled with the pedestrian commuters on Berger Avenue, going with the flow along the pavements which squared the Kleinshorn Palisades. He crossed Commercial Quadrangle, breaking away from the populated area, and headed out toward Fullerton Landways, where long electroglide drays imported produce from Landways' docking sheds twenty miles away in suburban Gabrielsgate. Produce to victual the city came in by sea and land. Precious few railroads were still in operation, for the high cost of maintenance had pushed the iron way into disfavor. Besides, Engineerings had not been able to design a reactor converter with a satisfactory safety guarantee. The administration had learned its lesson from the Vancouver disaster. Trucking unions had long ago sewn up the turnpikes and forced congressional expenditure on Top-Up Transport reactor tape all across the nation, the last act passed before voluntary dissolution of the Senate. Feeding and commodity supply of the culture-producing area, that is, the ten city-states, lay exclusively in the hands of the Freemen. Fullerton had the monopoly on New York.

There was no security round Landways' installations. Theft was unheard of. If you were a status hand, you didn't need to steal. If you were a casual, you knew you could be arrested and condemned to a research center, maybe even the infamous one on Nantucket. The drays, a hundred meters in length, ran in from Gabrielsgate, a junction from which arterial supply routes spread out into the producing areas of the hinterlands.

New York was not demanding, now that the city took pride in itself. Every jack and jill citizen of that jewel of the eastern seaboard was well fed and content. Clothing, in New York, was the one extravagance. Even that foible was officially condoned by the issue of credit ratings eight points higher than the national urban average. Food sorting was done in Gabrielsgate. Crops and manufactured goods arrived already separated according to season and locale. The huge, gleaming alloy cross-continent trucks were teamed by a four-man crew plus one reactor hand. The men were picked not for their nerve but their patience. There was never any hurry. What didn't reach New York today would reach New York tomorrow. Beef cattle and other livestock were handled in Chicago. Particularization, now recognized as the single most important economic event after the introduction of a national credit system, had sneaked into being in the wake of the Isolationist pogroms of the nineties.

Fullerton electric drays waited on the stems of the wide tarmac flowers that spread out from the tunnels. The electrics were comparatively small, traveling along the stock belts, charging at the same time as they picked up goods tabulated by area requirement. Statistics: no more, no less. Public eating-house cooks, supper-room quartermasters, and other licensed purveyors had first call on the fresh stuff. By the time Alexander got there, a couple of hours after dark, the quartermasters had prowled away with their shipments. Fullerton's electrics would be loaded, held on charge rails, and released at two A.M., 100 at a time, to purr through the streets to the local stores.

Gabrielsgate main center was strictly off limits to kibitzers. But Alex had often been to the dray-depot before, a favorite spot for epicures. Great, colorful, mouth-watering mounds of milk powder, sugar, assorted fruits and vegetables, ground coffee, wine kegs, processed meats, and egg constitute, yellow as pollen, regularly interspersed with cereal loads like mobile mountains, rolled out of the tunnel mouths. A spectators' gallery ran along the length of the stem, tee-branch sections lofting high over the transfer quays. It was a much more exciting spectacle than the Flannigan show which happened a long way offshore. Tonight, though, Alex hadn't come to ogle the foodstuffs or chuckle at the expressive hand-language of stevedores and drivers as they jostled for the best position at the base of the tunnel feeders.

The scene was bathed in pink light from overhead arclamps. It was too raw an evening for tourists. Only a couple of ardent ectomorphs in sealskin suits occupied the gallery. Alex nodded to them as he went past, heading down to the back of the distribution quays. Drivers and stevedores were not uniformed. Many wore bullhippers. Alex went on down the metal steps to the lane behind the quays where sibilant hoppers sucked up grains and dry powders and doled them into the sliding trays of local electrics. There was no waste, no packaging, though a few Fullerton Stores kept special returnable cases for their registered clients.

For five minutes he loitered by the railing, watching empty drays clumsily reverse, straighten, and come down, in strings of five or six, onto the tarmac ramp that dipped into the exit tunnel. He studied the scene for a while, then walked up to the cloverleaf. Here the drivers were most occupied in tending their small, squat vehicles. The power boxes toted the weight of laden drays well enough but, released of their burdens, behaved skittishly. Four drays came around. Alex sat on the railing. He did not try to make himself unobtrusive. He wagged his fist at the drivers and fashioned finger signs that he hoped were appropriate. The first three drays straightened, speeded up to cruising limit, and glided off into the tunnel. The last in the clutch approached. Alex glanced left and right. Right, he could see the tenders on the hopper mechanisms, but the loaders were blocked off from sight by the back trucks. It couldn't have been more perfect if he had spent a year planning it.

The dray trundled past, driver in his cab up front.

Alex lifted himself, squatted on the railing, frog-hopped, caught the top of the open dray, and vaulted over its eight-foot retaining wall into the long, boxlike interior.

The dray ran smoothly along the straight ribbon of tarmac. Alex settled himself, his back against the perforated inner wall through which the Gabrielsgate cleansing detail would shoot water at high pressure. The dray had carried wine kegs. The inside smelled of pungent spirit essences from the vineries of California.

The gantry flew overhead. Strings of arc-lamps, then the edge of the tunnel roof fled past. Sounds became loud but soft-edged in the dim recesses of the tunnel.

Alex watched the dayglow blocks flicker by, whipping away behind him. In ten minutes or so he would be in Gabrielsgate. Maybe he would get no farther. But at least he had tried. He had made the mammoth effort of will needed to break the inertia of capitulation.

When the dray slowed and emerged into the final mile's run up to Fullerton's huge silvery-gray warehouses, Alex vaulted out.

Right now he was farther from New York City than he had ever been in his life before, farther even than Newark.

He still had a long way to go.

With a stifled yelp of joy he sprinted for the cover of the maintenance sheds.

-: PART TWO :-

The House of Descent

THIS IS THE WAY
THE JAGUAR LEAPT,
PADS SO POISED
THAT EVERY ROCK
SEEMED SPRUNG
WITH SPEED,
ROOTS OF EVASION,
SPIRITS OF THE CHASE,
SHAPED FIRM AGAINST
THE CAPTOR'S NETS.
HOW DO YOUR PURSUITS
COMPARE? AS VECTORS
OF A HUNTED SOUL
RAISED TO DEFEND
HUMANITY, OR SIMPLE
SPURS TO DRIVE YOUR
FAINT EXHAUSTED HEART
ACROSS THE STEEP
ESCARPMENTS OF THE PAST?

Eugene Morello

: 1 :

OVERNIGHT Parima Lake had acquired a thin skin of ice, and high above to the east the Sierras were draped with the first of the winter snows. In deep shade under the pines sleet chalked the ruts that led from the cabin to the water's edge. The air was sharp as new-run alcohol. It tickled the back of the old man's throat as he carried a steaming coffeepot and tin cup onto the porch and set them down on the table. He fished a pouch of Makins from his vest and rolled himself a smoke. He lit it with a black iodized Eversure. Still discernible on the lighter's base was the thumb-chafed copperplate that Miss Jenny had had engraved there back in the year one. He studied the inscription wistfully for a moment before sliding the Eversure into his pocket. He did about the same thing every morning, like ritual.

November weather in the high country: he never did tire of the changes that the seasons brought, vagaries of cloud, climate, and perspective. He sucked on the smoke and coughed a little. Breathing at eight thousand feet was a trick he had learned; dragging on dry tobacco was something else again. But it sure was healthy up here, healthy as all hell. If he stayed in the mountains, he did not believe he would ever die. And what if he did? What did it matter? Shit, you grabbed what you had and got out with it. He would take plenty of good stuff with him across the Divide, back-packing it on his soul. But not this year, nor the next. No, not for a long time yet, thank you kindly.

If he climbed to the top of the ridge today he could look out to Mount Whitney and see just how much fresh snow the big fellow had collected in the last couple of weeks.

Sure, it would tire him, but in a good way, so he could sleep tonight, not lie in his sack milling over bygones, wishing that he had known then all that he knew now: though maybe that other life had been part of the learning, the hoppity-hip style necessary to a young man with more balls than brains.

The old man eased himself onto the porch chair, poured coffee, and drank. With a gnarled fingernail he picked a fishbone from between two of his eleven remaining teeth. He looked down what passed for a road, toward the factory town. He could not see the shanty lanes, generator stacks, nor much of anything beyond a half mile of dirt road. The folds of the land closed Dealersville off and downward-dropping pines stitched the middle-distance horizon. The old man could easily pretend there was nothing at all between him and the Pacific Ocean except the coastal ranges alive with bear and deer and small game, and maybe some redskins drifting down from the Colorado plateau for the winter hunting.

Redskins! Shit, he was confusing fact and fantasy again. The past now was nothing but fantasy, preserved within him like a corpse wrappered in aromatic bandages against the chemistry of air and sun and an excess of corrupting bacteria. Only *he* could watch the little deer come down to drink, see the redmen waiting in the trees with their delicate bows, poised, silent as leaves: though perhaps the deer were real at least. He had heard rumors in the store last spring that the animals were staging a comeback. Long ago the old man had relinquished the notion of making a comeback. He had given it up after the city, and the pain of his departure from it, had gotten steeped out of him by the mountains and the inturning strength of solitude. Now it was almost winter. November. Soon the rains would rake the Cordilleras from Alaska down to the volcanic cones of Mexico south, falling as snow above the timberline and blocking off the passes.

The old man drank his coffee and smoked the Makins and thought how within the week he must trek down to the factory town, show his release card, and pick up a season's supplies. It would take him a couple of days to haul the stores up to the cabin, five or six trips in all. He was too old now to fish the lake when the ice was as thick as a boiler plate, so he ate little and was sparing of his fresh supplies when the blizzards locked him in. The cabin was snug enough, straight pine sprayed with Talus Transparent Tar. The interior was paneled with Endural Board, pasted with a heap of five-century guarantees, by way of the factory contractor from whose yard he had filched the stuff soon after his arrival—or maybe he meant the factory's arrival, since he had been loose in the mountains for years before "Joe Dealer" picked the narrow, fertile valley as a crop-processing site. Endural might promise 500 years' worth of durability tacked inside an urban liner with walls eight feet thick. But up here, the land and the weather had means of squandering guarantees and he doubted if the boards would see out the twenty-first century.

The old man caught sight of the figure under the slanting pines—hat first, head and shoulders rising over the slope of the dirt road. The old man evinced no alarm or obvious interest at the stranger's approach. He supped his coffee a mite slower, and didn't move his head: that aside, he was as unstartled and unafraid as if the caller were expected. It might have been his boy coming up from the creek with a mess of fish or a trapped animal hanging from his belt. But the old man had no boy, no relatives, close or distant, in all the hinterlands and cities of America. Rover though he'd been for a spell, he had never crossed the seas to spawn or even just to be impotent. So it could be no kin of his that had come this high, though he knew that he was the stranger's target, sure as eggs.

He made no move, waiting on the porch, bent forward, elbows planted on the knee patches of his double-denim flocks, his small, patched face peering out from the wide winged collar of genuine, moldy sheepskin. The coat had been traded for in the Stillwater Mountains, bartered off a crazy Navaho who still believed that the gods might give the Indians back the plains, like all the videos of that particular season seemed to promise, and wanted two functioning sets to double the potency of his spells. How long ago was that? the old man thought, trying to keep his mind off the kind of trouble the stranger might bring. Eighty-nine years gone. Good Christ! How the years did roll. He had swapped for that coat just to dazzle smartly fashionable Studio Street and had wound up living in it for nine-tenths of the year, every year, like a second skin.

The stranger stopped, and wiped sweat from under his hatband. He read the poker-work sign nailed to a post beside the track, just the name and some ancient cabalistic symbols from the days of post-codes, then gave a spluttering laugh, incredulous, relieved, and joyous, and trotted the last couple of hundred yards uphill. The plastic goat-sack, slung across his shoulder by a length of nylon rope, bobbed eagerly. Thrown wide, the stained and tattered mock-leather bullhipper flapped like a bat's wings.

The stranger halted ten feet out from the porch step. He put his arms behind his back, kind of scholastic like, and stared all around, as if he expected to be plugged in the back from one of the cabin windows or the apertures in the bleached-out, broken-down walls of the old ore sheddings.

The stranger's eyes finally fixed on the old man—maybe because there was nothing much else to fix on—and he said, "Bellerophon?"

"Yup," the old man answered.

"Is this the only Bellerophon?"

"Only one I knows of, son."

"Then this is it." The stranger nodded. "Must be it."

"Coffee?" the old man said and shook the enamel pot hospitably. "I can heat up some fresh."

"Don't trouble," the stranger said. "That will be fine. Anything so long as it's wet."

"It's a far piece up from town."

"Yes."

"Come on hup here and set yourself down."

"Thank you."

The stranger was not so young as the old man had expected. He was very lean and tanned, and sure hadn't stepped out of a gyroped on the stump below the slope and come up the last half mile on the hoof just to make an impression. He was a traveler, if ever the old man had seen a traveler. The stranger clumped up the board steps. One heel of one boot was broken. He walked like a peg-leg, holding his balance carefully. Clover-hoofed Smartboys weren't designed for rough terrain. The pair that the old man had once owned hadn't lasted more than a month.

The old man poured coffee into a tin cup and handed it to the stranger who took the cup in the palms of his hands, lifted it to his mouth like a chalice, and drank the lot in a couple of long, greedy swallows. He sighed.

"Makins?" The old man offered his pouch.

"What is it?"

"Makins: tobacco."

64

"You wouldn't happen to have a Menthol, would you?"

"Hard to get round these parts."

"I . . . I'm not sure I could roll one of those right now." The stranger held out his shaking hand. Generously, the old man rolled and lit the smoke and handed it over. The stranger dragged on it and coughed. He asked for more coffee.

"You come a long way, son?"

"I didn't realize it would be quite so easy," the stranger said. "I don't mean actually finding this place—that was anything but easy—but traveling, you know. I thought there would be nothing much out here, except Bureau of Ethics' cabs and roadblocks and all that."

"You're from the city, ain't you?"

"New York."

"New York! Now that *is* a far piece."

"You know, I've hardly spoken to a soul in . . . five weeks."

"Reticence won't kill you," the old man said. "When d'you last eat?"

"Yesterday," said the stranger, without interest. "I really can't believe that I've arrived. I mean, one thinks of the hinterlands as . . . waste."

"How did you come?"

"In a Landways' freighter heading southwest. I didn't even know which direction to take for Bellerophon. But I wanted as far from New York as possible. Strangely, I had no problem at all getting into that freighter. It was full of empty wine kegs. I was high before I'd gone a mile. I couldn't see out, of course. I almost got pinched when the freighter stopped."

The old man let the stranger talk. It was what he needed. He had come here, all the way from New York, just to talk. It was symptomatic of urban innocence that he did not question whether it was safe to confide in the old man. Sure, the old man knew he did not exactly resemble a standard B. of E. handout on unethical factions, nor did he have the look of a planted hinterland agent. But the stranger didn't know that. The fact that it did not even occur to him, told the old man a great deal in a very short space of time.

"Yes, that was rather stimulating," the stranger went on. "I reeled out of that freighter in the dead of night in a place I'd never been before—I didn't even know where I was—and lay in a ditch, a real earth ditch, until daylight. A very strange experience. I felt like a child again."

The old man nodded understandingly.

"Where were you?" he asked.

"A granary town called Vermillion. The freighter changed crews there."

"In which urban area?"

"Kansas City."

"You must have been a long time in that truck."

"Too long. I was weak with hunger. You know, I've never been so hungry in my whole life. Now I think of it, I'd never been hungry before. I didn't think about risks. I just had to eat. I went to a restaurant, a diner, put my cards on the table, and waited for them to arrest me. Nobody paid the slightest attention. They fed me up to the meal limit and would have given me more if I'd insisted."

"How did you vector in on Bellerophon?"

The stranger paused now, wariness creeping into his eyes.

"Who are you?" he asked.

"I live here," the old man said. "You've nothing to fear from me, son. Keep talkin'. It'll do you good."

The stranger clammed up. He finished the smoke, dropped the butt, and ground it out with the broken heel. The old man waited.

"Actually," the stranger said, glancing behind him at the cabin door, "I came here in search of a friend."

"Who would that be?"

"A . . . a former associate of mine."

"Uh-huh!"

"Morello: Eugene Morello."

"Uh-huh!"

"Is he dead?"

The old man shrugged.

"Why was I sent here?" the stranger asked. The planes of his face were hard and swarthy. Black stubble beard made him seem handsome in that ruthless way that had been all the rage back in the first decade of the century, in the wake of the wars. He reminded the old man a lot of the only real close friend he had ever had, not counting Miss Jenny. The old man experienced a slight tremor of pain at the memory of that son-by-adoption who had been dead now for five decades. He studied the stranger closely.

"Maybe I should introduce myself," the old man said. He

searched, found his former voice, and put it onto his tongue. "My name is Dowd Hartmann."

He was not altogether surprised when the stranger punched him in the mouth. That sudden angry gesture told him the rest of what he needed to know.

Blunt had come at last.

: 2 :

DOWD HARTMANN, the bull figure of the twenty-first century's great cultural revolution, looked sadly down at the broken tooth in his palm. His tongue explored the jagged edge that remained above his gum.

"I really can't apologize enough," Alex Blunt said. "But you must understand how difficult it is for me to believe what you say. How can *you* be Dowd Hartmann?"

"I'm Dowd Hartmann, okay."

"But you died, what, almost five decades ago."

"You saw the body?"

"No, but . . ."

"A video, perhaps?"

"No. But you were old even then."

"I'm about eleven years your senior, Alex," the old man said. "I got caught in the chasm, you see, had the youth squeezed out of me old-style, and not enough pull with the new establishment to persuade them to hand me immortality like an olive branch. I did manage a couple of quickies, that's all: boosters bought illegally. God knows what good they did me, or if they'll have any permanent effect on my longevity. To be honest, I don't give a shit."

"What age are you?"

"I was born in '59: 1959."

"It's incredible!" Alexander said. "I just can't believe it: Dowd Hartmann!"

"Eat your fish."

Obediently Alex Blunt wiped up butter gravy with a heel of warm bread and popped the piece into his mouth. Though his mind was spinning with shock, his palate had noticed that the fish tasted magnificent, totally unlike any of the fish dishes, larded with rich sauces though they were, that were served with fanfare at the Appledore. He made no comment. He lit a smoke and drank hot coffee, seated still on the porch in the crystalline noon light of the High Sierra Nevada, in the former mining hamlet of Bellerophon.

"You don't look at all like the yellowpress graphics," Alex said.

"Never did, son. What'd you expect? Ain't nobody nine feet tall, five feet broad, and with a jaw like a snowplow."

"But what happened, Mr. Hartmann?"

"Dowd: you better call me Dowd."

"Why are you here? Where have you been for the last fifty years?"

"Now let's you and me have a nice long conversation, son, a real old-fashioned gabfeist. Do you remember that inanity? Gabfeist! Jesus H. Christ!" The old man shook his head. "Anyhow, suppose you tell me how you got from this hick grain town in the middle of Kansas City zone out to here, and how come you managed to find Bellerophon. Did Gene give you the vector-points, or what?"

"Gene gave me nothing." Alex frowned. "Well, perhaps he did. I really cannot be sure. That's part of what I'm doing here, looking for Gene's trail to discover if he left any answers strewn along it."

"Not Gene in the flesh?"

"I think Gene may be dead."

The old man worried the broken tooth some more.

Alex said, "To answer your question how I got here: I became quite emboldened by my first contact with the hinterland. It's really astonishing how little genuine information is fed into the urban centers about what it's like out here. I had no idea, for instance, that one could travel comparatively freely, that the credit system was so casual. That's not what we're led to believe at . . . at home."

"You ever talk to anybody from outside New York before?"

"Of course; I've met Visionist clients from Washington, from the Frisco-L.A. zone, from Chicago."

"The big ten," the old man said. "They're urbanists."

"But one can apply for a Gypsy ticket."

"That's like applying for an exile visa," Dowd Hartmann said. "They let you out—but you ever try getting in again? They don't picket the borders any more. They don't have to. Try eating, try buying something, anything, inside any urban zone with a card that has veto treatment. They'll fling you out so fast your hair'll smolder."

"Is that what happened to you?"

"Never mind what happened to me awhile. I'm still trying to figure out just how smart you are."

"I called a colleague from Vermillion, a wordsmith in the K.C. zone."

"Uh-huh?"

"He programmed his information ZIGTRAC for me and came up with this town out of historical records."

"You hopped another ride?"

"Three, in fact. I had no idea that 'Joe Dealer' had quite so many factories. There must be ten Dealersvilles in this part of the world."

"Tab land usage," Hartmann explained curtly. "Did you ride into town, the town below in the valley, our particular Dealersville?"

"No, I discreetly disembarked on the outskirts. It was a pretty run-down sort of vehicle, an electric. It crawled in from the Denver zone, another Dealersville, believe it or not."

"I believe it," Hartmann said.

The shadows of the pines had shortened and the tracers of sleet were nothing now but moist red ruts set against their own hard ridges. All the contours seemed to run on down to the lake or the creek that fed on past the lake. Even the route up the arroyo dipped away at first from the cabin. Only the rocks, jutting yellow as tusks and granite red in layers and slabs above the scrub, lifted the eye southeastward to the saddle above which the Sierras were painted over the width of the sky. It was cold on the porch of the pine cabin, a dry, invigorating cold.

Alex Blunt sat back from the table, holding the tin coffee cup. He squinted into the clear, bright, hard light.

"Do you want to talk to me?" he asked.

"Sure, I don't mind saying a little word now and again."

"Why was I directed to this place?"

"I can't rightly say if you were sent, or sent for. Summoned or dispatched," Dowd Hartmann told him.

"Is Eugene Morello dead?"

"I *really* don't know, son. I ain't clapped an eye on him for four years."

"But you saw him then?"

"He came here three, four times in all. Stayed quite a while once."

"Was he alone?"

"Always."

"But he must have had a Riss-Interlink with him."

"What the hell is a Riss-Interlink?"

"Video device, a transceiver. Like the old voiceprint units, only not so cumbersome."

"That!" said Hartmann. "Yup, he had one. Goddamn it, that was all he had. He hauled it on his back, too. He worked over there in the second shack, four, five hours every morning, religiously—you should pardon the expression."

"Why did he come here, to this . . . this part of the hinterland?"

"To consult me."

"Eugene *knew* you were alive?"

"That he did."

"He never told me."

"Was there any reason to tell you?" the old man said.

"We used to argue about you sometimes. The peculiar thing is that I was on your side, and Gene was . . . well, let's say opposed to your part in the founding of the cultural revival."

The old man, caught in some other thought field, did not respond. He gazed out over the valley, his eyes blue, washed-out. He had forgotten the tooth. It lay in his palm like a small amber bee.

"I've been waiting for you, Alexander Blunt," the old man said, at length. He spoke softly, all trace of the imposed twang gone, the banjo sound. His tone was crisp, but low, energetically sad. "I've been waiting four years for you, Alex. Eugene told me you would come, that you would ask for him. This was as far as he was prepared to lead you—to me, to old Dowd Hartmann."

"But why here?" said Alex. "We conversed literally every day. We were partners. Why this ridiculous method, this chase sequence?"

"Who designed your connection?"

"Florian—of New York. You remember Florian?"

"Too well," Hartmann said. "That's why Gene did it. That's why he got me involved. He left the cross here, like on a map, knowing that when you were ready you would come; that when you came I would stop you."

71

"Stop me?" said Alex, a shade anxiously.

"Give you pause, shall we say."

"Listen, sir, I . . ."

The old man slapped his palms on his thighs and got to his feet, brisk and decisive. In that motion there was the echo not of the past as Alex recalled it, but of the yellow-press depiction of Hartmann and his cohorts as men of action, of instant decision. That part of the fiction at least had been truly caught.

"You look spry enough," Hartmann said. "Let's go."

"Go where?"

"The top of the ridge," Hartmann said. "I want to look at Mount Whitney."

"Why?"

"To see how long we've got before we hafta leave."

"Leave?"

"To look for Eugene, of course."

"Both of us? You're coming with me?"

"Sure."

"After fifty years you're leaving here?"

"Yup."

"Just to help me?"

"Why not? One thing's for sure," Dowd Hartmann said, "it's the last thing I'll ever do, and I want to do it right."

Dowd Hartmann said, "If you really want to know what happened, I don't mind admitting—I sold out to the conglomerates."

"But you worked for the conglomerates," Alex said.

The younger man was seated on a davenport in front of the fire, his hands trying to kneed some suppleness back into his stiffening muscles.

The afternoon's trek had taken it out of him. He felt relieved to be here, though, in full control of his thinking processes. The madness that had possessed him in New York had gone during the course of his journeys from New York to Vermillion and on down the chain of Joe Dealer factory towns. The only phantasmagorical sensations that overtook him from time to time were comparative, a balancing of the rich, new experiences of this strange westerworld, the country of the hinterlands, with his upbringing in New York. He assumed he was undergoing a form of birth trauma. Meeting up with a boyhood hero in living flesh, was another aspect of the fantasy.

How did that Hartmann epigram go? *No fantasy is ever idle*.

True or false?

True, of course.

Hartmann was making supper over a log-fed stove, gnarled hands expertly flattening and shaping the canned steaks, palming them onto the skillet.

The old man said, "Sure, I worked for the conglomerates. Remember, son, the conglomerates were only collecting their power in those days. Their authority was not so absolute then as it is now. I didn't work for any one company, either. I free-lanced, moonlighted, flitted through the demarcations. I was considered a rogue, a bit of a heretic. At first I was tolerated, then I was used, and, when the Freemen's Club founding group got together, I was supposed to be roped into that corral as a kind of tame bronco. The only thing was that they couldn't be sure of me and my allegiances. There was dissension in the stratospheric ranks of the organization. They already had Robert, you see. They thought he'd be enough."

"Robert Lambard, you mean?"

"What more did they want?" the old man went on. "They had Robert in their weskit pocket to flash like a gold watch whenever they needed to impress the public."

"Robert Lambard was always his own man," Alex snapped.

Hartmann shook his head. "It only looked that way. Robert was bought, paid for, and wrapped up like Christmas candy. It's the solemn truth. He flew too fast and too high. He kind of lost his strength up there. I did the best I could for him, but it was too late."

"I don't understand."

"I loved Robert like a son." Hartmann turned from the stove, a second steak lying limply in his fist. "I taught him to respect the power of the word. I trained him to pillage only the best sources and to put together with style, force, and imagination. The Marchat format was originally my idea, God help me."

"But the Marchats were wonderful."

"Wonderful for the Freemen."

"Lambard gave everybody a rough ride. Lambard was no respecter of status," Alex declared.

"Sure, but in the end, Robert made the folk who counted look good. He *seemed* to rattle them, shake them up, but

73

the Freemen's boys always came out cleaner than they went in. Not so the others."

"You mean even the Marchats were rigged?"

"Everything was rigged." Hartmann sprinkled herb powder on the steaks and nudged them around in the skillet with a wooden spatula. "The propaganda machine moved into top gear. I gave it the respectability of an art form, isn't that what they say? Jesus, look at how the comix-cuts caught on, with me as a kind of Super Spellman, a dropper of deathless epigrams, two *bons mots* per episode, able to change lives by a few well-chosen words. All crap, of course. But the principle was sound, so sound that the Freemen used the so-called cultural revival to rope and hog-tie the whole of America. *Stand still while I talk: listen and stand still.* The audience was captive, society made static, the village mentality fed on cultural pabulum sweetened by the promise of a long life span."

"Longevity *is* a reality, Dowd," Alex reminded him.

"Five years in an isolation ward in a Bureau sanatorium is a friggin' *eternity*, believe me, son." The skillet spat as Hartmann flipped over the steaks. "What counts ain't how *long* but how *well* you live."

"Isn't that a little . . . banal?"

"Banality has always been the lifeblood of popular culture, Alex. How the hell do you think I got to be a popular hero—by pretending I was an artist, an intellectual? Shit, no, I didn't raise the populace's sights; I just equated entertainment with art, and lowered the whole surrounding standard. Creativity, as such, has always been a dirty word. The mediotocracy has always been top dog. I just gave it a new kind of respectability. I'm not proud of it, by the way. As Stratten said in the dock, when charged with killing President Campbell: *It seemed like a good idea at the time.*"

"I think you've just insulted my profession."

"Laureates," said Hartmann, "are no better than greeting-card scribes. Your so-called great epics—yup, I've seen and heard a few—have no more substance than sugar-floss. They work well, give the desired effect, link with great precision to sound and image. The best of them stand upright on their own, like a row of kumquats. But they typify to perfection the Freemen's dictum: *Reduce and conquer.* When all nominal 'art culture' becomes a product of human psyches conditioned from birth to accept values that are socially and ethically impeccable, then the dog in your soul barks noiselessly and his teeth decay through lack of use. Everything becomes propaganda, ground down so fine that even the simplest minds respond as desired. I did it first. I helped pave the way for extreme manipulation."

"But the Right of Termination faction . . . ?"

"Ain't no such animal," said Hartmann.

He slid the steaks onto heated plates and ladled gravy over them. He had a pot of Fluffies warmed up, and a side dish of Bronson's Broccoli. He put the food tidily on the plates and carried them over to the table.

Alex ate hungrily. He was beginning to come to grips with his new personality. Hunger and its satisfaction were part of it. He was given a glass jar full of a colorless, fiery liquid that Hartmann called Corn Likker, better than the best bourbon Alex had ever tasted. He did as Hartmann did and mixed the drink with equal parts of branch water from a big plastic jug. Hartmann seated himself opposite his guest. The log fire blazed, casting light upon the two men, drawing the cabin walls tightly round them, and, somehow, adding spice to the eating. Alex came to grips not only with appetite but also with the precepts around which Hartmann's talk had ranged. He guessed that the old man was feeding him, piecemeal, scraps and gobbets of a whole radical philosophy.

Mouth full of hot Fluffies, Hartmann said, "Since no word or combination of words, no image, symbol, slogan, or fusion of intangible subsensory reagents is *quite* harmless, then it stands to reason that a skillful technician represents not only a valuable tool of the All-City State, but also, as an individual, a threat to that State."

"If he gets out of hand, you mean: rebels?"

"Correct."

"Morello rebelled?" asked Alex.

"Morello was never one of them."

"But I've known Gene since graduation, almost," said Alex. "He was always pretty much his own man, but his work was . . ."

"His work was the projection of a superficial talent," said Hartmann. "Inside, Gene remained his own man."

"Yet they let him travel. Wasn't that dangerous?"

"As it happened—yeah. But Florian was vain enough to

75

think that he could sweep up some of the heretical elements in the hinterland."

"By using Gene?"

"Right."

"But Gene proved too much of a fox—so they killed him?"

"We can't be sure," said Hartmann.

"Do you think," Alex asked tentatively, "that those . . . er, messages on my unpowered Riss-Interlink were really from Gene? How did he do it?"

"What's the other explanation?"

"That they came from Florian, from the Bureau."

"Pretty devious stuff," said Hartmann. "Why would Florian bother?"

"To ruin me?"

"He didn't, though, did he?"

"It's a pretty elaborate scheme," said Alexander. "Florian could have got rid of me much more easily. Then there was the business of Miss Abbott, my minder. Why kill her and try to make me take the rap?"

"Let me bend your ear with a couple of parables," said Hartmann. "The first is a memory from my days as a student of, among other subjects, entomology. Put a wasp in a mason jar and funnel in smoke and what will happen?"

"I imagine that the wasp will suffocate."

"In ninety-nine cases out of a hundred, the wasp suffocates."

"But there is a rare exception?"

"Right: there are occasional smart wasps. They don't go buzzin' round the bottom of the jar. They aim for the aperture through which the smoke is being funneled and, if they don't get too dazed, wriggle free through the smoke hole."

"Yes," said Alex, thoughtfully. "I can see meanings behind that."

"The other parable is actually history," said Hartmann, "real, genuine, finger-lickin' history.

"It's what happened to Robert and me, an illustration of how goddamn devious those sons of bitches in the corporate structure are. First off, they had Robert doing just what was required of him. They had him as their front shield, their culturalist badge. They vetoed my elevation to the exalted ranks, and consequently splintered the remnants of the Gang. They bought out Pinkie, and Jason.

Charlie Blake died of natural causes about that time. They got rid of Roger Whitcomb by shipping him to Chicago to start up a plant. Roger went along innocently, and found he couldn't backtrack. Miss Jenny and I were taken into custody—only they didn't quite call it that. We weren't getting any younger, so we were told we were in need of proper care and attention. Robert Lambard was fobbed off with that lame excuse. But, after three years, even Lambard got curious and started asking questions. Now, though they had no use for me, they still had a use for Robert. They made me a deal. I would cool the boy's zealous search for truth by convincing him that I was going along with everything voluntarily. In return I would be paid off, released with a nice new face, a wallet full of valid credit, and a traveler's ticket. The same would hold good for Miss Jenny."

"And you accepted their terms?"

"Yeah."

"But why, Dowd, why?"

"I banked on Robert realizing that I'd never buy a gag like that. And I was right, son. Oh, sure, Robert pretended to play along, too. But he was never much good at pretending. He saw us safe out of New York, Miss Jenny and me, not together, then he went a touch crazy. I didn't have to say or do anything to prompt him. All that status which had gone to his head blew off like cloud from a mountain. I still admire his guts, if not his method."

"What did he do, Dowd?"

"Made himself a Marchat, the Marchat to end all Marchats."

"Who was the subject?"

"Robert Lambard was the subject."

"What?"

"Robert Lambard in conversation with Robert Lambard."

"But how . . . ?"

"The technique was easy enough. He'd been around studios so long he could do anything. He could even fix the goddamn coffee-vendor, so I'm told. Anyhow, what he did was put the pieces together on a batch of equipment he had stashed away in an apartment in Queens. He matched the visuals there, printed out the evidence, like, then he hijacked a studio. Studio C in the Pentecost Memorial."

"God Almighty!"

"Neato, as the kids used to say." Hartmann's food was forgotten, cooling on the plate. "So, working the dog-watch for three consecutive nights, Robert taped a four-hour spellbinder, the juju, the ultimate kibosh on the plans that the Freemen had for us, a complete exposé of schemes in embryo and programs already accomplished."

"Did he complete it?"

"Sure thing. Now that really *was* dangerous to our Founding Fathers. If you create a tame folk-hero of the video, a vox populi, and all of a sudden that voice begins to speak the truth, then the world's going to listen, and the world's going to sit up, and the world's going to be jolted into starting to think. Once enough of the goodfolk of America *begin t*o think for themselves, then the end is nigh and only force, not persuasion, will keep the power where it happens to be at, namely with the Freemen."

"But Lambard couldn't have hoped to commandeer a Universal wave band, not without exposing his material," said Alex.

"Oh, Robert knew that. That's where he made a fatal error of judgment. He went in for *honest* blackmail. He gave them an ultimatum: broadcast this Marchat, un-edited and intact, or I'll pull out of the show in mid-season *and* blab my reasons to every yellowpress rag that'll listen; a few underground presses still operating then."

"So they killed him."

"Uh-huh! At first they pretended to go along with him. They set up the broadcast, even drew off the handbills, the whole fanfare. Meanwhile they had Miss Jenny locked away again down in New Orleans, and me in Frisco-L.A. They told Lambard exactly what would happen to us if he insisted on broadcasting that Marchat."

"But that was bluff, wasn't it?"

"Cunning," said Hartmann. "They knew Robert would be suspicious if they just sat around on their keisters and did nothing. Robert wasn't one to balk at sacrificing a couple of old buddies in the cause of truth. I respected him for that. I'd taught him to be ruthless."

Hartmann paused to rinse his mouth with whiskey.

"Miss Jenny killed herself. It took three attempts. She tried ground glass—and they gave her a new stomach. She ran a manicure file through her left breast: they gave her a

78

new heart. She jumped through a window on the eighth floor, and the nurse who tried to shoot her was promptly shot for his stupidity by an attending surgeon. Miss Jenny broke her back and both legs. They patched her up once again. But she was a determined old lady, our Miss Jenny."

"How did she finally do it?"

"The need for self-sacrifice was long past," Hartmann said, quietly. "Robert was already dead and there was nothing two old-timers like Jen and me could do. But she had only one means of beating the goddamn system. If the system wanted her alive, then she would cheat them of that. She always believed that her life was her own. She'd have liked to have lived forever—but only on her own terms. How'd she do it? She blew half the hospital to hell and gone. Nobody knows to this day how she smuggled a vial of aeroglyccrine—stabilized nitro—into the sanatorium. But she did. She had no means of detonating it, though. So she made them do that for her. After her eighth-floor leap she'd had a hollow bone-substitute graft in the thigh, the femur. She pilfered a hypo and shot the whole ampule into the bone. Next time they wheeled her along for some nice muscular-radiation treatment . . . *bazoom.*" Hartmann lifted the Corn Likker glass, took a small mouthful, wiped his chin with his wrist, and softly repeated, "Bazoom."

"But what about Lambard? Is he really dead?"

"Yeah, yeah: Robert's dead all right. On the surface it was just like they said it was. He was lasered to death on the Pentecost steps by John Demoines Fraser Black, a genuine genetic throwback. Friend Black was another poor slob. He believed what he was told to believe and he was told that Lambard and his kind were responsible for changing the world so fast and so radically that guys like him, like poor slob Black, were no-count citizens, that every minor grievance Black suffered could be redressed by plugging poor Robert. Black was the perfect subject. Brainwashed by all the filth that the media had poured at him until he believed everything he was told. You can do anything with a mind as pliable as that. They made sure that Black got access to a lasergun—a very sophisticated piece of weaponry which Black had learned to use in the Street Artillery in the last of the civil uprisings. See, he

79

was as four-square as that, Alex. Four weeks before the Universal wave band was about to be contaminated with the truth, Black lays for Robert and plugs him. They didn't even have to use the back-up men."

"But I studied the scenario: there was no evidence of collusion," Alex said. "Black was a loner."

"An *official, educational* scenario?"

"Pardon my naiveté," Alex said, sincerely. "I'm having a little difficulty in jettisoning almost a century of history in the course of one day."

"Naturally, the Big Marchat was canceled. Instead they broadcast the Eulo-ceremonies, with purple flags and dyed carnations and all the rest of that funereal crap."

"And you?"

"I was flung out of the All-City State, a retired casual. I was, in effect, dead and buried. Most jacks and jills thought I'd gone to that great big four-color printing press in the sky. Didn't you?"

"Yes," Alex admitted.

Hartmann pushed his plate aside and concentrated on drinking his Corn Likker for a minute or so. "They just let me slide off into the hinterland," he said, at length. "I was puzzled at the time, and then I ceased to fret about it. I had a new face, a new name on my cards, enough to feed on. I settled here."

"Logically, they must have had a reason for allowing you to roam free."

"I was a spent force, of course," said Hartmann, "but I admit to a certain nagging curiosity over the years. I finally figured out why."

"May I ask—why?"

"Florian lost face in that debacle fifty years ago. He was only an apprentice then, a deputy Freeman, and it must have occurred to him that he was never going to make it to the Club."

"I'd forgotten that Lambard was Florian's baby," Alex said.

"Florian had to wait, and sweat, for his chair at the Club dining table and his gold statue. Fabrianno, Florian's foster father, hung on three decades past normal retreat. That was the Club's way of making Florian squirm for his error."

"But he did make it."

"Sure. But he hasn't forgotten. He'll never forget. It's a loss of status, of power, and that's what Freemen play for. It's their sole, whole, unadulterated, and absolute reason for living—power."

"So Florian kept you alive—just in case?"

"That's about all I know," Hartmann said. "The rest would only be conjecture."

"I think you've left something out," Alex said.

Hartmann peeped at him over the rim of his glass, blue eyes winking in the firelight. "Like what?"

"How come Florian gave Morello a long rein, and why I was permitted to find the smoke hole, and why I was driven, or drawn here, and . . ."

"That'll keep: all that'll keep."

"Where do I—we—go from here?"

"South again."

"So you do know where Gene Morello's hiding?"

"Nup," said Hartmann. "I don't even know for sure that they *didn't* get him. I can only do what Gene asked of me last time he was around these parts."

"Which was?"

"To keep a weather eye open for Alexander Blunt, a native New Yorker, Bachelor of the Laureate Class, who might stumble in someday in search of his partner's hide."

"What else?"

"Not much."

"Don't I even get a clue, a trinket to put under my mattress to sleep on?"

Hartmann chuckled. "Push: push: push. Got no time, son, have you?"

"More than you have, old man," Alex said.

"Yeah, that's a fact," the old man said.

He groped at the thong around his neck and fished up the Makins pouch. He opened the purse neck and put his stubby fingers inside. For a moment, Alex thought that the old man was merely rolling a smoke; then the right hand came out and turned at the wrist and twisted palm uppermost, fingers opening. Hartmann blew off crumbs of dust-dry tobacco.

"What's that?" asked Alex, curious and eager, grinning in immediate response to the tiny artifact in Hartmann's hand.

The figurine, modeled in an ocher claylike substance,

was hardly more than an inch high. It represented the head of a tiny man, with a flattened ornamental headdress, elongated ears, and a wide infectious grin. He seemed to be all teeth. Even the blanked-out almonds of the eyes were strangely full of merriment.

"Take it: study it," said Hartmann.

Alex took the figurine, placed it on his own hand, and held it up close to his face.

"God, that's beautiful," he said admiringly. "How old?"

"Oh, that little 'un is a copy, about a hundred years. It isn't even clay: some kind of fake mix. Very hard." Hartmann retrieved the miniature. "The original's six, maybe seven hundred years old."

"A parable in stone?"

"Sure," Hartmann agreed. "Four years back Eugene left it on my mantelshelf. No other hints, just the Totonac head. I figured it out, though. Mythopology was another of my special subjects. Gene knew that."

"Tell me about it," said Alex.

"Scholastic experts assure us that the indigenous peoples of Central America—what *used* to be Central America— were a pretty down-in-the-mouth bunch. The Spanish historical brochures confirm this theory. When you think of it, we've gotten most of our stuff through the Spanish filters. These little figures with the big, happy smiles, however, tell a different story."

"To what culture do they belong?"

"Totonac—the Folk from the Land of the Dawn. You know what these heads express? Joy! That's what we really know about the Totonacs. We have a little data from early Franciscan missionaries and other contemporary sources, but it's really invalid. The Totonacs go back beyond the conquests. How far back? Nobody knows. In the midst of subjection and humiliation, they laughed at life, with that joyful expression which their sculptors didn't create, only copied. Ain't much Aztec blood lust in their scrolls, little enough hatred, vengeance, and destruction. Some, but not much. They must have been steeped in mysticism, abstract and metaphysical symbols, and yet they always remained alive to humanity, to the fact that life is just one big joke that you laugh at even while the yoke crushes you and the dictators grind you into the dirt. Maybe they knew that something would remain and endure of their culture in spite of the conquerors."

82

"Had Gene been to the place where the Totonacs once lived?"

"I expect so." Hartmann put the little clay-simulate head carefully back into the tobacco pouch and tugged the strings tightly. "Melancholy contentment is not the inevitable lot of mankind, son. We dug up some other facts about those old Amerindians, you know. For instance, we have some authentic data on the *tlamatini*, the Followers of Truth, and their wonderful youth-songs about Netzahualcoyotl, the poet-king of Texcoco."

"Where were the smiling heads found?" interrupted Alex.

"Remojadas."

"Where's that?"

"The Gulf coast: Veracruz."

"Then that's were we go," Alex said. "That's where Eugene Morello wants us to go."

Hartmann pursed his lips and nodded.

"How do we get there?" asked Alex.

"Tomorrow, I'll show you," Dowd Hartmann promised.

The last cabin in the Bellerophon cluster faced northwest. It was staggered back from its neighbor on the southen flank of the earth square, its narrow upright door looking across to the home cabin. On the outer wall, though, well screened by scrub slopes, were two larger doors linked by a metal bar fastened with a magnolock. Grass and weeds blocked the bottom of the doors and spiders had laced webs across the hinges. Hartmann stood in the pool of sunlight before the doors and fiddled with the circuit-breaking plate that he had brought with him.

It was an hour after dawn. Cloud was still down upon the Sierras and a chill mist filled the Dealersville valley. The sun, however, laid a spot on Bellerophon and Alex, dressed in a simulated Mutton jacket, was glad of its warmth.

Hartmann had wakened him before it was light. He had washed in a bucket and put on the clothing that Hartmann had laid out for him, rough-country garb that made him look more like a no-status hand than ever, yet roused in him an atavistic urge to tackle hard tasks and physically exacting chores. The men ate breakfast without speaking. Alex helped Hartmann wash up the crockery and put it neatly away in the cupboard by the hearth. The hearth fire was out, feathery gray ashes broomed away. The stove was extinguished and the coals shoveled out into the yard and rubbed into the dirt. By the door of the home cabin dunnage sacks of heavy yellow plastic and bundles of bedding had been laid out. Alex knew that they would begin the journey that day, but he did not know how. Veracruz, way down in Mexico, was too far for the old man to trek on foot. Even dogged Dowd Hartmann must realize that. To travel was not the aim: the aim was to arrive. Only at some distant destination would he find out why Morello had lured him into the central regions of the continent.

The magnolock sprang open. Gleefully Dowd Hartmann swung the double doors, pushing them wide against the grass.

Alex was standing off to one side.

Hartmann beckoned eagerly with his forefinger.

Alex came around the front of the shack and looked inside.

The machine was massive, square, and high, with two plexiglass windows like eyes shielded by goggles, and a grid that looked much like a mouth.

"Behold," Hartmann said, "the last Mitsukisan Mastodon in captivity."

"It must be all of a century old."

"Not quite," Hartmann said, proud of his museum piece. "One of the last off the production line, though. Registered 2011. It had maybe one year's running, if that, before the knell of personal transportation sounded. God knows why the guy bought it when he did. Maybe, like me, he was a kook with an unfulfilled longing to bolster his masculinity by sitting up there in the cabin and scaring the shit out of other road users. Maybe he just needed a monster like the Mastodon here in the high country. It was here when I arrived, neglected and beginning to rust—though the Mitsukisan did build for long life. In spite of its shape, that lovely brute'll shove in forty old miles in an hour and drink only a half-pint or so of petrofuel in the process, plus minimum gas."

"What does she burn?"

"A real cocktail: kerosene firing, with a methane gas infiltrator when the engine cooks up power. She sounds like a goddamn calliope and she's probably a potential fireball, though the tanks and pipes of the fueling system are all double-lined and armor-insulated. There's an ejector button on the dash that shoots off the methane canisters and kerosene tank in case she decides to lumber over a cliff with you inside."

"How much fuel do you have?"

"Enough to carry us to Veracruz," Hartmann replied. "I made the methane in my own organic breeder tank. Found over thirty old canisters buried round the site, plus nine full ones in the shed. Fourteen-gallon cans of kerosene under the floorboards. I've topped that up over the years from my annual credit supply which privileges me to a half-gallon per annum."

"When did you drive her last?"

"Nine, ten years back," said Hartmann. "I got nervous about running her so near the town. I didn't want to run the risk of having her confiscated. She's mine. I keep her good. Jesus, I admit I'm even fond of her."

"I can understand that," said Alex, thinking of his former attachment to the Riss-Interlink. "Listen, Dowd, can we get away with this journey? I mean, if we troll along Landways' turnpikes for—what is it?—a couple of thousand miles, we can hardly hope to go undetected. That Mastodon is anything but inconspicuous."

"You're still clinging to the urban's image of the hinterlands," Hartmann told him. "They ain't as sewn-up as you imagine, son. Anyhow, I know how the land lies. I charted the routes on a sheaf of maps I brought with me when I kicked out of New York, good, old-style, detailed maps. We'll shy clear of urban centers and main exporting towns. In the little burgs there's always a chance that some Bureau stoolie will blow the whistle on you, so we'll be cautious and go when we can by desert tracks and mountain trails."

"In that vehicle?"

"That's what she's built for. Those Nips sure knew how to build good."

Hartmann fondly patted the brow of inch-thick steel that frowned over the alloy grill. The Mastodon engine cowling stood higher than he did, from steel-shod carbon tires to hood latches large enough to have come from a maritime museum.

"She'll eat it," Hartmann said. "Won't you, sugar. You'll soon shake the stiffness out of your springs."

The truck had an ambience that went with Alex's new

image of himself, the amalgam of masculine roles that he now wore as snugly as hand-forged armor. Stepping close to the vehicle, Alex inspected the squat, deep-tread tires, the crescents of bolts and bray-headed rivets, laser-welded double-safe seams, and the all-around stalk fender of curious teak-colored alloy. Two, perhaps three, thousand miles across the hinterlands of America in the Mastodon. He felt excitement at the challenge, a kind of four-color, crude-print sensation like being rollered out in one's own comix serial.

Grinning, he peered around the prow at Dowd Hartmann.

"When do we leave?" he asked.

"Soon as you like," Hartmann told him.

"Okay, old man," Alex said. "Let's pack and shove off."

Dowd Hartmann chuckled.

"If you shake it, son," he said, "we can hit the trail by noon."

The old man dropped the last of the cereal sacks into the back door of the truck. Alex grabbed it by the ears and wove it up the narrow aisle between roped and tarpaulined methane canisters and kerosene cans. The fuel was padded with all the foodstuffs that the old man's credit would allow, plus bedrolls, cooking pots, and much other gear. Dunnage bags were stacked high against the inner alloy partition and even covered the plexiglass window.

Now that he had examined the interior of the Mastodon Alex understood the true meaning of durability. She was built like one of the guerrilla Leviathans which, he dimly recalled, had been capable of flattening guardposts as if they were birds' nests, and had created a thunder in the city streets through which they passed to support the civilian uprisings.

Alex climbed out of the back and hopped to the ground. He looked nervously down the track toward the Dealersville junction. The factory was only a quarter mile away, though the trees still gave adequate cover.

"What did they say in the store?" he asked.

"Didn't say much: they figure I'm up to something, though."

"Did you tell them you had company?" Alex said.

"Nup," said Hartmann, also glancing back. "Listen, let's heave the lead, son. We've got all we need now."

The men climbed into the cabin from separate wings, Dowd Hartmann taking the wheelside. Maps were clipped to a navigator's plinth by Alex's deep, padded seat. The old man paused, his hands, in heavy leather gloves, passive on the wheel. He had driven the vehicle down from Bellerophon as cautiously as if he were running her over the scum ice of Parima Lake. But now there were other factors, not just the unfamiliar feel of the wheel, the pulse of the engine, and the chug of automated transmission already plugged into the low-gear synchronizer. There were beginnings, and endings.

Dowd Hartmann looked good, seated high over the wheel, gnarled and determined, salted with rich experience of unknown terrain and not afraid of the hazards it would disgorge. He took a lungful of air and reached for the panel switch which would choose Reverse and, with an audible whining hum, jet power to the wheels.

The Mastodon sat up a little, and you could feel it bite into the earth. Hartmann punched the brake block on its angled podium. The weight of the truck sagged forward a couple of inches, then took up. With Dowd fisting the wheel, she curved backward, crowding arid shrubs by the track's verge to bathe her roof with russet leaves and a rain of needles from an isolated pine.

Hartmann threw the switch once more.

Dials and gauges and the digital data strip with its bold white-on-black numerals and alphabet letters came alight as Hartmann's gloved thumb tripped a tumbler and his fist slid the gears into forward contact.

Mingled with the scent of the trees, and the sweetish aroma which rose from the factory vents, was the clean, flushing odor of kerosene. As the Mastodon began to haul uphill, though, that smell was replaced by a warm, metallic effluvium which prevailed so long as the truck was in motion. It somehow made Alex's blood sing.

It took ten minutes to crawl four miles uphill to the second junction, hardly a junction at all, only a branch track running awry from the main stem. Settling now, Hartmann turned the wheel and steered the steel-browed beast into the wilderness, heading on a binnacle bearing of SSE along the base of Bellerophon's dog-leg ridge. Gears meshed and adjusted below the transistored box and the springs gave a bucking shake as the massive structure hit rough.

Alex glanced at the old man.

Dowd Hartmann was grinning.

Yes, Alex thought, the sculptors of Remojadas would just love this guy.

: 3 :

DISTANCE WAS NO OBJECT to the fortunate Freemen. They controlled space and, consequently, time, utilizing them for their own advantage and, by extension, for the continuing benefit of mankind. Leased from the All-City Transport Department, Cadillac Replicas carried the Freemen from their offices about the city to the stately structure on Manhattan's tip, not 1000 yards from invincible City Hall above whose portals, indelibly stippled into the stonework, was the hapless legend: *You Do Not Have to Fight Within These Walls*—legacy of New York's penultimate mayor, a gentleman not noted for his wit.

City Hall was now used as an interdepartmental warehouse for high-value cargoes. It housed imported wines, genuine Virginia tobaccos, refined Dutch gasoline, and many nonindigenous pharmaceutical necessities which were filtered out to Montagu Centers across the eastern seaboard. The warehouse was guarded by the cream of the graduate crop of the Westchester Bureau Academy. In the opinion of most Freemen, the site could have been left wide open without danger of infiltration: no layman really understood the value of its contents. Inquisitive citizens tended to regard the Hall only as the luxury larder of the Freemen's Club in nearby Campbell Plaza. But City Hall was more than the Freemen's larder. It was also their power magazine. None of them wished to take the slightest risk with its security.

Modeled on the ground plan of the now-submerged St. Mark's square, Campbell Plaza was synonymous with the Freemen's Club. Subtle troughs and outward-sloping tiers of fine aquamarine marble protected the area. Only

89

from a distance could tourists watch the Fathers come and go up the canopied ramp which led from the Cadillac lot under the frescoed arches.

At ten A.M., NY-ST, on that bleak December morning, there were no kibitzers as Florian, under an English umbrella, hurried from the limousine up the ramp into the bullet-shaped external capsule which would jet him ten floors to the Penthouse Hexagonal. Within the great committee chamber the Freemen met every Friday night to discuss the affairs of the week and to plan for the future, a program concentrated entirely on preserving the status quo.

Though the democratic principle still prevailed in America, and all 400 of the nation's Freemen had equal voice and voting stock, for the sake of expediency pressing local matters were handled by the area "Montagues"; that is, by the two Freemen who jointly controlled and managed the Montagu Centers, Booster Stations, and the whole complex procedure of acquisition, manufacture, distribution, and administration of Endurance Serum. The Serum had first been successfully processed by the late Professor Alfred Montagu, an expatriate Englishman, in the Lavater Research Clinic in Oregon, to which sanctuary the professor had been lured by the promise of big money.

New York's own Montagues, Furneaux and Faulkner, hospitably greeted Florian on his emergence from the elevator hatch. Flanking him, they led him past the day-porter's booth into the Hexagonal chamber. By chance, all three men had elected to wear London Style morning suits and two-inch band collars with Freemen's cravats, not too full, displayed in the vees of the dove-gray weskits. All three pairs of black calfskin shoes squeaked just a little as the trio crossed the enormous antique Wilton carpet and seated themselves at the circular table where such business, by tradition, was usually conducted. It was this very table, sixty-one years ago, that Faneuil had been admonished in the biggest scandal ever to shake the Club and had voluntarily exiled himself to the Transalpine Embassy in Zurich where he now worked out his second century as a purchaser of art-treasure rights, a menial post without power.

The black box was put in full view upon the table as an indication that the Freemen intended to record the proceedings. Florian had anticipated that they would. As the black box was on direct link to a pitch analyzer, he realized that he would be obliged to keep himself in total control if he hoped to fool the sensitive machine, let alone Furneaux and Faulkner.

Now on the brink of the last phase of life, Furneaux had a thin, beaky face and very slender, elegant hands. In fact, he was distantly related to Alfred Montagu, via a chain of cousins, though this ancestral claim could be made by ninety percent of the nation's Freemen. Montagu had not been one of your postdynastic Englishmen and battalions of blood relatives had accompanied him on his emigrant flight. Most of the family had married well or in some way made social capital out of Alfred's genius. Certainly Furneaux resembled the Montagu clan survivors with that aesthetic, ducal skull, and heronlike frame. He also wore London Style better than anybody else alive.

Originally Faulkner was a hand-hammered Pennsylvanian. He had the bluff manner of a fourth-generation legal eagle and the habit of folding his arms and standing spread-legged like a philosophical colossus. Though a couple of decades younger than Furneaux, Faulkner was one of the very few Freemen on the All-City roster to have purchased his status. Faulkner sported a genuine saberslash mustache and groomed his long, dark hair into ravenstail held in place by a proprietary fixative. His morning coat had sateen lapels. His gray weskit was braided with peachstone thread. Dead center of his cravat was the silver stud that marked him as the father of a child.

Faulkner had snuck in under the legislative wire by coldbloodedly impregnating the sixteen-year-old granddaughter of Cyril Montagu, the family's marketing exponent, twenty-four hours before the Preservation Bill became law. He had thoughtfully acquired an eyewitness notary's statement to prove time and date, thereby avoiding charges of breach of Ethical Behavior in the process of securing himself a son, Blake. In time Blake would assume his father's name and be elected a Freeman. Faulkner made no bones that he intended to retire early from public life and devote his energies, and welter of credit connections, to perfecting cybernetic judicial systems that would prove absolutely infallible.

Faulkner switched on the black box.

Furneaux said, "We would be grateful if you would explain, Florian, why one of your Laureates has been

91

permitted to travel by irregular means, and without proper authorization, out of New York."

Florian said, "It was done with my knowledge: indeed, at my instigation."

"Quite!" said Furneaux, dryly. "Why?"

"To obtain information on the circumstances surrounding the death of Eugene Morello."

"There are channels, you know, Florian," said Faulkner.

"I did not err," said Florian. "I planned the circumvention of Bureau channels."

"Why?"

All flowery conversational hypocrisies were swept aside at this level. Florian's voice timbre was negative, perhaps a shade acerbic. He had decided that to act guiltily was to court too full an investigation into all his sundry schemes. His plump, pink features were implacable. He could have been scanned by a whole bank of sensors and still have passed through their probes as honest.

"Why?" said Florian. "I will explain why in one moment, gentlemen. First let me outline the progress which I inaugurated three decades ago and which, if you will bear with me, will soon come to a successful and indisputably beneficial conclusion."

"You may explain, Florian," said Faulkner, "in any way and at any length you choose. We're entirely at your disposal for the rest of the day."

"I am after Narvaez," Florian stated.

"Narvaez?" Faulkner and Furneaux repeated in unison.

"I feel that the Bureau has lost the opportunity of stemming the revolutionary faction in the central part of the continent and, if I need an excuse for taking it upon myself, I'm anxious to protect the papyrus harvests in the Yucatan Peninsula, from which course, as you know, the main documentation and distributor centers are provided with their staple supply."

"Narvaez hasn't threatened the papyrus," said Faulkner.

"He has no army," said Furneaux.

"Yet," said Florian, cryptically.

"There is absolutely no scenario for military, even for Ethical revolution," said Faulkner. "There is no Mexican junta to overthrow. Never has been. Since the unfortunate cessation of the renovation program, our Central American sector has been passive. As you may recall, it was decided that, in view of its historical precedents, all Central and

92

South American terrains would be controlled from defocalized bases, that no urban reconstruction would be undertaken. Narvaez has never been a serious threat to us, and never will be."

"I—we—cannot understand your obsession with Mexico, Florian," said Furneaux.

"I would hardly call it an obsession," said Florian. "My interest stems, I suppose, from heightened historical awareness due to my youthful studies at the Toynbee. I will plead guilty, gentlemen, to a belief in the intrinsic vulnerability of the body corporate."

Furneaux gave a simpering smile. "By others less acquainted with your background, Florian, that statement might be construed as heretical."

Florian said, "To paraphrase Gorgon Tasker: *Heresies may come, heresies may go, but put bread on my table and clothes on my back and I will refute them all by total indifference to the fate of my ethical soul.*"

"Tasker was not infallible, Florian," said Faulkner. "Why, the fellow wasn't even Caucasian."

"I'll now explain why I want Narvaez scotched," said Florian, "and my long-range, long-term plans for the cleansing of Mexico."

"The cleansing of Mexico." Furneaux raised his brows in an expressive arch. "I did not realize that Mexico was in need of cleansing. However, do continue."

"The Bureau and the three Institutes cannot—repeat cannot—program Narvaez's movements, a situation that has obtained for almost thirty years.

"But without Serum boosters Narvaez cannot last long. He will be into middle life by now," Faulkner said. "He may even be dead."

"No, he is very much alive," Florian went on. "Many parts of the middle continent are not merely hinterland but waste—jungle, swamp, arid deserts, burned-out plague spots, and the carbuncle plains of nuclear skirmishes. There is, as we know, a profusion of mineral and other riches buried in Mexico in addition to relics, ancient and modern. A single Narvaez type in control of such a treasure house of potential power might be dangerous. At the very least he could cut some of our supply lines. Since the Bureau and the Institutes lost him and showed no inclination to find him again, I took it upon myself to do so. I

93

pride myself that I have now tracked him down—not a month too soon."

Faulkner stroked his mustache thoughtfully. "What do you mean, Florian: not a month too soon?"

"Revolt is simmering, gentlemen," Florian said. "Narvaez is preparing to strike."

Faulkner glanced at Furneaux, but the latter was apparently unimpressed.

Faulkner said, "Strike where, at what, and with whom?"

"He is in the Veracruz region," said Florian. "He has a small army with him, spread throughout the coastal area but ready to his call . . ."

"The target, Florian," interrupted Faulkner impatiently. "What is his target?"

"The Booster Station at Veracruz."

"If this is true," said Furneaux, "then obviously he must be stopped."

Faulkner growled, "I don't believe you, Florian."

Florian spread one pink palm to the ceiling, as if testing for rain. "Will you wait for proof, Faulkner? And risk the loss of the only Dissemination Center in southwest Mexico?"

"Your source of information, Florian?" snapped Furneaux.

"Eugene Morello."

"But . . . ?"

"Morello was killed by Narvaez, nine weeks ago," said Florian.

"We were led to believe that Morello had taken his own life," said Faulkner.

"Morello was an agent," Florian said.

"Belonging to whom?" said Furneaux.

"He was *my* agent," said Florian. *"My* on-the-spot 'undercover' man in the central region. I regard the Bureau's indifference as culpable in this affair."

Furneaux wetted his lips with the tip of his tongue. "If what you say is true, Florian, then indeed the Bureau is due for censure."

"Why did you not bring the matter before the Club?" asked Faulkner.

"The Club does not altogether favor me," said Florian. "It is unlikely that I would have been taken seriously. Can you, in honesty, deny that, gentlemen?"

Furneaux made another simpering, noncommittal sound.

Faulkner said, "It's quite true, Florian. The sympathies of the Club as a whole would have leaned to accepting the Bureau reports."

"When Morello was assassinated," Florian said, "I knew that the information he had been passing to me was accurate. He was a brave man, a daring man, in a society that does not altogether favor daring."

"How did he communicate?"

"Through a Riss-Interlink Portable Transceiver," said Florian. "Ostensibly, he fed his work into that to be revised and edited by Blunt, his partner. In fact, we tapped off Morello's original messages intact. They contained a simple code. That was the important part of each transrecording—the parts that Blunt invariably edited out."

"Rather ingenious," admitted Furneaux, grudgingly.

"So," Faulkner said, "you sent Blunt after the killers?"

"I did," said Florian.

"A strange choice," said Faulkner. "I've met Blunt once or twice. He did not strike me as being a suitable choice for a situation requiring 'daring,' and possibly ingenuity."

"Blunt is perfect for the task," said Florian. "He has been schooled for thirty years. On the surface he is as foursquare a Bachelor as you can find in the All-City State. But beneath he is cold, ruthless, and utterly dedicated to tracing the assassins of his beloved partner Eugene Morello."

"Blunt and Morello did not much care for each other," said Faulkner. "That is common gossip."

"Gossip should never be taken at face value," said Florian. "I scripted it that Blunt and Morello should *appear* to be incompatible. I had hoped that I would never have to put Blunt into the field, and I have deliberately kept him in the dark about Narvaez . . ."

"He knows nothing?" said Furneaux in surprise.

"Nothing."

"Then how can he function?" said Furneaux.

"By instinct."

Furneaux looked slightly pained: instinct offended him. His professional pride would not allow the acknowledgment that instinct still existed in his fellow men. The Montagu Centers had wiped it out.

Florian said, "Blunt has not been Serum boosted for five years."

"On whose authority?" demanded Furneaux.

Florian realized that he was close to overstepping himself. He had one card still to play: the Magus card. He played it now, boldly.

Stretching out his hand, he deliberately switched off the black box. A red light blazed and the device droned to indicate that it had not been coded out verbally. Florian would leave Faulkner to eradicate that piece of evidence.

Florian said, "I am surprised, gentlemen, that you have not asked me the most pertinent question of all."

Faulkner growled again. "How does Narvaez know that the Veracruz center is a target worth taking? And, Florian, how did *you* first draw wind of this danger?"

"I regret to inform you, my friends, that one of our colleagues is a traitor."

Furneaux slumped back into the club chair, aghast. Faulkner rose, the chair tilting away from him. He folded his arms across his chest.

"A Freeman? A traitor?"

Calmly, Florian said, "Possibly not a Freeman, but certainly a high-placed executive in the Bureau."

Faulkner glared at Florian. "I trust that you have proof of that accusation."

"No, I have no proof at all," said Florian. "That's why I have chosen to handle the matter personally. It is my prerogative to do so, gentlemen, as—loosely speaking—it can be said to affect my department."

"A disloyal executive is a matter of grave concern to us all," said Faulkner. Furneaux still seemed stunned by the enormity of Florian's suggestion. "It should have been raised at a Friday meeting."

"And," said Florian, "what if one of our members *is* a traitor?"

Slowly groping behind him to position the chair, Faulkner sat down again. He looked at the apertures of the black box, then activated it. "Transmission suspended," he said. The red light went out and the droning clicked off.

"Yes, Florian," he said. "I appreciate your dilemma. But do you trust *us?*"

"I might say that I have no option but to trust you," Florian told the Philadelphian. "But the truth is, gentlemen, that I welcomed this opportunity to put the affair before you, and you alone. If Montagues cannot be trusted then our whole society is doomed."

"I would . . . like . . . need . . . proof," muttered Furneaux, "to put to the Friday meeting."

"No," Florian said. "I would urge you to hold off before bringing the matter to light within the Club. You may be assured that once I can point the bone at somebody and back up my accusations with substantial evidence, then I will immediately do so. This is not the kind of power-wielding situation that I relish, my friends."

"Do you imply that one of our officers is using this Mexican bandit, this Narvaez, as a tool?" said Faulkner.

"That is my belief," said Florian.

"But . . . but . . . how will we discover the truth?" said Furneaux.

"By laying hands on Narvaez and making him talk."

Faulkner was nodding again. "And who will lay hands on Narvaez for us?"

"My agent in the field," said Florian.

"You mean, Alexander Blunt?"

"Precisely."

"Where is he now?" asked Faulkner.

"Now," said Florian, "I imagine he is halfway to Veracruz."

"Alone?"

"Oh, yes," said Florian. "Quite alone."

: 4 :

DOWD HARTMANN DECIDED to risk the broken-surfaced turnpike, trail of drovers, rovers, and raiders, the outlaws and *bandidos* who had trotted forth and back across the fluctuating border of North America and the States of lawless Mexico. The Mastodon bypassed sad little shanty-towns, negotiated unsafe bridges over steep-walled canyons and broad rivers, chopping the corner off old Arizona, hooking away into the desert in the neighborhood of Phoenix and Tucson, forging on across the base of old New Mexico to the notorious spot where El Paso and Juárez had once scowled at each other across the scorched hallmarks of fission skirmishers who had waged long and reeking battles across the slow old river, motivelessly blazing away with napalm and—later, when other lunatic factions ran out of causes and trooped to join the fray down south—with lasers and prop-mortars and two-man missile dischargers. Then the plague came on the desert wind and strangled the handful of madmen who remained entrenched in deep-dug bunkers twelve miles apart, and gouged out their lungs as they lay moaning on their bedrolls hugging their ugly weapons to their chests and still crying, pointlessly, for blood.

Not surprisingly, nobody much came this way now, not for seventy years or more. Landways' haulers had themselves a brand-new highway stemming off from Chihuahua on a line west of the Casa Grandes, through the old Sonora territory to Nogales and Tucson. The ancient drove roads were barely navigable, cracked along the spines, cleaving through blistered rocks and charred barren prairies; for the most part, though, no worse than they must have been two centuries ago in the galloping days of legend.

Alex tolled off the route along the thread of the Rio Grande, heading on down the shelving foothills of the Sierra Madre's southern flanks on abandoned feeders into Monterrey. He had shed his Hurons, though he dragged them on again to sleep for the nights were very cold. Fourteen, fifteen hours a day Dowd Hartmann drove the Mastodon, sometimes peaking it to forty MPH but most often creeping and sneaking at ten and fifteen over rubbled roads or scything wide into sand and stony scrubland. He drove tirelessly, talking all the while with indefatigable eloquence in his role as mentor to the maverick who had given him cause to ride out again across the landscapes that, in a half dozen seasons in his prime, he had grown to love—carbuncles, plague holes, and all. He indoctrinated Blunt in history, political philosophy, economics, geography, and a smidgen of religion. He informed him how the Freemen had come into power, growing out of vast conglomerate corporations which, through the shrewd application of cash-money, had effectively steered America's destiny into ignoring the rampant lawlessness and encroaching poverty that gutted the pride and resilience of the nation. He told how, in a welter of insurrections and guerrilla invasions, the conglomerates had secured a grip on sources of essential supplies; how entertainment was gradually transformed into propaganda; how the electoral system was undermined by corruption; how the Isolationists, fueled by corporation money, won the day, and how that day was turned into night by famine, sickness, and war all across the land. He told how, at the end of that period, the Washington Government had finally admitted that the old system of democracy was no longer valid and had indicated a willingness to hand over the reins to the Founding Freemen who were lurking in the wings. He told Alex how political economy had then become a matter of mastering the arts of multiplication and division, addition and subtraction having become redundant.

Alex had asked for an explanation.

Hartmann said, "The Freemen had already imported the Montagu family from England. It was the development of Montagu's Endurance Serum that really changed the world. Partial immortality. Think of it, Alex. To a sick, weary, demoralized people, suddenly the offer not only of healthy stability, of enough to eat and the assurance of peace to eat it, but the promise of a couple of hundred years of living, and the hint that at the end of that time the paramedical boys would have perfected a means of injecting you with a couple of centuries more."

"That's the power, then?" said Alex.

"Nup," said Hartmann. "The power stems from the Serum, but it's not the Serum itself. It's what the Serum *does* that makes the whole hell-bound system work."

"Health and happiness?" said Alex. "Hell-bound?"

"Don't you see yet, son? The Serum is administered to *every* child, woman, and man in the civilized world. It not only furnishes health and a long life, it also weeds out the human so-called failings of greed, avarice, sexual desire, aggression, and all but the most acceptable ambitions. In the hinterland there are no social strata. That's for the city gents, a pecking order, a ladder to the executive washroom; the definable hierarchy, an invention of the corporate state which the Freemen could not bring themselves to live without."

"The Montagu Serum does all this?" asked Alex, dubiously.

"Think about it," said Hartmann. "Bachelors of this class, that class: status hands. How many mothers do you know?"

"It's done for our good, our benefit. There just isn't enough raw material to go . . ."

"Ten American cities," Hartmann interrupted. "Each urban area has a controlled population of a quarter million; a grand total of two and one-half millions. Outside the city-states the booster registers give a hinterland census, accurate to within one percent, of another twelve and a half million, covering the whole land mass from Nome to Panama."

"So?"

"In the 1988 census the gross population of metropolitan New York alone came to more than that."

"It's common knowledge that we were overcrowded. That's what led to the high criminal behavior rate and the awful rise in anti-Ethical factions."

"Balls!" said Hartmann. "This huge continent was built to accommodate more than fifteen million. The point, Alex, is that fifteen million is a nice, neat, round number, and readily controllable. Fifteen million units are kept real passive by the boosters. All the old human foibles are consequently reduced. Revered Hebraic proverbs just don't apply any more. *Thou shalt not covet thy neighbor's wife's ass:* it don't mean a thing. The cynics—when there was still room for cynicism—used to say that the jacks and jills just got what they asked for, that they were wide, wide open for that kind of state dictatorship, sheepherding on the grand scale. Yup, maybe the cynics were right. Instead of booze, narcotics, games of chance, simulated skill sports, violence, sexual grafting of all kinds, coffee klatches, conventions, lodges and unions and guilds, we now have a small stable society divided into three distinct layers. *And kept that way.* The Freemen, the status hands, and the casuals: it's as simple a structure as you can get. And it works. Life is so pleasant that you don't need the PTA, the Knights of Columbus, the country club, the myriad substitutes for the Cosa Nostra that were the threads in the fabric a century back, yardsticks by which to measure your identity. You don't need them now because your ego, to use the archaic term, seems secure."

"But that's marvelous," said Alex. "That's the Golden Age. What's your . . . your beef, Dowd?"

"Secure like corpses in coffins," Hartmann said.

"A cruel and unfair analogy."

"Sure, there's some good mixed in the bad."

"Agreed," said Alex. "We all of us, even casuals, have security, a roof, space to ourselves, food in our stomachs, and 200 years of health."

"But not vigor."

"What's vigor got to do with it?"

"Vigor is change: vigor is progress: vigor is some little horseplayer along Fifth Avenue feeling like God because his pony came in on a longshot in the fourth at Hialeah. Vigor is a Polack teamster blowing his roll on a hooker and a snootful of Jack Daniels in a weekend rave. That's vigor."

"That's ignorance."

"Bliss."

"Balls!" said Alex, cribbing the expletive

"The human condition should be bedded in the so-called vices, the ignorance, the laziness, the aggression, the greed, the selfishness. Out of that broth grows progress. Where the hell are we going now?"

"Monterrey."

"I don't mean that: I mean, where the shit *is* progress?"

"Don't ask me."

"Nup," said Hartmann. "I ain't asking you, Alex. I'm only asking you to ask yourself."

"Ask myself what?"

"What are you—Bachelor, Laureate class—doing here?"

Alex hesitated. He looked blankly through the big windscreen at the long, granular stretch of cracked tarmac which ran ribbon-straight toward a ripple of distant mountains. The sky was vast and baby blue and the cactus plants stood up tall and gaunt. There was no apparent sign of life; yet he could feel life. Even with the absence of figures in that panorama, he could still feel the pulse of life—within himself. It was a whole new bagful of sensations, each one linked like capillaries to that source pulse.

Defensively, he said, "I was forced out of that system by circumstances."

"But circumstances, like the birth rate, are under total control," said Hartmann. "Breakouts are summarily dealt with by the B. of E. or one of the City Institutes. Listen, son, the Freemen allowed the world to burn itself out. It wasn't that they did much, they just didn't do anything to prevent it. Look at Mexico, for instance. War, plague, famine, floods, earthquakes, volcanic eruptions—there's nothing new in those scores. This time out, though, we did nothing. We didn't feed the hungry, cure the sick, evacuate the stricken areas, rehouse, repopulate, and then rebuild. We let well enough alone; let natural wastage occur. We adjusted the technology to keep the population figure down to two percent of what it had been. We applied all our considerable know-how to shrink the frontiers. We can keep a mere fifteen million alive forever, provided we keep them apart. The natural resources of this continent are so overprotected that they will last out the goddamn universe, never mind our solar system. It's the Golden Age all right, gotten by the Midas Touch."

"I didn't study mythopology."

"Forget it: forget it, son," said Hartmann, impatiently. "The further we move from the fixed spiritual points that have obtained in one form or another from the time the first Java Ape Man sunk his teeth in a fricasseed neighbor and liked the taste so much he made the delicacy taboo; from the first rap in the mouth with a knucklebone for getting too fresh with a female anthropoid, from the first slave-master to the last pensioned accountant in the meanest Wall Street brokerage, the further we *drift* along the channel marked out for us by the Freemen and their kith in other national zones, the more difficult it will become for us to return. Soon, when my generation, Alex, is quietly expiring in front of a video-screen, exchanging one kind of sleep for another: soon, in a century or less, it'll be too late. Nobody will remember how it was before. They will believe, as you believed, that the old times were the bad times and that passivity, contentment, security, and a two-, three-century descent from birth into death are all that man has to hope for. Jesus, son, don't you see how we're being robbed of our capacity to struggle, to suffer pain and grief and the anguish of desire? Eventually we will be born without souls and that'll be how it is until the sun cools and sucks in on itself and quietly draws the planet to its jet-black bosom."

Alex said nothing.

The sun sat low on the western horizon, streaking cirrus clouds that had gathered on the edge of the twilight with gold flame, scarlet, and a beautiful, glistening blue, like the colors of a dolphin's back. Even as he watched, it threw out a dazzling coronet of fire. Hartmann thumbed down the dimmer-switch and spread a smoky amber stain through the plexiglass. It was easy now on the eyes, but the landscape had changed, excluding where the two men were. Though they traveled on through it, they were no longer a part of it.

"It won't always be like that," Alex said, softly. "Surely something will go wrong. Somebody will . . . will come along who's different."

"Look around, son, and hope that the next guy will be less indifferent than you: huh?"

"What do you want me to do about it? I'm not the guardian of the goddamn future," Alex snapped.

"Can you be sure, son?"

Alex opened his mouth, and left it open. Dusk was flooding across the desert, its all-encompassing shadow visible even through the tinted glass sandwich.

"I only want to find out what happened to Morello."

"That'll do just dandy," Hartmann said, grinning. "You can bet that circumstances will take it from there."

"Let's camp now, Dowd: I'm tired," Alex said.

In fact, he wasn't tired at all—but he was uncertain. He

wanted to do some thinking, solitary, motionless thinking. The truth was that he was no longer sure that he was still playing a role. He was in process of becoming someone else.

For some unfathomable reason, Dowd Hartmann was counting on that.

Florian crossed the low-eaved foyer and entered the bee-hive entrance into the servicing basements of the Florian Building. There was no big deal down there, nothing that interested parties, which meant the rest of the Freemen, could fail to uncover by inspection. But Florian, broad-caster of all sorts of news, views, and entertainments, did not see fit to broadcast just what he kept at the root of the building in addition to pressers, shredders, thermal-extractors, and storage cylinders. The main room lay behind a baffle wall of sea-green concrete. It was as broad as a baseball diamond and as long as a basketball court, though the analogy was meaningless since both sports, and most others, had long since been supplanted by games in which the participants had no opportunity to commit acts of physical and psychic violence, to say nothing of squandering energy.

At Florian's approach, the jade door slid open. He entered the basement section briskly, cloaking anxiety with eagerness. Some anxiety was left over from the interrogation with Furneaux and Faulkner an hour ago, but subtle additions were made by the proximity of Volpe and Slattery, two gentlemen whose auras made most folk uncomfortable and who, consequently, worked and lived as close as Siamese twins.

Isolation helped plate their consciences and increase their restrained hostility. In every outward aspect, however, Volpe and Slattery were models of social propriety. Their names appeared on all the right rosters: they turned up punctually for their boosters and shared the same credit rating to the last pack of Menthols. They had a mutual minder to tend their luxurious liner up on Central Park West, but neither man had ever clapped an eye on her, nor she on them, which was probably just as well. The pair had been with Florian since their college graduation, a hundred seasons ago, and had proved hilt-loyal to the Company and their benefactor.

Volpe was descended from a Middle European literary

critic and belletrist, a rarefied hatchet man who had driven many a turn-of-the-century poet to drink, despair, and death, but had not apparently passed on his sterile talent as a litterateur to his only son. Volpe had golden hair and zinc-colored eyes, rather like the young woman into whose belly he had plunged his knife only a couple of months ago. He also had a broad, handsome, virile throat. You noticed the throat, all strong and veined, before you remarked the face, which really did not match up to the promise of its supporting column, being flat and plain and slightly shorn away in the region of the chin. The skull was too small in circumference for the wedge-shaped, muscular body. It might have been the unhappy result of one of those infamous transplant experiments of the 1990s, only Volpe would have been too young then to have endured nineteen hours under the scalpels with his own head in a jar while the new one was persuaded to adhere and function. No, Volpe's brain was his own, the thoughts in it his own, too, except for those he elected to share with Slattery. Nobody ever knew what went on between the pair, except that when they talked within earshot the subject was usually about death in one of its less inevitable manifestations.

Slattery was a second-generation Anglo-American-Irish-Teuton, a fascinating ethnic stew which had given endless hours of amusement to the biogeneticists in the Women's Block in Folsom, where Slattery had been born minutes after his mother had been executed for treason. (A real neurotic militant with the moral sense of a squid, the judge described her in his address to the jury shortly before pronouncing sentence for her part in the Albuquerque Massacre.) The Celtic part of Slattery seemed to be in constant rebellion against the Prussian. Only the gelatinous shell of genes inherited from a Boston grandfather and Bristol-born grandmother, on his mama's side, prevented the other halves of his primitive personality from spilling out all over the prison orphanage. In a previous century Slattery might have become an enduring legend by dancing on the gallows tree at an even earlier age than William H. Bonney, though it's questionable if he would have had as much fun getting there. Slattery was born joyless, without a heartsfold (medically attested: microslides on record) in his brain. Shorter than national average, he was dark haired, dark eyed, and had a soul like a hold in a coal cargo boat,

105

if he had any kind of soul at all. If circumstances had shaped his destiny differently he would have been a natural for the lead in Shoball's *The Temptation of Mephistopheles;* only the adult Slattery, like the child, would not have uttered a single note much less a word of the lyric in case it was recorded and later used against him. Slattery walked in silence like a small, swarthy, secret, hostile cloud.

Even Volpe, his noncorporeal lover, had never been treated to a sentence of more than five consecutive words. It didn't matter much to the success of their professional partnership, which seemed blessed with a sinister composite intelligence that resulted not only from being on the same temperamental wave band but from 100 seasons' arduous practice in the arts and skills for which Florian had adopted them, educated them, and given them status; arts like that of totally silent entry into an occupied liner, and skills like that of dipping a nine-inch steel skewer through the abdominal wall of a sleeping female so that the first angled thrust killed her stone dead, and the second, third, and fourth drew just enough blood to etch the scene vividly in the mind of her male companion.

"Good afternoon, my boys," said Florian, breezily. He always breezed in the presence of his wards. They were such a physical pair, in an almost ethereal world, that their solidity disconcerted him. "And how are we today?"

"We are well, Florian, thank you," Volpe said.

They waited.

They had turned in unison on Florian's entry and stood like two figures on a single cross, the Firebow Mercury pistols upright in left and right hands, Slattery having been born a sinistral among his other natural attributes.

The roar of the eight visible inches of thickly falling water behind the targets (required to absorb and disperse the velocity of the mercury balls) set up a strange vibrating echo in the basement offshoot that housed the range.

Florian was almost tempted to raise his voice, something he did not do often. He glanced toward the targets, which could only just be picked out by the naked eye due to a prismatic arrangement that greatly increased the focal perspective so that the manshapes were only an inch high against a distractingly active thread of water.

"Would you . . . er, like to demonstrate for Uncle Florian?" he tentatively requested.

The young men pivoted at once and, as the Firebows'

aligners grazed and steadied on the targets, squeezed the trigger wires. Everything was simultaneous, men and weapons in complete harmony. The inch-high manshapes exploded into the narrow waterwall.

Almost at once a video-screen on the blank wall of the range lit up, showing frame-by-frame the last moment's travel of the two phosphorescent balls and their splash, at precisely the same millisecond, onto the manikins' painted sternums. Jagged fragments of brittle plastic starred out, then, driven backward by the spreading mercury, retreated into the rippling curtain of water.

Volpe and Slattery pivoted again, saluting with the long-barreled pistols, their faces devoid of all pride in their remarkable accomplishment.

Florian laughed uneasily. He would have patted one of them on the back but neither could stand to be touched. The video was repeating the feat of marksmanship, a slow ballet of beautiful, harmless violence.

"Unerring skill," Florian said. "Absolutely unerring." He meant "deadly" but wouldn't say the word.

Still the pair waited, like androids, to be instructed and set in motion. Slattery's eyes were hooded a little and Florian gave his attention to Volpe, who was the spokesman and the less unapproachable of the two.

"How would you like a trip?" asked Florian, rubbing his hands as if to encourage enthusiasm.

Volpe almost nodded.

"The central belt: Mexico," Florian went on. "Have you visited there before, boys?"

"Yes," answered Volpe.

"Now when was that? Ah, yes, I remember, back in the summer of '49: that business in Hidalgo. You . . . er, won't find it quite so uncomfortably hot at this season. Besides, you are going to the coast, to the seaport of Veracruz. It's quite cool and pleasant at this time of year, I believe. Linens would be best, however, with a nice warm jerkin or a sweater for evening wear. I expect you'll be there for several days, perhaps even a week."

Florian paused, vainly hoping for a response.

None was forthcoming. He went on, "You will report to Smolkin in the Florian Station there. You will travel on a Landways in place of two of the crew. You *can* drive? Yes, of course you can. You will travel directly. The Landways' freighter is an express, returning from Gabrielsgate with the season's tapes for the outpost relays. That's all it will carry: the tapes—and you."

Volpe said, "Equipment, sir?"

"Hum!" said Florian. "Pack light stuff, I think. It's a watching brief but you may be required to . . . ah, conduct a . . . ah . . ."

"On whom?"

"A fellow called Blunt, Alexander Blunt."

"Who will finger?" asked Volpe.

"Smolkin. I will confer with you and pass my instructions through the Studio."

"Understood."

"Incidentally," said Florian, "I advise you not to ignore Narvaez. You remember Narvaez? I don't want any . . . er, accidents to the principals until you have studied the situation and reported back to me."

"But Blunt is a potential target?" said Volpe.

"Indeed," said Florian. "Sooner or later, they are all potential targets. But I must have the package first. After we have the package, the ROT faction may strike again, if you follow me. Bring in Morello, too."

"Understood."

"Oh yes, there's one other: an old man, Dowd Hartmann," Florian said. "You can take him out at any time. He has served his function. I no longer need him."

"Narvaez, Morello, Blunt, and Hartmann," said Volpe. His voice had a knell-like quality. Just behind him on the video-screen the plastic breastbones splintered yet again under the onslaught of the slow silver balls.

: 5 :

As the Mastodon dove deeper into the Gulf Coast states, Dowd Hartmann fell silent. It was not that the springs of his eloquence had dried, merely that the changing landscape stunned him with ruminative wonder. It occurred to him that perhaps some divine destiny had at last come into its own, that the great central belt of the American continent had been created to end thus, half wild, half tamed, the debris of tribal dynasties indiscriminately smeared by time and climate into a vast pastoral fantasy.

Even the meager scatterings of people—mestizos, Indians, and criollos—were like part of the land, not owning it nor owned by it, just mutely tolerated. Peons all, they were held in thrall by an utterly indifferent god who permitted no glimpses of heaven, promised no celestial rewards. The prevailing spirits had no tangible calendars and rites, the silken ropes of promise by which previous conquistadores had bound the vanquished. The only conquistadores were now Time and Nature, deities who, in the guise of rain, heat, and storm, viruses, bacteria, and hostile spirochetes, had withered the populace and made it, like the earth, ripe for regeneration under the Freemen's studied regime. There were no more fiestas, no gaudy markets. The last civic monument had been unveiled seventy years ago. Trumpets, marimbas, and guitars had been tossed aside to rust, or broken and burned to ward off the bitter cold. Though that period of physical anguish was over, not much replaced it in the hinterland, only squared crops of timber, maize, sugar cane, wheat, coffee, and fruit, the tidy abundance required to fuel the husbandmen and provide the lordlings of the city-states with all life's little luxuries.

Among the ancient halls, temples, pyramids, tombs, courts, colossi, and eternal steps lay other ruins of stone and stucco, all that remained of churches dedicated to the worship of the Virgin and Her Son. Cheek by jowl with sacred wreckage stood abandoned hotels, peeling and awry, overgrown haciendas, rugged airstrips and deserted ore towns, the flat-patterned hulks of cities on whose outskirts only did the keepers of the crops dare live. Baroque cathedrals, office blocks, and graceful aqueducts slid and sank piecemeal into tilth, less enduring than the oxidized tanks of neglected oil refineries and the rusted towers of sulfur works. Between the arable plantations everything was given over to the agave, mesquite, sagebrush, saw palmetto, and the Joshua tree, patrolled by the ubiquitous vultures who thrived under every god, or none.

Out of this Mexican vista old Papan and her daughter Xochquetzal emerged in the soft, rain-wet December dawn, stepping noiselessly from the pearly mists that enveloped the jungle road down which, in a barbarous thunderstorm, the Mastodon had churned to lose itself in the narrow, creek-horned valley of Tajin.

Dowd and Alex had been straggling on in search of a back-door route to Veracruz when the headlights of the Mastodon had suddenly lit on the gigantic staircase of the Solar Year. Hartmann had braked, astonished, and, raking the steps with the stalk lamps, had tentatively identified the place as the Pyramid of Niches.

"Where the hell is that?" asked Alex.

"Near . . . Jesus, I don't know where it's near."

"Which site is this?" Alex said.

"El Tajin," said Hartmann, peering. "I recognize it, I think."

"We can't backtrack at this hour, in this goddamn weather."

A peal of thunder reverberated hauntingly over the surrounding hills and the matted jungle which encroached on the ruins and in many places absorbed them completely.

"I'm beginning to suspect that these maps of yours aren't accurate, Dowd."

Hartmann shrugged and switched off the truck's drive systems.

"You may be right, son," he said. "We'd best hole up until morning, maybe even until the weather clears. One thing's for sure, ain't nobody going to locate us here."

They slept in the back of the truck. The ground was puddled and splashy with mud between the stones and neither man, not even an old mythopologist, was keen to prowl about the ruins by torchlight in search of a snuggery to stretch out in.

By his wristband, it was a quarter of seven when Alex struggled out of his sleeping sack and, yawning, slipped from the truck to relieve himself. Fastidiously he walked a little way from the Mastodon to do so, staring up at the shrouded ruins. Only the huge principal temple with its soaring staircase of 365 steps and its balustrades which reminded him of human vertebrae, all dripping with moss and weed, stood out from the insidious vegetation. Hartmann had told him what he could about the history of the archeologists' fight to redeem the whole site from the arms of the jungle. But that kind of endeavor had foundered, like so many other enterprises, in the face of famine, war, and plague, and the jungle had stepped in quickly again to claim its own.

The creeks which flanked the valley basin were brown torrents and the dirt road down which the Mastodon had inadvertently strayed swam like a creek. All around the hills the mist clung: the *chipichipi*, Hartmann called it, the Jalapa mizzle, which spilled from the highlands forty, fifty miles south. They were close enough to Veracruz to make a swift run in—assuming they could find a route out of the valley. For the last couple of days, though, Hartmann had been advocating caution. He was more apprehensive at this stage than he had been throughout the trip, yet denied that he had a valid reason for nervousness.

Spanning the ruins and, more particularly, the fringe of jungle country around them, in search of an exit, Alex finished his business and, drawing up the collar of his Mutton jacket, lit a hand-rolled smoke with difficulty in the drizzle.

When he turned he saw them. He felt no embarrassment, no fear. Unlike the rest of the peons whom they had passed, the girl and the old woman did not back away. They stood at the corner of the ruined plaza against a gray-green backcloth of dense jungle. Quickly Alex glanced around the perimeter of the clearing in search of other Indians. But there were none, only the girl and the crone, as motionless as bas-relief, side by side at the base of the temple.

A fine green-dyed rebozo draped the girl's shoulders,

covered her bosom, and tucked into the leather belt about her waist. Beneath it was a skirt of a different green, raggedly hemmed at her knees. Her legs and feet were bare. The old woman was clad in a poncho of ocher wool, heavy and all-encompassing. On her head she wore a strangely anachronistic hat, a broad-brimmed, high-crowned affair of still-white felt with four gaudy plumes sprouting from the band. Beads of moisture clung to the brim, like ornaments of glass. Her beaked, wrinkled brown face glistened, her eyes, too, like glass, very bright.

Alex felt curiously calm.

He lifted the cigarette to his lips and drew in a long pull of smoke, staring at the couple who, for all of three minutes now, had remained stock-still.

From the door at the back of the Mastodon Dowd Hartmann studied the strangers. By chance he was dressed like them, barefoot, a blanket draped round his shoulders.

Born and bred an imperialist, Alex called out, "You speak their lingo, Dowd; ask what they want."

In plain, crisp American the old woman said, "What is the name of your conveyance?"

Hartmann answered, "It is called a Mastodon."

"And where would such a conveyance be built these days?"

"In a country to the east," said Hartmann. "By a company called Mitsukisan. But not 'these days,' ma'am. Built many seasons ago."

"How many?"

"Seventy years, maybe more."

The peons that they had encountered so far had shown no trace of hostility, indeed almost no energy at all; yet, for a moment, Alex suspected that the couple might be the vanguard of a raiding party with their eye on the Mastodon. He could understand why they might covet it, if covetousness had not been excised from human nature. The opening gambits obviously had some point. He hoped Dowd would be smart enough to interpret them.

Dowd said, "Unless I'm mistaken, ma'am, the young woman with you is of the Totonac blood, and the lineage is very pure."

The old woman said, "That is so."

Dowd said, "May I show you something?"

The girl came forward. She walked lithely, slightly—and rather endearingly—duckfooted. She had strong, smooth

112

legs and carried herself very straight. Her hair was dusky, her eyes a strange, rich brown. The shape of her face was almost heartbreakingly beautiful. Unfamiliar emotions seized Alex as he watched her cross the muddy plaza toward Hartmann.

Dowd had come down from the Mastodon, barefoot like the girl, rain sifting and soaking his faded shirt, settling like cobwebs on his grizzled hair and beard.

They met, the old man and the girl, directly below the base of the Staircase of the Solar Year, in the blue-gray-green light of dawn. It should, by rights, have happened on a beach near Veracruz, that portico to the wealth of all Mexico and all the things that the outworlders desired, and did not understand. Totonac girl in Totonac temple, protected by the aura of a century of centuries: she would come to no harm here. And neither would they, Alex thought; not from this girl, nor the wrinkled crone. There was no evil in their presence, only a subtle, almost fragrant mystery, like the pollen of the flower of the vanilla plant.

Dowd Hartmann held out his hand, palm open.

The tiny sculptured head sat there, grinning. The girl gave no sign of recognition but the old woman came forward, too, now, walking just as straight and almost as gracefully as her companion. It was difficult to gauge the hag's age. These days, nobody showed how old they really were. Dowd Hartmann held out the figure for the old woman's inspection. She smiled fondly in response to the smile on the Remojadas sculpture.

She said, "I am Papan. The girl here is called by the name of Xochquetzal, which means Flower Feather."

"I will call her Flower Feather," Hartmann said. "If that is permissible, ma'am."

"It is permissible."

"Are we the men?" Hartmann asked.

"You are the men."

"And is he alive, or dead?"

"Alive," the old woman said.

Suddenly Alex realized that they were ambassadors from Eugene Morello. How they had found them, how long they had been in Gene's sights, he did not know and could not begin to speculate. It had been a long haul down from Monterrey. Had Gene established some sort of scouting network all across the northeast and, if so, how did his spies report to him?

113

Dowd Hartmann said, "Where is the man?"

"Not far from here," the old woman replied. "Close to the township of Poza Rica."

"How long will it take us in the Mastodon?"

"No length of time. We will guide you."

"That is gracious of you, ma'am," Hartmann said. "Will you ride with us?"

"We will ride."

The old woman gestured. The girl went forward to the Mastodon. Alex was tempted to hurry forward and gallantly open the passenger door for her, but he restrained himself. Perhaps some ancient formality was involved, or a hierarchy, which prohibited such displays. He had a lot to learn. Now that he had learned one truth, that Gene was alive and that the messages spooled through the Interlink had been fakes, he found all the corollary questions of less immediate importance than making contact with the girl.

Flower Feather: the name suited her. Gene had chosen his emissaries with typical flair. Though he had worked with Morello for almost thirty years, Alex realized that they would meet now as strangers. Circumstances had changed him radically in this past month. He was prepared to admit that the former Alexander Blunt had been so four-square that he could not recognize his friends, let alone his enemies.

Dowd came toward him.

"Can we trust them?" Alex asked.

"Oh, sure, we can trust them."

"How did he do it?" Alex inquired. "How did Gene know that we would wander into this particular dead end? Or did you rendezvous here deliberately?"

"Nup," Dowd Hartmann said, frowning a little. "I only followed my nose. I had the feeling, though, that if he was alive at all he would contact us. That's the way it is down here in Mexico. That much hasn't changed, nor has your partner's penchant for drama, I guess. Who the hell else would find a purebred Totonac girl and an old condor with a name like Papan to welcome us?"

"What's so special about her name?"

"Papan was a sister of the second King Montezuma, a princess royal, *Papantzin*. She died young. Only she didn't stay dead. She was restored to life, and given the gift of prophecy as a compensation."

"It's probably a common enough name."

"Sure." Dowd Hartmann turned away.

Alex caught his arm. "What are you driving at, Dowd?"

"Call it imagination, son, but I'll wager you the Mastodon and my last half-ounce of Makins that Gene Morello didn't track us down."

"You mean . . . ?"

"She did it," Hartmann said. "That old Aztec, *she* put the grabs on us."

"But how?"

"Don't ask!" Dowd Hartmann said.

Two hours' driving coaxed the truck from the valley of El Tajin and crawled it eleven miles to the outskirts of the former industrial center of Poza Rica. The stealthy overhauling of the jungle had improved this place, raking down and burying ugly gas stacks and sulfur-stained silos, gantries and tanks and towers, together with the metal shacks of chemical-company workers and the bungalows of foremen and executives. Farther east the roofs of the main town buildings stood stark under falling rain. The Mastodon swung south at a crossroads in the deserted suburbs and crept on down the flanking wall of a wide freshwater lagoon.

It was snug in the cab. Alex sat thigh by thigh with the Mexican girl. With the exception of his single night with Miss Abbott, this was the most intimate situation he had ever been in with a person of the opposite sex. He did not think of it that way, accepting her with an awkward fusion of respect and anticipation.

She had shucked off the rebozo. Beneath it she wore a faded denim shirt with small ramshorn buttons down the center. Her breasts, full and succulent, made Alex forget that he was an impotent Bachelor of the Laureate class—whatever the hell that meant down here—so that he found himself squinting at her smooth, coppery arms and the solidity of her flanks under the tightly-tucked skirt. If Flower Feather was aware of his ungallant inspection she gave no sign of it. She was, however, neither aloof nor distant. When questioned about the route, she answered him in that same American accent as Papan used, with just a trace of prolongation on the vowel sounds.

How long had she lived in these parts?

Many years.

How long had she known Eugene Morello?
Several years.
Where was her home?
She traveled.
Was the old woman her mother?
Only a friend, a companion.
What was the weather like in Veracruz?
Variable: hot in summer, and often humid.
Had she traveled out of Mexico?
Never.

The important question—was she Morello's girl—was too pointed to ask at this stage. In fact, Alex did not frame it in those terms; not yet.

Shifting his leg to enjoy the warmth of her thigh, he peered out at the dismal landscape of the industrial suburbs and at the huge, flat gunmetal-gray reservoir around whose shore the Mastodon plowed relentlessly, bucking over the fissured concrete and into deep puddled potholes.

Up ahead a pier jutted out into the still, rain-speckled waters. A slender walkway ended in a floating platform on which was erected a drilling rig of white alloy and a cluster of shacks of the same durable material. The shacks were windowless, like Dutch barns perched on metallic piles linked by wooden catwalks. A broad-beamed barge, cloaked with a tarpaulin, and a fiberglass skiff were moored to the bollards at the back end of the rig, the skiff bobbing slightly on the lift of invisible currents.

The sea, Alex knew, was distant. What purpose the minature maritime rig could have here, he could not guess. He had no opportunity to ponder the question. The Mastodon slowed, swung out onto the apron of concrete, and came to a halt.

On the middle span of the pier a man in a white linen suit was seated on an oil drum under an improvised awning of oily black canvas. Even at a distance of sixty yards Alex recognized Eugene Morello, alive and apparently well. His heart skipped a beat in the sudden excitement of the moment. He felt a compulsion to fling open the door and rush forward, clamoring for explanations, for some answer to the mystery of what he was doing here in the middle of the Mexican hinterland. But he had learned enough to remain calm, apparently composed, even without the environmental trappings of little

116

old New York and the Freemen's State to hold his emotions in check.

Morello rose and came out into the drizzle, strolling on up the long walkway across the lagoon. Under the white linen jacket was a midnight-blue shirt with a winged collar, open at the throat. On his head, perched on a mass of curly brown hair, was a cream felt hat like Papan's, cocked raffishly back from his face. The face itself was bronzed by the sun, definitely copper-colored. A mammoth brown mustache curved around the corners of his mouth. The beard—how many seasons ago had that been in vogue?—had gone. The square, naked chin protruded arrogantly.

As he came to within ten yards of the Mastodon, Morello raised his arms and spread them in an effusive gesture of welcome.

Alex buttoned open the truck's offside door and pitched out. Landing, sprawling, he picked himself up and ran the distance between himself and his partner.

Morello was crying, "Hey, old buddy, old lad. Come to poppa, old friend."

Alex reached Morello, fastened his fists on the linen lapels and yanked the man hard in against his chest, yelling into his face, *"What the fuck do you mean by dragging me down here, you sonuvabitch? What the fuck goes on?"*

Morello smiled, fleshy nose tip to tip with Blunt's.

"Simple, old buddy," he said, suavely. "You've come here to kill me. And I figure maybe you will."

–: PART THREE :–

The Phoenix of Veracruz

TELL ME THE MIST-DRAPED MOUNTAIN LIES
UNCAPPED, A GATE TO THE WORLD BEYOND,
AND I, IN MY FAITH, WILL CREDIT YOU
WITH VISION DEEPER THAN THE HEART CAN
HOLD AND ALL THE SPOILS OF MAN RECORD.

Alex Blunt

: 1 :

HARVARD AMARYLLIS SMOLKIN claimed that he lived in but not on Mexico. The riddle involved inside-type knowledge that the Voladores Hotel on Capricorn Avenue was built on a raised concrete platform to provide a safeguard against hurricanes. The Voladores was no longer a hotel. Freakily, it was the only building of any stature left standing after terrorist leader Craig Leland's hijacked nuclear submarine self-detonated and wasted a good eighty percent of *Bello Veracruz*. Shortly after the Settlement Plan got underway, Florian took over the Voladores and converted it into a Studio Dissemination Center to cover the Central American belt. Externally the fourteen-story building was almost as it had been ten minutes after the Leland sub jetted off in a mushroom cloud, pitted, scarred, and frescoed with smoke. The windows though had been replaced with six-sill bricks and all the entrances, bar two, fitted with fireproof, mobproof, laserproof, weatherproof, double-plated Vulcanian steel stitched onto the structure with rivets like an ocean tanker's bulkheads and sealed with triple coats of Transparent Tar. From the domed roof, like the horns of a stylized snail, the D.D. discs directed sounds and images in graceful, preordained parabolas all across the land to dump down in factory cantinas, peons' shacks, and the thatched huts in which a few burro breeders sulked down in Quintana Roo. The Voladores served in all almost a hundred thousand receivers, from A-frame Diablophonics to Tuckaways tiny enough to be stowed inside a man's hat.

Being the only White Man, City-Bred, Freemen-Ap-

121

proved Executive Technician in the whole of that vast tract of hinterland, Harv Smolkin had plenty to keep him busy. In fact, H.A. had not set foot on Mexican soil since he had first picked his way over the cobbles to the steps of the Voladores 241 seasons ago. He stayed strictly indoors out of choice, a prisoner of his fear of the realities that lay outside the walls, of the three-dimensional world that could never compare with the taped versions on which he suckled and thrived. The big, dissolute spaces out there could not be governed and condensed by programming a simple-system ZIGTRAC computer. Everything outside Florian's Voladores Studio, so H.A. thought, was wild and frighteningly libertine—which shows how much H.A. Smolkin knew about life in the twenty-first century.

Harvard Amaryllis Smolkin had been named in memory of his father's alma mater, the Harvard Business School, and after his actual mater, Amaryllis Hope Alkes, youngest daughter of the Alkes of Rembrandt County, West Virginia. Harv's mother had eased herself out by tippling a noggin of paraquat when poor H.A. was only twenty-two years old, and his father—Smolkin' Joe to the columnists—was having women four to the basket bedwise and making a roaring success of the ensuing melee, more than he had ever done with the lone Alkes dove back in his ivory castle in Vermont.

Ol' Smolkin' Joe, a scholarship boy from the Bowery, had ridden the stigma of his humble origins hell for leather across the entertainment industry of New York. He had won the distinction of solo credit on every gosh-darned script of the world's longest-running soap opera, "Maury's Girls," the everyday story of three sisters, Kate, Constance, and Barbara. After Poppa Maury was mercifully martyred to sagging ratings in the series' eleventh year, the girls took off for the city and settled to their respective courses with real, everyday tenacity. Kate was a criminal lawyer bucking for D.A., Constance an international model, later movie queen, and Barbara, hausfrau-cum-helpmate to a blind novelist who earned his gingerbread teaching English, nights, in a Harlem high school and, over the years, did more to abet the segregationists' cause than the KKK at its zenith. "Maury's Girls" was built into H.A.'s chromosomes like a predisposition to epilepsy, together with every kind of pictorial nougatine from the days of Marguerite Clark through Garland and Doris Day to Ann Nilkin and petite Becky Luckhurst. Smolkin was probably the only American alive who did not suppose that Pickfair was some kind of scented delousing powder. Not that such names cropped up often in household parlance, only in H.A.'s dreams, along with a million similar oddments concerning the luminaries of Hollywood and Old Broadway; tittle-tattle, tootsie-fruitsie, the gossipaceous nightstuff of the Grandma Moses of nostalgia.

It was H.A.'s task to feed the pabulum of yesteryear to a nation that had only reluctantly emerged from cultural darkness and had, so H.A. thought, been so startled by the light that it had retreated again posthaste. At least that was the little guy's rationalization of the fact that the ZIGTRAC selector canceled out Van Johnson as being a meaningless sexual symbol to a contemporary American audience. Violence was out; love, lust, and lingerie were out; social realism was out—and that didn't leave too much. What H.A. couldn't show to the public, however, he greedily kept for himself. Daringly, he fashioned his dreams of it, even slipping so far toward heresy as to imagine himself holding hands with Margaret O'Brien and, one warm spring night, kissing Veronica Lake on the cheekbone. For the rest, the quarterly quotas arrived by transit Landways from New York or Florian's sub-office in Frisco-L.A.; Harv built them into programs and fed the automated systems which kept the stuff spooling out, then retired to his personal video for his private screenings.

H.A. Smolkin had been a year short of thirty when his old man had run his big, sleek G.M. Auroch sports coupe over an acoustical trip wire, later proved to be a booby trap set by the N.Y. Evangelists' Kamikaze Squad. The Auroch's methane tanks had exploded instantly, sending Smolkin' Joe off to join his missus in nirvana. Underage Harv was taken into protective custody, made a ward of the city, his inherited estate managed by an uncle from his mother's side, an Alkes who later became a Falkes, and a Freeman. When the Community Property and Credit Bill was finally legislated, the loss of a half million bucks didn't worry H.A. too much because he was already where he wanted to be, in Florian's Academy, learning computing, data processing, the chemistry of celluloid, and all the other subjects that the course required. At the age of forty, Harv graduated to the post of Junior Executive Archivist in the Florian Building in Queens. At the age of forty-four he had so proved himself that Florian promoted him, with special instructions, to a solo spot down in Veracruz, the Voladores—the Lighthouse of Central America, as Florian eloquently called it—and H.A. shipped out for his one and only leg of travel on a Flannigan freighter to Tampico, laden with preselected movie goodies.

Life in the Voladores was almost perfect. The ecosystems, though not sophisticated, functioned adequately, and his minder, Miss Spears, attended to all his requirements and saw that food was stocked in the hotplates when he wanted it. Miss Spears had been with him a long time. He had never actually seen her, though, for she came and went like a leprechaun, being always where he was not. Once—just once—he had felt an inclination to make more than professional contact with her. Again on a soft spring night, he had deliberately left a tape of *Roman Holiday* running on his night-table set in the vague, fond hope that Miss Spears would, perhaps, respond. She did: she replaced Greg and Audrey with B. of E. DOC.-1719-CA.—*The Parable of the Grapes*—and that was the end of Harv's halfhearted flirtation.

In addition to Miss Spears, H.A. Smolkin governed a three-man team of maintenance engineers, one of whom—Bosun Jones—Harv regarded as "the mandatory nigger," a piece of outmoded prejudice left over from his grasshopper days in TV studios at his father's knee. Occasionally he met up with one or another of the crew, but not often, daily communications being made through audiophones or by taped messages. Once every year, a special medical crew from the local Booster Station entered the Voladores and stuffed H.A. full of health and contentment—a concession to his importance as a status hand, a gesture arranged by Florian.

Florian was H.A.'s only real contact with the outside world. A small video-phone, ranged on a satellite, gave him access to Florian's personal office—and also gave Florian year-round, round-the-clock access to Smolkin. The messages could hardly be said to come thick and fast, but come they did, occasionally, and H.A. acted upon them as best he could. He was not unduly surprised, then, when, one December day at high noon, the door of the computer room on the ninth floor slid open and two gentlemen from New York entered his sanctum.

Harv Smolkin was not, however, entirely prepared for the arrival of a couple of torpedoes like Volpe and Slattery and his first thought was that he had gotten (himself) into another fine mess. The last, and only, mess he had ever gotten into had to do with the unauthorized copy-printing of Angostini's *Swann's Way with Women* from the *Codex Prohibitorum* in the Ogham Archives. But he had been a callow forty-one then and Florian had forgiven him. This present situation, however, previewed as something much more unpleasant. He suddenly felt like a Tibetan monk confronted by Ronald Colman, sure of himself, but suspicious of how far authority, confidence, and the advantages of locale would carry him in the face of the vast and varied experience of his strange visitors, hit men if ever he saw them.

Sweating under his cobby-shirt, he rejected at once the role he had elected to play, based on an anthology of character parts by Cedric Hardwicke. He revised his manner to emulate Jack Adams, the most famous psychopathic hero of them all, a pebble-eyed vigilante who roved the range from Fraunces Tavern to East Gun Hill. Adams's special crowd-pulling gimmick was his skill in tearing out villains' tongues with his forefinger and thumb, though his way with dialogue made Coop seem like a blabbermouth. Harv found, though, that he could not cope with the impersonification in the presence of two guys who might have taught Jack Adams his party piece. Besides he wasn't dressed for it, being caught sloppily collegiate, like eager Mickey Rooney.

H.A. propelled the gliderchair along the banks of keys which fronted the ZIGTRAC and, in a twinkling, polished off the day's work. He swung the chair out in a pirouette and stepped off as it came to rest about five yards from his guests.

"Messrs. Volpe and Slattery, I believe?"

"You Smolkin?" asked one, Volpe.

"I am he."

"Where's Blunt?"

"Narvaez has not reported to me yet."

"Why not?"

H.A. shrugged "Being a revolutionary isn't easy, you know."

"Don't give me that crap," said Volpe. "Where's Hartmann?"

"I assume he's with Blunt."

"Where?"

"Look here, gentlemen," said H.A. helplessly, "I'm only a relay station. I disseminate culture through standard communications channels and collect and rephrase the odd message or two."

"Shit," said Volpe.

"You'll find the cloakroom there, and the lavender door, same floor, is your suite," Harv said. "I hope you'll be comfortable, gentlemen, and as soon as . . ."

Slattery and Volpe set down their rectangular suitcases, reached into their breast pockets, and brought out packs of Menthols. They flicked the bases of the packs and lipped the filters, tapping the packs away and cocking their wristbands to light the Menthols' tips. Through the peppermint smoke they studied H.A. Smolkin with basilisk dispassion.

Sweet Jesus! thought Harv, sweating like a lawn sprinkler, they *know* what I've done. They're hit men for *me*. Holy Mary, Mother of God! I am about to be *found out*. He fought for control of his mouth which had become unzipped at the corners. It was okay if they were *only* hit men. It would take a Bureau Interrogator to get him to actually *admit* to anything. There was no reason in the world—cool it, baby—to suppose that Florian or some other Freeman had rumpled him. They *might* be ZIG-TRAC experts come to filter the whole program, all 9,457 reels, plus the 780 partially completed miniature tapes that he had rescued from oblivion, restored, recorded, and stashed on the second floor. If they *were* ZIG-TRACKERS then it would only be a matter of time before they discovered the one unrecorded, unclassified tape—disguised as the fourth reel of a COM.DOC. three-reel feature, *Extinct Species of the Canadian Northwest;* that fourth reel, miniaturized, running ten times as long as the dreary DOC. on the whooping crane and the slate-colored junco; that fourth reel, capable of sending him into a white-tiled ward in a sanatorium for the rest of his natural days, or until they wrung the truth out of him with hypoglossal nerve probes, a process H.A. knew would take all of five minutes. He cursed himself for allowing

126

Morello to talk him into it, and cursed Florian for introducing the greaser, Narvaez, into an otherwise stable situation.

"What's wrong, Smolkin?" asked Volpe.

"Nothing. But listen: I mean, look, I can't be held responsible for Narvaez. I mean, he comes and he goes as he pleases. You—the Bureau—have Veracruz staked out and it always takes Narvaez a little time to thread his way into the town, except when he's holing out here, and he doesn't do that often. It's not as if I *know* Narvaez well, or anything. I mean, he's not a *friend* of mine."

"He's sweating," Volpe remarked.

Slattery grunted, darkly.

"I mean, I can't order this Mex about, or anything," Smolkin dribbled on. "I kinda got the impression that he was doing *us* a favor, anyhow."

"We'll wait," said Volpe.

Harv's small paunch stuck out over his snakeskin belt. He wiped his hands on his pants. "The ... the ... lavender door," he said. "Re ... red door if you wanna freshen up. It's separate systems. I'm s ... s ... sorry."

Volpe and Slattery lifted their suitcases and carried them out of the hexagonal computer room, heading on down the corridor, step in step, until the door puffed and blotted them out of Harv's sight.

He swayed, then called out for the glider which hissed over and nudged itself affectionately at the back of his knees. He sank into it, plucking at the Menthol that the armrest erected, already lighted. He dragged on the cigarette and let his head rest on the cushion.

The glider, unbidden, took him on a gentle tour of the room. Harv closed his eyes. It was sixty years since he'd last smelled the sour stink of fear, his own fear. He didn't like it one teensy bit. He wished to God that he'd never gotten into this, though it had seemed like nothing at the time and had titillated his collector's instinct, giving him, equidistantly, some kind of private power to gloat over in secret in his bedroom.

No, really, he never thought anything would come of it. Morello had assured him that it wouldn't.

But Morello had deceived him.

Now he understood the spot he was in, not only being one of maybe six people in the world to have *seen* the goddamn thing but actually being the temporary cus-

127

todian of Robert Lambard's Last Great Marchat; the gasser; taped dynamite.

"Holy Mary, Mother of God," he began again in the manner of Barry Fitzgerald, hardly moving his lips at all.

: 2 :

OPIUM, Morello explained, had become the religion of the people. The whole human community from Cape Horn to Ellesmere Island spent their lives more or less stoned to the eyeballs with the gloop that was injected into their bloodstreams via the Montagu Serum. In addition, liberal credit on Joe Dealer items and liquor proved that they too were effective narcotics. With the exception of the contents of Freemen's bonds, all manufactured quasi-alcoholic beverages were merely diluted, adulterated derivatives of tequila, chemically treated to simulate a variety of different wines and spirits. This piece of information put Alex's epicurean nose out of joint. He wondered what his fellow *bons vivants* in the Appledore would think if he ever got to reveal the truth about the supper room's famous cellars.

Morello went on, "No, *I* didn't send for you, Alex. You were drugged, rendered receptive to hallucinogenic suggestion for months, maybe even years, before Florian lit your fuse with that fake Interlink scenario. When our contact went dead, I figured he was up to something and that I could expect you on my doorstep eventually."

"All of that . . . that business—my madness—was actually arranged?"

"Absolutely," said Morello. "Every detail, including your 'escape.' "

"Even the death of my minder, Miss Abbott?"

"What's one minder more or less," Morello said.

129

"But why me?"

"To blow your mind, to shoot you out of New York, to make you a fingerman."

"I don't understand," Alex said. "The Freemen have dozens of trained agents on tap through the Bureau. If they wanted you, Gene, why didn't they just come after you, track you down?"

"It isn't the Freemen. It's only one particular Freeman."

"Florian?"

"Our father; yep."

"But what does he hope to gain?"

"Power."

"And to make amends for his error with Robert Lambard," said Alex. "Dowd explained some of that."

"Florian couldn't care less about making amends," Eugene Morello said. "He's a traitor to the Freemen's Club. He wants *all* the power, every last scrap—and he thinks he knows how to get it."

"How?"

"Eat your dinner, lad."

Venison steaks, barbecued over a charcoal fire, were served medium rare, with sweet potatoes and peas. Alex, Dowd, and Gene already had demolished enough to feed a dozen mouths in any big-city restaurant. For afters there was a dish of maize pudding flavored with fruit and honey. The girl did the cooking on the grid and on a large tin stove heated by a gas cylinder.

The inside of the main building on the abandoned oil rig was Morello's den: a rough table, chairs, a mattress, a number of items of clothing, and the Portable Transceiver with a sheet thrown over it like an old-fashioned bird cage.

Alex attacked the pudding, spooning deeply into the soft, sweet meal.

Morello had changed. He looked larger, younger, and infinitely more healthy than before. His skin was smooth and tanned and his muscles bulged under the shirting. He was, now, a figure worthy of emulation, original enough to provide an archetype for ciphers back on Broadway and Fifth Avenue to copy. It seemed fitting that he had found a companion as beautiful as Flower Feather.

Outside, the rain made a soft pattering on the roof of the shack. The girl was filtering coarse coffee grounds through a cloth. The fragrance of the brew filled the air.

Alex's initial anger had quickly diminished. He was still wary of the setup, though, not fully convinced that the complicated charade was not an invention of his partner rather than his boss.

Alex said, "Go back, Gene. Explain from the beginning."

Gene said, "Florian has been power-crazy for decades. He knows that any peer group, like the Freemen, is ripe for takeover. The history of revolution in a nutshell. Military organizations were a favorite breeding ground for dictators. The corporate structures of the twentieth century fostered war and crime for their own power and profit, giving us the Presidents, Mr. Big, Godfathers, Papa le Grand. Anyhow, it was Florian's original aim to set Robert Lambard up as a national hero, to promote him into the Freemen's Club, then manipulate Bob, like a puppet, into a position of absolute power."

"The Freemen wouldn't have stood for it," said Alex.

"It would have happened so gradually that they might not have been aware of it. Once Florian had gained knowledge of *all* the Freemen's secrets, gained access to the ultimate secret—how the Montagu Serum is made—then he would have been in an ideal position to close his fist on New York. Once he had New York, he would have attracted aberrant power-hungry members from the other Clubs, divided the 400 All-City Freemen into warring factions, from which he—being more prepared than the others—would emerge victorious. It was a long, long-term project. But he did, after all, control the propaganda machine; a big plus in his favor. Back in the old days, when little guys with guns and libertarian principles tried to overthrow a government the radio station was always their first target. Gain control of the communications circuits and you have a louder voice than your opponents. You can 'make the news.' "

"Bob Lambard wouldn't play, though," said Dowd.

"So Florian had him shot," said Alex. "Wasn't that pretty stupid?"

"The Freemen forced Florian to it. It was a major setback to Florian's plans, the more so as it delayed his entry into the Freemen's Club and his gaining legitimate control of the communications network." Morello lit a cheroot, a tight roll of honest tobacco leaf. "But Bob

Lambard was smarter than even Florian imagined. Bob Lambard's Great Marchat Exposé Show *wasn't* destroyed. Lambard had the foresight to make a full version on microtape into which he incorporated every shred of evidence against Florian, against the Freemen, against the system. That was the grail, the bargaining factor that Florian failed to snatch while he had the chance. Lambard smuggled it into hiding a week before they obliterated him."

"But what's its value now?" said Alex. "Bob Lambard may be remembered and respected by some of us but he's not the hero he was fifty years ago."

"The tape tells all," said Dowd Hartmann. "Everything."

"So Florian, to save face, must retrieve that tape?" said Alex.

"Nup, not to save face. The Freemen don't even know the tape still exists," said Dowd. "Even Florian wouldn't have known of it if. . . . Shit, *I* told him. *I* squealed."

Morello glanced at the old man, fondly. "In the hope of saving Miss Jenny, Dowd. You wouldn't have done it otherwise."

Hartmann shrugged. "Maybe not."

"Anyhow, you didn't tell him *where* the tape was hidden."

Dowd grinned. "Bet your britches, I didn't. I told him that I didn't know, and goddamn it, the idiot *believed* me."

"Where is the tape now?" asked Alex. "Do you have it?"

"I . . . well, I think we'd rather keep that secret, Alex, if you don't mind," Morello said, apologetically. "In this game knowledge really is power."

"What game?"

"Revolution."

"But whose revolution?"

"Revolution to Florian," Dowd Hartmann said, "means the overthrow of the existing state of government and its replacement by a system of dictatorship: one man in the driving seat, a president, an emperor, call it what you like, even king. That's him: that's Florian. It's a time-honored and almost laudable ambition, son, to rule the whole fuckin' world yourself."

"But revolution to us—and it's *our r*evolution, Alex— means encouraging the process of cyclical change, restoring the order of humanity in all its disorder, all its

132

sweet confusion," Morello said. "The planet now is a mortuary, the Freemen's Club the dead end of evolution. Christ knows how we'll go, what'll happen. But you can't let progress end with a whimper."

"It isn't that bad," murmured Alex.

"In a century, in two centuries, in a thousand years," said Morello, vehemently, "there will be no fundamental change, only a fossilized race. I'm not going to argue with you, Alex."

"You never did," Alex said. "You just bawled me down."

Tactfully Flower Feather began to serve coffee from a large earthenware jug. Morello reached for his cup thankfully, glad to be out of that area of discussion.

Alex said, "All right, Gene, so it's your revolution. But how come Florian let you go, and then, seasons later, decided to send me after you? It makes no sense."

"I am a Florian agent," said Morello, sipping coffee.

"You're working *with* Florian?"

"Not now," Morello said. "Way back. He cultivated me, groomed me to his way of thinking. The trouble was that I never really agreed with him. I was always, I suppose, just naturally perverse. The cessation of the booster shots threw me into the proper state of mind to examine every word that Florian flung at me, every whisper. He arranged our dissension, arranged my Gypsy ticket and sent me out into the hinterland to see what I could vacuum up."

"That was also my brief," Dowd Hartmann said. "That was the reason I wasn't knocked off at the time of the Lambard assassination. But he didn't trust me, even though he'd broken me. He put Gene onto me in case I caused trouble."

"The Riss-Interlink served a double function," Morello said. "It was also my source of contact with Florian. He has agents everywhere."

"How did he know you'd gone over the top?" asked Alex.

"That little sonuvabitch Narvaez," said Morello. "He's been a troublemaker, old-style, since the day he was born. His Mamma kept him hidden out in an old silver mine up north and refused him registration. He grew up without subjection to the Serum, ran around the border towns

133

making crowing noises and looking for banks to rob and women to rape—which was pretty crazy because none of the women even knew what the hell he was doing to them and considered it, maybe, a little bit painful and unpleasant, and certainly anti-Ethical, but nothing more than that. There are no sexual deviations now, at least none worth talking about, and you can't rob the credit system by brandishing a handgun. But Narvaez really was—and is—a genetic throwback."

"He decided to foment a revolution of his own," Dowd said.

"He has about thirty men and women, all middle-aged cripples, that he calls his army," Morello went on. "He has targets marked out across Mexico and he's certainly fed us an occasional scrap of interesting information. But Florian decided to use Narvaez for his own ends. He had me bribe him."

"With what?"

"Immortality."

"Pardon?"

"Once every year I shove a fucking great needle into Narvaez's arm, and tell him he's going to live forever. The—call it 'çourse'—of injections numbers twelve. Narvaez has had eleven. The price of the last shot, due this month, is the whereabouts of the Lambard tape. Florian has finally figured that we have it or know where it is. Every time he activates his home video he must sweat drops of blood in case we've found a means of broadcasting it."

"Does Narvaez know where the tape is?" asked Alex.

"No, but it was Narvaez who fed Florian the information that I was acting on my own, working against him as well as against the established regime; what they used to call a double agent."

Dowd Hartmann took over. "Florian lost Gene 'bout four years back."

"But we've worked together since then," said Alex.

"I rigged the Interlink," Morello said. "And I kept moving. Florian couldn't put a proper fix on me, and he couldn't send in a Bureau task force to smoke me out without explaining to the Club how he had gotten into a jam in the first place. Private agents and armies aren't legal so Florian's manpower resources must, of necessity, be limited, otherwise he might arouse suspicion. He used Narvaez as an excuse. He cast around for a four-square fingerman so innocent, so nutty, that the Freemen might just accept Florian's cockamamie story and give him time to lay his claws on the Marchat tape."

"Have I been followed, then?" asked Alex.

"Florian directed you to Bellerophon," Dowd Hartmann said. "He made it easy for you to get out of the city, forced you out. It's only a guess, mind you, but I figure you've been deprived of Serum for three, four years to make you unstable."

"So that's why Miss . . ." Alex began. He bit off the sentence, flushing.

"Sure," Dowd Hartmann said. "Prompted, maybe, by a strong dose of hormonal stimulant."

"But if I've been followed here, Gene, then Florian knows where you are?" said Alex.

"He's known for months that I'm holed out in Mexico: Narvaez told him that much, passing messages through the Voladores in Veracruz. But Mexico's a big country. Florian can't pin me down. Not even Narvaez can pin me down. Besides, Florian daren't assassinate me until he has the tape."

"So what's my role?" asked Alex.

"Florian sent you off mad as a hornet. But Florian knows that you won't kill me, no matter how mad you are. He's hopeful that maybe you will put the finger on me even if I do a lot of talking to you."

"Because we hate—hated—each other's guts, Eugene?"

"You've been changed, Alex, haven't you? You've been fashioned and molded like clay."

"All right: so?"

"Even if you don't fink on me, Florian figures that I'll confide in you, eventually. Then he'll have you lifted, and break you."

"But why go through this burlesque? Why not lift *you* straight off?"

Morello smiled, the heavy mustache shrugging on his upper lip. "I'm not so easy to find. Besides, Florian knows he can't break me. But you, Alex: *you* he figures he *can* break, like a twig."

"The bastard," Alex shouted. "The fucking low-down bastard."

He looked furiously from Morello to Hartmann and across at the girl. She was watching him, too, but he did not feel ashamed either of his filthy archaic language or of his wrath. He thumped his fist on the table, making the pudding bowl leap and cups rattle.

"I'll show him. Break me, can he? Manipulate me? Jesus H. Christ! Let him try," Alex stormed.

Hartmann gave a dry chuckle.

"Like a bone-dry twig," he said.

"*Snap!*" Gene Morello said, and laughed uproariously at his partner's discomfiture.

Viva Narvaez! the portly, grape-eyed, draggle-assed Mexican bandido hollered in his head. *Viva Narvaez!* Echoes rang thinly in the crown of his huge, ragged sombrero, like the jingle of tarnished half-dollars dangling from the brim and the crop of saintly medallions which his Mamma had given him years ago and which he had forced his woman, at gunpoint, to stitch to the hems of the leatherette weskit, which he called a *bolero*. All the tiny, tinny, clink-clank sounds, including the chinking of his plastic spurs, merged into an anthem of acclaim which only he heard. He acknowledged it with a swaggering gesture that didn't quite come off since he was huddled behind a hump of adobe wall in the place of stones that used to be *Bello Veracruz*'s most attractive square. He didn't dare peek his lank bootlace moustachios over the ridge in case some treacherous dog spotted him and yelled for the Bureau's *federales* to haul him off to the scaffold and make a martyr of him, while the women in his army straggled down out of the hills to croon sad songs and weep, and the whole country rose against the *gringos* who had hanged their saintly Pancho.

Something like that went through Pancho Narvaez's brain as he grubbed deeper into the dust and waited for the shadow of the Voladores Studio to fall across the square as the sun sank into evening.

Something like that went through Pancho Narvaez's brain most of the time, though the irony was not always so pointed.

Hey-ey-yah! Maybe he should have risked riding openly into the blackened, largely ruined town, guns barking, big chestnut-brown stallion curving its muscular neck against the sawing rein, with silver buckles on it, of course, flung himself off at the door of the Voladores and gone stalking in, blazing off the locks with his guns. Trouble was that the doors of the Voladores were sealed by some bewildering force. A cannon couldn't have blasted them open, let alone one man—even Pancho Narvaez—with the brace of Colt Navy Replicas that Morello had gifted to him to celebrate his first Immortality Shot.

So, Narvaez, Scourge of the Hinterland, skulked in the deserted Plaza Capricorno until blue shadow gave him a wedge of token shelter to scuttle along and flatten his back against the wall of the Voladores. He hugged the corner, all fourteen stories of the Studio leaning over and peering impassively, then, Colts in hand, snuck on around the gable and, with eyes darting like demented roaches, slithered into the arched doorway and rang the bell.

The dude was big and strange. Nobody ever actually opened the door *to* Narvaez. He was startled, this time, to find himself confronted by a person, a *gringo,* not even Harv Smolkin, whom he could handle, but a pea-headed crop-haired blond with shoulders like somebody had rammed a longhorn up the back of his jacket and a smile of welcome on his face that made Pancho's blood turn to ice.

The dude chopped Narvaez twice, once across each wrist—the motion like that of an ambidextrous sugar-cane peon wielding a pair of machetes. He caught the Colts before they could hit the rubberized floor. Next, though the motion seemed simultaneous rather than sequential to the *bandido,* two forefingers and two thumbs closed on the roots of his moustachios, yanked him off the stoop, jerked him straight across the foyer and into the elevator thirty feet away. Pancho's belly buffered against the concave back of the jet-el and he began to sink slowly down it like a hunk of seaweed abandoned by a wave.

The dude frisked him, tore off his Velcro-lined gun belt, found and confiscated the melon peeler in the top of his boot, the mustache clippers in his *bolero* pocket, and even the tinderbox on his hip. It took five seconds, by which time the jet-el had soared to the thirteenth floor and Pancho was being reined out again by his facial bootlaces and skidded along a corridor to a tiny, closetlike chamber full of weird-looking devices.

In this chamber were Harv Smolkin and another dude,

an urban area type whose expression spelled real bad news, a kind of *periódico* of personal disaster.

Pancho Narvaez had some dignity left, some sense of style allied to a knowledge of what, as *un hombre duro,* he was required to do.

Dropping to his knees, he bent from the waist and kissed the bulbous toes of the urban dude's Smartboys with a fervor that used to be reserved only for cardinals' rings and slivers of the True Cross.

"Hi, Pancho," said Harv Smolkin, from a niche between two of the machines. *"Cómo está usted?"*

"No me siento bien. Estoy enfermo. Necesito un médico," mumbled the revolutionary pathetically.

"Shut your hole, greaser," the blond dude told him. Feverishly Pancho Narvaez bussed the boot toe again.

The small, black-haired, simian *gringo* did not seem to object, though it was hard to tell because the expression of the guy was as bland as polished lingum.

"These two gentlemen have come all the way from New York, Pancho," Harv Smolkin explained. "They'd appreciate a little word with you, if you can spare the time."

"I got all the time in the world," Pancho Narvaez assured them. "Take all night, you like, *amigos.*"

The blond hauled him to his feet, spun him around, and pushed him against the bruin. The bruin's thumbs locked across his shoulders, digging through the leatherette, the cotton, the wool undershirt and layers of fat to find nerve threads that Pancho didn't even know he had under his clavicles.

"Where's Blunt?" the blond said.

"Blunt?"

Pain burrowed across Pancho's shoulders and bored into his skull so that he felt as if his sombrero had been smitten by a lightning bolt: his forearms and all his fingers *zizzed.*

Pancho shouted, "I don't know who this Blunt guy eeeees."

"Where's Morello?" the blond said.

"Morel . . . ? Yea, sure I know Morello. I not know where Morello eeeeeeees."

"Blunt is with Morello," the blond informed him. "We want them."

"I get them: I get them."

"Within twenty-four hours," the blond said.

"Twenty-four hours?" Narvaez shrieked. "Mexico, she eees a big country. I no be able get . . ."

"For Christ sake, Pancho," Harv advised, "don't argue with . . . with us. Lissen, it's important. If you want your Immortality Shot—which I've got downstairs—then I really recommend you to do your very best to comply. I mean, this isn't just you and me any more, my friend."

"Okay: okay: okay."

The blond said, "You know about the package?"

"Si, si: yea, I know about the package," bawled Narvaez. "I spen' ten years tryin' to fin' out where the package is gone."

"Then you're not trying hard enough, am-ee-go," the blond said.

The bruin's thumbs rested idly on Narvaez's shoulders.

"Anything goes, now, Pancho," warned Harv Smolkin softly. He was sweating, too, almost as much as Narvaez. "It's not just a question of you getting your Shot, it's a question of . . . uh, a matter of life and death."

"You have one day," said the blond dude, holding up his forefinger. "Tomorrow night at five, you be here, with the information."

"Then you'll get your Immortality Shot and you can leave the rest to us," Harv promised.

"I don' know if . . ." Pancho Narvaez paused to scream.

"Do it, greaser," the blond said.

"I do it. I do it."

Three minutes later, Pancho Narvaez was running across the plaza again, arms dangling limply, his empty Velcro gun belt hooped halfway down his ass.

The Bureau of Ethics' officer for Veracruz watched him from the window of the bunker, chuckled, and lazily returned to his video show.

Pancho Narvaez was a joke.

By tomorrow night, however, Pancho Narvaez might be a dead joke. Pancho Narvaez knew that only too well. Yelling inside his brain, he hobbled rapidly on through the quiet twilit suburbs toward his encampment in the hills.

Florian's pink face coalesced out of the granular scattering of colored dots that entered the eidophor projector from inner space and emerged with startling clarity, pore by pore and hair by silken hair, on the screen at the end of the little public viewing room. Side by side on swaybacks in the center of the center row Slattery and Volpe sat upright at the image of their master.

"Good evening, boys," Florian said, in perfect sync.

"Good evening, sir," said Volpe and Slattery, also in perfect sync.

"Is all going well?"

"The Mexican has promised delivery by tomorrow evening," Volpe said.

"How on earth did you manage that?"

"He wants the Immortality Shot," said Volpe.

"And he'll deliver the package?" said Florian eagerly.

"Yes."

"You mean, he's *got* the package?" Florian's eyes were crossed with ardor.

"He will have it, or precise information as to its whereabouts, by tomorrow evening," said Volpe, confidently.

"And Blunt, and Morello?"

"What are your instructions, sir?"

"Once you have the package, my boy, you can remove whomever you see fit."

Slattery nodded appreciatively.

Volpe said, "All the principals?"

"Yes, all of them," said Florian. "I'll contrive to explain how the New Yorkers died in a state of Ethical grace, warding off the forces of rebellion in the hinterland."

"We bring the package to you, sir?"

"Directly. To nobody else, my boy. Into my hands."

"Understood," Volpe said.

"I'll contact you again tomorrow," Florian said. "In the evening; to ascertain that all is going well."

"Yes, sir."

"Good night, boys."

The huge image faded, Florian waggling his fingers in farewell as the atomized parts of his portrait floated down from the encircling satellite and the beam emptied through the projector and dispersed to an ivory blank.

Volpe and Slattery sat quite still.

"How many do you want?" Volpe asked.

"All of them," said Slattery, garrulously.

The Mastodon growled and lurched over the highland track. It was hardly even a track now, only a meandering clearing of the trees where palms gave way to spruce along the vegetation line which charted the contour of the foothills of the Sierra Madre Oriental thirty miles inland from the gulf shore. Hartmann was driving, the passenger bench occupied by Morello and Alex Blunt. Flower Feather and old Papan were stowed snugly in the back. The luggage now included Morello's Riss-Interlink Portable, a stuff bag of personal belongings, and three long wooden crates so heavy that it had taken the men all their strength to transfer them from the tarpaulined barge, along the pier and into the Mastodon.

It was night now. The darkness was pierced by the fanning beams of the headlights. Rain had ceased, the insect drone of the twilight diminished into silence. For the winter season it was comparatively mild, the sky pricked with stars above the tall trees. Alex felt more alive than he had ever done before, filled with steel, too, tempered by his outburst and the realization that Florian, even Morello, considered him something of a weakling, useful only as a pawn.

He said, "I've got a couple of questions, Eugene. Will you answer me?"

Morello said, "If I can."

Alex said, "What do you really want from me? Am I here as a scapegoat, or as a catalyst?"

"I'm not sure," Morello said. "That's the truth, Alex. I tell you though, I'm *glad* you are here. I've waited for your arrival with anticipation. It relieves me to have you here."

"I find that hard to accept."

"You're the trigger," said Morello. "As I explained this afternoon, Florian wants *us* to make the first move. He figures we'll make it soon, and he's prepared. He has, he thinks, forestalled anything that we're liable to do."

"It's the Lambard tape, isn't it: that's the crux of the whole show?"

"Yep," said Morello.

"Won't you tell me why it's so important?"

Morello paused, then said, "The full tape is much more than a mere exposé. It contains a blueprint for the overthrow of the Freemen. Somehow—I don't know how—Bob Lambard found out where the Montagu Serum is manufactured. Whoever controls the supply of the Serum controls the continent, maybe even the inhabited world. Booster Stations, warehouses, chemical-supply depots, and, of course, the Breeder Cell Clinics, are all important. But there's one place, one center, where the Serum is actually produced— the rest of the stations are merely outlets of one sort or another—we need that."

"But you won't tell me where?" said Alex.

"Not unless I have to," Morello said. "It's not that I don't trust you, Alex, but if you know nothing then they can't wring anything valuable from you. And that might be important when you step into that Studio tomorrow."

"You're sure this Mexican bandit will do as you ask?"

"I may be mistaken," Morello said, "but I think that Florian's front-runners have put the screws on Narvaez already. He's out looking for you, Alex. You're the end of the thread by which Florian hopes to unpick the whole pattern of revolution, to steer his way to the Lambard tape."

Dowd Hartmann said, "Tell him the rest, Gene."

"You're my safeguard, Alex," Morello said. "Dowd is too old now."

"Yup," Hartmann murmured. "Far too old."

"I can't step into the Voladores Studio myself—yet I must have that Studio, and all its facilities."

"To beam out the Lambard tape."

"Yeah, that's right. We have the bullet, but we don't yet have the gun."

"Florian won't be able to keep it from the Freemen then."

"I don't care about Florian, Alex," Morello said.

"Once that tape is exposed to the public, then you'll have every Bureau unit in America descending to wipe you out."

"If they can find me."

"And me?"

"You're my backup, Alex," Morello said, quietly. "If by any chance I am disposed of, then you're the one guy I'd trust to continue the program."

"Revolution?"

"Right. What's your next question?"

"So far, Florian has used guile, cunning, bribery, and all the soft persuasive arts. Now he's going to use force— right?"

142

"Right again," said Morello. "Force is at least honest. Force is open: a shown hand. We want that to happen."

"What do we use in our own defense?"

Morello said, "The ancient arts, Alex."

"I don't understand."

"I found the girl, Flower Feather, and the old woman, Papan, only after a long search. They represent forces that the Freemen believe they have suppressed. They represent the kind of wisdom that nobody holds in high regard now: the power of the mind, not of the laboratory; the driving forces of the spirit, not of the credit rating. They are, if you like, the true liberators."

"A girl and an old woman?"

Morello glanced across at Hartmann whose face was lit from below by the blue-green glow of the dash-control.

Hartmann said, "They lie across the chasm from us, Alex. What they represent is all that we have forgotten. They are the spiritual tool-builders, architects of the psyche. Don't be fooled by appearances, son. Papan and the girl are *our* weapons. Florian has no knowledge of them."

Alex felt a strange crawling sensation in the pit of his belly and the hair on the nape of his neck rose slightly as if somebody had breathed coldly upon it.

"How . . . how old is she?" he asked.

"The girl is twenty," Morello said.

"And the old woman?"

"As old as you wish her to be," Morello said.

Alex said, "How is that possible?"

Dowd Hartmann answered, "Look outside, son: what do you see?"

"Darkness."

"What's in that darkness?"

"Trees, rocks, sky, mountains, I suppose."

"Invisible to us, but nevertheless solid and real."

"What does that mean, Dowd? Another parable?"

"Would you believe me if I told you that Papan is 600 years old?"

"No," Alex said, "I wouldn't believe you."

"The body she uses now is 100, maybe 110 years old, but the active soul, the being within her flesh, has walked through the gates of five lifetimes."

"She claims. . . . No, she *is* the daughter of the great

Aztec leader Montezuma; Papantzin; princess, prophetess, sorceress."

"A descendant, you mean?"

"No, she ain't a descendant. She *is* Papan, the princess who conquered death, who died and returned, who does not die but lives on, returning again and again into the world and . . ."

"Jesus, you're crazy," Alex blurted out. "You're both nuts."

"It's true, Alex," Morello assured him.

"How do you know? How can you be sure she hasn't taken you in with some . . . some conjuring trick."

"Because I believe," Eugene Morello said.

"Well, I don't believe," said Alex heatedly. "What the hell *have* you seen to give you so much faith?"

"Later: we'll tell you later, son," Dowd Hartmann said.

"No, wait," said Alex, anxiously. "What of the girl?" How old do you claim she is?"

"Just twenty," said Morello.

"And what's so special about her?"

"She's the guide," said Morello.

"Guide? Guide to where, for Christ's sake?"

Hartmann revved the engine. The odor of kerosene became strong in the cabin. Alex realized that they would not answer him, that his skepticism, his scathing rebuttal of their assertions, had debarred him from sharing their secrets, at least for a time.

Though he blustered and feigned irritation at his comrades' claims, within him was a gnawing hunger to be, again, that spiritually innocent—not marked with the naiveté of a status hand in the All-City State. But innocent, virginal in his soul. Was this the revolution that he had been drawn into, not by his own volition, but by the perfidious scheming of men who wrestled for power of a different sort each from the other? Both hoped to satisfy that hunger by the zealot's creed, Florian by taking all unto himself, Morello by reopening the locked castles of the psyche.

"We're almost there, Gene," Dowd Hartmann said.

Morello put his hand on Alex's arm. "You sure you want to go through with this?"

"What goddamn choice have I," Alex growled.

"It means conviction, commitment. Are you prepared for that, and for what may follow?"

144

"Yeah! Hell, why not? I'm nobody's man, right now. I'm a freewheeler, a traveling soul. *Ain't* that kerreck, ol' man?"

"Kerreck, son," Dowd Hartmann told him.

"I don't set much stock by all that mystical and metaphysical crap you've just handed me. It isn't necessary. I know what you want: you want me to be the fall guy."

"Like Lucifer," Morello said.

Hartmann drew the Mastodon to a gradual halt, its blunt snout slightly uptilted. From the screen, painted with light, Alex could see rugged, whorled rocks and the bright-green sprays of spruce-tree boughs. He felt there should be an omen too, a bird or beast in the frame—but there was nothing. The steep slope even cut off the stars.

Dowd Hartmann said, "This is as far as we dare go."

Morello leaned across Alex, opened the passenger door, and dumped a Moonglow hand torch into his lap.

Alex climbed slowly from the cab into the pressures of the forest and the hill. The clean wind ruffled his hair. He could smell the moist odors of the night. A sound behind him brought him around.

The girl stood by his side, against the flank of the truck. She said, "Are you afraid?"

"Yes."

"Of what?"

"Jaguars, buzzards, and men," Alex said ruefully.

"They are all the same here," the girl told him. "We will protect you."

Alex's face hardened. He could not discard his skepticism in a moment.

"Papan will protect you from jaguars and buzzards," Flower Feather said.

"And from men?"

"We are all of mankind," Flower Feather said. "We have no protection against ourselves."

"Thank you," Alex said, curtly. "I will ponder on that profundity as they strip the flesh from my bones and roast me over a slow fire."

Turning quickly, he activated the Moonglow and by its wide spread of light began to pick his way along the track heading due south in the direction they had told him to go. He glanced back only once, briefly. Hartmann had

145

killed the Mastodon's headlights and he could see little of the men inside, only the soft silhouette of the Totonac girl against the truck's metal flank. Turning again on his heel, he struck off quickly into the foothills, alone.

: 3 :

DOWN THE RAMPARTS of the Sierras, from the volcanic crowns of Orizaba to the *milpas* that ringed the desolate outskirts of Veracruz, a sudden contour plunge carried the land through a variety of weathers and ecological communes the like of which was to be found in no other part of the All-City State of America. An hour's ride from the ruined cloisters of the hacienda where he had parked his burro brought Pancho Narvaez out of the flats, through pockets of growth and cultivation and into the pine-tree wilderness. It wasn't deep country. It lay close enough to what had been the city for the trees to be stunted and the old banana-thatched huts of yesterday's peons to remain scattered here and there among tangled twentieth-century plantations.

In a clearing, hard against a frowning cliff three, four miles up rock-strewn slopes from the semijungle, Narvaez had made his camp for eleven years now. He imagined himself well hidden and secure. But a Boys' Own Patrol of Westchester first-year students could have captured his whole ailing band without firing a shot.

The burro was the last of twenty-eight. The remainder had been slaughtered and devoured by Narvaez's carnivorous dependents in compensation for the fact that every healthy body around them would outlive them by a century and a half. Pancho had held the loyalty of his rebels only because they were, collectively and individually, too stupid to have minds of their own. They had been indoctrinated into believing that they lay beyond the pale of science, medicine, and such newfangled things as credit ratings. In fact, they could have quit Narvaez at any time

147

and registered with the Bureau in Veracruz where amnesty awaited them. As the Bureau did not see fit to woo the comedians in the hills, however, none of Narvaez's ageds realized that they might rejoin the Establishment just by requesting admission. If Pancho suspected the truth he kept it to himself. He strongly refused to be manipulated by the Bureau. If he got immortality it would be on his terms and for himself alone.

The appearance of the two missiles from New York, however, really worried Pancho Narvaez. He feared for his life more than the survival of his life-style. Something too devious even for his devious intelligence was brewing. Though he was loath to confess it to himself, he had the hollow feeling that he might wind up being sacrificed, not even martyred, simply swatted off the board. After twenty-five years of cat-and-mouse, it looked like somebody had brought in the dogs. This sudden climaxing of affairs made him sick to his stomach, the more so as the last, vital hypoful of Eternal Life waited down there in the Voladores, and he was helpless to claim it.

The burro trudged up the final quarter mile to the encampment. Though there were many vacant huts and abandoned villages in the vicinity, Narvaez preferred to live like his spiritual antecedents. The camp was a squalid collection of wigwams and turtle huts, fashioned from thick black-and-yellow argofoam sheeting. The whole area stank due to lack of sanitation and a profusion of smoldering domestic fires whose smoke did not seem to have the energy to rise above head height and consequently formed a low, reeking ground mist in the clearing.

The rebels—mostly fat, unhealthy women—skulked about, thinking only of how to fill their bellies or obtain the Sheva root which would prevent them becoming pregnant when taking pleasure with one of the *bandidos,* an occurrence that didn't happen too often, only when Pancho managed to bring them Likker or wine. Most of the females had chewed so much Sheva root in their lives that their metabolisms had rioted and produced outlandish, ugly swellings on their bodies in compensation for the babies they could not have. Only four children had ever been born in Pancho's camp. All of them had died in infancy.

The eleven men, none under fifty—old-style lifecount— were lethargic and defeated, too. They spent most of their time asleep or cleaning the bulletless carbines which Pancho had stolen from an antique store in Cordoba many, many years ago.

The *gringo*, however, did not appear to realize that the guns were as impotent as the *bandidos*. He sat motionless on an upturned jerrican, meek in the face of the weapons. Maybe he was scared by such a show of ruthless force.

The watch fire flickered. The *gringo* turned his head. He was young, but no boy, and handsome and had taken much sun. He wore Huron pants and a Mutton jacket. A Moonglow torch was clipped to his belt.

Pulses quickening, despair and fatigue sloughing off, Pancho heeled the burro into the encampment and stiffly dismounted. He tried to swagger but he was too sore and too eager to find out what development the *gringo* might represent, good or bad. Certainly, the scene was original enough to tickle his imagination, to augur good for Pancho. It was an eternity since they'd last taken a prisoner.

Jingling, hitching up his gun belt—unfortunately empty —Narvaez stalked forward and, tipping back his sombrero, sneered at the stranger.

"How you take him, Pedro?" he asked of a lank mestizo who stood guard with his—empty—Ithaca Supersingle Shotgun. "You run him down?"

"Are you Pancho Narvaez?" the stranger asked, making to rise.

Pancho kicked him, gently, with the side of his boot to make him sit like a good leetle *gringo*, and said threateningly, "Who you think I am, *amigo?* I am Pancho Narvaez, and you had better not forget it."

"And I am Alexander Blunt," the stranger said. "And *you* had better not forget that, *amigo.*"

Narvaez's jaw clicked and fell open. He clamped it shut again with an effort, staring at the stranger, struggling to understand the miracle of his deliverance.

"Blunt?" he said.

"Alex Blunt."

"He had no food on heem," Pedro said, dolefully.

"Shut your mouth, you fool," Narvaez grated.

The women had gathered, not close, but thickly, making a circle around the center of the clearing. The event of the stranger had interested them but not until their leader returned did they dare display their curiosity openly. From their stations on the rocks, three male guards, who had somehow kept awake tonight, also watched.

Pancho Narvaez stooped and peered straight into Blunt's face.

"How you come here?"

"Looking for the great Pancho Narvaez," said Blunt.

"You found him now."

"I need your help."

"My help? You come from Morello?"

"I know where Morello can be found."

"Lotsa dudes say that: Morello not so easy to lay by the heels."

"I know exactly where he is."

"Where?" Narvaez hardly dared breathe in case this vision of redemption vanished like a mescaline phantom.

"Tontala: the Temple of Tontala."

"Why you tell *me* this?"

"I want him taken," Blunt said. "I want him taken, and I want to see him killed."

"You his friend?"

"Jesus!" Blunt said. "No, I'm not his friend. I'm his goddamn partner, and I hate the guy's guts. Can you take him, or do I have to go down into Veracruz and report myself to the Bureau?"

Blunt got to his feet. Pancho Narvaez no longer had the temerity to bully the stranger. The Mexican stepped humbly back.

"Well?"

"This is the truth?" Pancho said. "You hate Morello, and you want him keeelled?"

"I told you. I want to *see* him killed—personally."

"Okay! Okay! I help you."

"Can you take him?"

"Not myself: no, not myself. We are not enough."

"Morello has one man, one girl, and an old woman with him," Blunt said. "You have twenty *bandidos*."

"But Morello . . ." Pancho Narvaez began.

"*Well?*"

"Trust me?" Pancho Narvaez pleaded pitifully.

"What's your offer?"

"I take you into Veracruz. I got . . . better *bandidos* there; *amigos*. They can do what you want. Do it fast and sure, I give you my word."

"What's in it for you?" Blunt asked.

"I get the . . . the reward. You get Morello. Okay?"

"When?"

"We leave at sunrise: okay?"

Blunt hesitated. "Okay."

In spite of himself, Pancho Narvaez threw his hat in the air and yelled in glee. He was saved: for posterity, he was saved. By five o'clock tomorrow afternoon, he alone in all Mexico would be truly immortal—and then he would really make trouble for the *gringos*.

Flinging his hat in the air again he yelled out in triumph: *Viva Narvaez*.

Phlegmatically, the stranger called Blunt rolled himself a smoke.

On the plateau of Tontala many past *kulturs* had met and merged. Dominant among them were Totonac and Aztec, the latter a creeping tendril of the mystico-military caste of Tenochtitlán, the former perfumed by the influences of wandering gurus from Texcoco, the *tlamatini,* followers of Truth. Out of such uneasy matings the character of Mexico had been bred. From it Christian missionaries had shaped a garish religion of forgiveness, fructification, and resurrection drenched, in all its trappings, with innocent blood and the smoking remnants of retributive sacrifice. Catholic priests, however, had had little truck with Tontala. It was too ancient, too mottled to have attracted them in large numbers. In its vicinity were no beds of cement stone, no sulfur diggings, no gold or silver ores, no fields under or upon the earth to enrich the worshipers by whose tithes the Jesus cult prospered and increased its power. In the late eighties, Tontala had been the scene of considerable archaeological activity, teams of collegians chipping and brushing, scraping, measuring, and recording, under the false impression that the secrets of that enigmatic place could be unearthed and interpreted by scientific calculation. But Tontala was an experience that could only be grasped by sacrificing the identity, by plucking off the petals of the soul and bathing the psyche in *all* that it contained, the invisible paradoxes of barbaric cults dovetailed with spirituality as ethereal as any to be found in history. Tontala, Dowd Hartmann said, was also a catchment of styles and objects, housing on its long, narrow shelf of subtropical jungle, a ball court, a temple, a Pyramid of the Sun, a dozen giant colossi, and a welter of undecipherable

151

friezes, steles, and huge ramrod masks to gods and skyborn strangers long, long forgotten.

It was to this place that Eugene Morello brought the Totonac pureblood and the Aztec prophetess, riding them in on the kind of chariot that ancient sculptors, painters, and graphic delineators would have adored, with its blocky shoulders, goggled visage, and prognathous fenders.

The Mastodon ground on slowly, with the stately, powerful thrust of a conqueror, pawing up over the southern rim of the ball court between fallen columns and tumbled carvings. Growling throatily, it advanced onto the grass-carpeted arena in which lithe athletes had once competed in the game of life, using a rubber ball for the soul, staking victory against shameful decapitation. Feathered serpents, skulls, flying machines, and stone knives waited symbolically on the base of the plinth, a platform as high as a man. Onto this deck the Stormbringer, lost now in labyrinths of time beyond recall, would be conjured to ordain his own and weed out the weaklings of the warrior race by demanding their hearts in payment for defeat. Into the same well of sacrifice, however, went all sorts of men; believer with atheist, soldier with poet, players of the ball game with those who regulated the destinies of the players, priests and musicians of one race culled out and condemned by the rulers of another. But in the waters of that well all soon became one, blood mingling with blood, until the red and ocher dust clouds came and silted over the well and choked it and all quarrels were lost and all souls fused in amnesia as the races died out.

To Tontala, with Papan, Eugene Morello brought the materials of a dozen different destinies. He was prepared for every fate on offer. After all, as an upright son of a twenty-first-century All-City State, citizen of the Freemen's beautiful New York, he respected the intrinsic power of the word. He knew precisely what it could do, how it could cut the strongest bond, pierce the toughest hide, penetrate the hardest human heart. Propaganda, sloganeering, and advertising were but the pale, unhealthy flowers of the tree of ritual, a tree so thickly rooted in the rich soil of time that no man, not even a bard, could ever shake it loose. He, Eugene Morello, did not wish to try.

In the back of the Mastodon were Papan's ageless tools; a tobacco calabash, a snakeskin drum, an obsidian mirror. He would use her this night and tomorrow to predict and

152

shift the future. Prophecy, he had learned, always took account of the interventions of prophetesses. There was no better than Papan, old though she had become in this era of this life. It would soon be time, the old woman had informed him, for her to change her shape, to enter the womb and emerge once more smooth and innocent and unstained, yet with the knowledge of all lives patterned into her in ways that no Bureau geneticist could comprehend. Not only did he utilize his faith in the incarnations of Papan, Gene Morello also had a purpose for Flower Feather. She was the counteragent, fertile as the maize plant, soft as cloud, young as tomorrow's dawn. From her loins, now that she was ripe, he would spawn sons balanced on the rope of his instinctive aggression and her mystical understanding of the beneficent world. He had not taken her yet. He had still—somehow—to prove himself. She, in her turn, had only to wait.

It was very close. Gene Morello sensed it. Dawn and dusk touched like the horns of an old bull. Tonight, tomorrow, he would study the future with the instruments of the past—and fashion the present accordingly.

So far he had acted only against Florian and the ideals of the State. Now he would do more than counter a theology of others' devising. He would create his own, foster it in triumph. Since his first arrival in Mexico thirty years ago, he had realized that this must be his life's work. All the happenings since—though he had responded to them as a man—dwindled to trivial preparation. Even the necessary hardware of the Voladores Studio, the know-how of little men like Smolkin and Blunt, the incredible exploitable naiveté of Narvaez, were rendered spectral, less tangible than his inspired dreams of cyclical revolution.

"Stop here, Dowd," Morello said.

Hartmann phased out the engine.

The headlights seemed strangely ineffectual. An eerie phosphorescent light hung in the air like a gas and backlit the ringed ruins of Tontala.

Behind him in the rear of the truck, among the travelers' dunnage, the old woman stirred. In the silence, Morello could hear her clearly, the low, satisfied crooning sound that she made when she was deep in another life. Perhaps, he thought, she has been dozing. But he knew that that was only his rationalization of a state he did not under-

153

stand. Papan was no doubt more awake than he would ever be.

"What the hell is that?" Dowd Hartmann murmured.

"Papan is singing," Morello answered.

"What kind of song, son?"

"A war song, I think," Morello said. "We're committed now, Dowd, at last."

"And which of us will die?"

"We'll find out at dawn."

"How soon is that?" Hartmann asked.

"Shortly," Morello said. "Very shortly now, old man."

Obsidian, a vitreous bottle-glass rock, had long been revered by the peoples of Mexico, as flint was by the tribes of ancient Europe with their elf-arrows and thunder-stones. Obsidian had even been elevated to the status of a god, Tezcatlipoca, deity of the knife, life-giver, food-getter, drawer of blood, and later of the magical raising of storms, a divinity of the wind. But obsidian had other purposes than those connected with hunter and warrior. From its dark flakes mirrors were cut and polished, scrying stones in which Tezcatlipoca observed the doings of mankind, and his priests and acolytes were permitted brief glimpses of the future.

An obsidian mirror was one of the objects that Papan carried through the gaseous half-light just prior to dawn. She wore the robes of an Aztec princess, loud, large-patterned, and a headdress sewn with obsidian beads and the plumage of falcons. Slung on a thong about her bony shoulder was a priest's calabash containing packets of herbs and finely ground powders.

Flower Feather walked behind the old woman, carrying the small serpentskin drum. The girl was clad in a scarlet skirt emblazoned with full yellow flowers. A cloak of feathers—waxwing, cardinal, woodpecker, crossbill, and stork—covered her nude shoulders and breasts.

In file the woman and the girl crossed the diagonal of the ball court and ascended the staircase to the Pyramid of the Sun, upon whose flattened summit the House of Ascent stood intact, a shelter for visiting gods from the sky. It was not cold, even in that season, at that hour, as if thunder lurked in the clear skies behind the mass of the mountains.

Morello and Hartmann did not accompany the Mexicans. The men waited by the base of the Pyramid. In silence they watched the woman and the girl climb the staircase and, like copper shadows against the porous stonework, enter into the dark aperture and vanish from sight.

Long minutes passed. Hartmann smoked. It was utterly still in the subtropical forest below the plateau. In the mountains above there was no sound except the faint, glassy tinkle of a stream fanning over rocks. Insects, birds, any small animals which had escaped the wildcat hunting of the period of the famine, when whole species had been eradicated, made no noise.

Into this silence the drum sound dropped like a pebble into a deep well, sending faint vibrations rippling out from the mouth of the temple on the pyramid summit, a light, staccato note tapped out with the fingertips upon the small, tight disc of snakeskin stretched across the gourd. She would be cross-legged, Flower Feather, seated discreetly in a corner of the empty chamber, the gourd clasped between her smooth thighs, her elbows raised to give flexibility to wrists and fingers and to enable her to cock her thumbs down for that slightly louder point to the rhythm. At no time in the short pulsing sonata did the drum speak loudly. It coaxed, enticed, persuaded; it did not command.

Hartmann looked up unblinkingly at the staircase, at the paring of pitch darkness which was all that was visible from the ground of the door of the House of Ascent. Morello stared at the earth for a while, then, standing slowly, swung from the hips and scrutinized the east.

There was no dramatic serrated edge for the sun to splinter, no cloud to give body to its rising. On that day of the winter solstice, it came from far beyond the rim of the plateau, spreading light frugally along the grass carpet of the ball court at whose extreme edge the men waited. It was not to the Pyramid that the sun gradually slanted its rays but to the deck of the Stormbringer, crawling redgold staves of light across the arid grass. It was odd that there was no dew, no apparent moisture. The blades of grass were stark as spears in their own shadows, each individual leaf outlined. The massive consolidated shadows of the walls, like turquoise doors opening vertically from the surface of the earth, the burgeoning shadows of the warrior colossi, even the fan-shaped geometric shadows of the Pyramid's stone steps, all seemed heavier than lead against the myriad prickling brightnesses of the lawn.

At precisely the instant that the first finger of sunlight

155

touched the steps of the plinth the drum ceased. The light lay, trembling, like furrow filled with molten metal, bronze not gold, then crept upward to the dull lump of the altar stone. Spreading from its source point a hundred million miles out into space, it blocked out the graven images, giving them, briefly, life. A flickering snarl, a sneer, ferocity, and a tender, hollow-eyed awe were lured from the weathered stones as the light passed across the faces.

Dowd Hartmann had got to his feet.

The firmament was stretched tightly over them, sprinkled with visible stars like pinholes in colorless membrane that reddened and deepened as if suffused with blood.

Out of the clear sky rain fell, an abrupt, shocking storm, which rode wildly across Tontala. A single blast of wind flattened the grasses, crackled into the pines, and bellowed away into the mountains dragging the rain skirt with it. Glistening wetly, the ruins picked up and absorbed the colors of the sun. The grass sparkled. Droplets clung to Morello's hair and beard, beaded like obsidian the brim of Hartmann's hat.

The men swung compulsively with the axis of the storm, staring away after it to see the stems of rain rattle into the northwest, into dry deserts and the icy screes of the Sierras. When they looked again to the House of Ascent, Flower Feather was descending. Carrying the drum under one arm she assisted the woman, old, ageless, death-cheating Papan who hobbled and whimpered as if she had undergone some brutal torture within the holy house on the Pyramid's shorn-off peak.

Morello ran up the steps and lifted the bundle of woman flesh, wrapped in her ornate robes. He carried her carefully to the bottom of the staircase and on across the grass to the butt end of the ball court and laid her at the base of the Stormbringer's dais where the sun now was warm.

The orb hung clear of the earth, resting, like a ball, upon the edge of the long court, framed neatly between the stumps of fallen columns.

Papan's eyes were opaque, her brown skin as thin, veined, and yellowish as tobacco leaf. She gave out little puffing breaths, her chest heaving, as if she had swum a long distance underwater. Her left hand clutched Morello's collar.

"Did you *see*, Papan?" he asked, anxiously.

"I . . . saw."

"In the mirror, Papan?"

"I saw in the mirror."

"What? What did you see, old woman?"

"It will be well. It will be triumph."

Morello gave a soft, leonine roar. "Ah, God!" he sighed. "I'm glad."

"It will be triumph for your soul, Eugene," Papan continued, staring directly up into his face.

Morello cradled her more tightly in his arms, frowning. "My . . . my soul?"

"You must give up your body, my son," the old woman told him.

"Die?"

She lifted her shoulders, shrugging. "That word will do."

Frightened, Morello glanced around at the girl.

She shook her head.

Papan said, "But it will be triumph, in the end."

Morello's beard brushed the wrinkled brown cheek. "How can it be triumph when I'm . . . dead? How can it be?"

"There are others more important than you," Papan said. "I thought you understood the way a man drops down into destiny, stirring the waters of life around him. I thought you understood."

Morello bit his lip. "I am arrogant, mother. I am full of pride and anger and hurt. I would have the triumph for myself because I thought that it was my triumph and that there could be no other kind, that a victory without me would be no victory at all."

"It is not so, Eugene."

"Yes, I understand now. Is it . . . is it Blunt?"

"It is."

Eugene Morello put his hand down upon the Aztec's withered breast and wept.

: 4 :

PANCHO NARVAEZ allowed his prisoner to ride the burro. Thus Alexander Blunt, Bachelor of the Laureate Class and Citizen of New York, came into Veracruz, a shade saddle-sore but otherwise relaxed, while his Mexican captor was quite tuckered out trotting along, panting, by the animal's moth-eaten rump, juggling a big ox-hide water bottle and a—loaded—Winchester Rim-Fire .22 Long Rifle Caliber Semi-Automatic Carbine, a weapon that, in twenty-first-century terms, had all the stopping power of a wet spitball and whose barrel Slattery could probably have bitten off as if it were candy. But the Winchester was good enough to keep Blunt in order, and the New Yorker rolled meekly on down into the wasted city, hanging onto the reins some-times and sometimes to the mule's ears or mane, pro-tected from the chill of morning by a borrowed poncho and from the heat of noon by a nibbled brown sombrero that Pancho had excavated from the banana-box clothes closet in his plastic Potalla in the hills.

Four hours and forty-eight minutes before Volpe had any right to expect the bandit to rendezvous, Narvaez dragged the burro past the broken trough at the wall of the Bureau bunker, with scared glances at the slotted win-dow behind which he could see the shapes of the Bureau officers—they knew enough of the secrets of the Voladores not to interfere yet—and, gibbering in Spanish at the mule, who understood only four words of that language, invoked the beast to the steps of the Florian Studio Center and helped Blunt down.

Volpe opened up.

Narvaez had refreshed himself with a long pull from

the water bottle which contained a brand of tequila flavored with cocoa beans, sold locally as "Copacabana Scotch." It tasted lousy but it washed the dust from his brain, and brought mobility back to his hip joints, so that he managed an unctuous flourish for Volpe, a dandified sweep of the hat to present his captive in all his glory.

Blunt did not seem awed by Volpe.

"Is it you I deal with?" he asked, still on the step.

Volpe's eyelids flickered.

"Step inside."

"What's your name, and your status?" Blunt demanded.

Narvaez had the niggling suspicion that all was not as well as it should be.

"I got him," Pancho declared, inching his plump body between the men. "I want my reward."

"Yes," Volpe said. "That will be arranged."

Blunt said, "Come now, sir, your name."

"Volpe."

"Florian's man?"

"Listen . . ."

"Can you put me in direct touch with Florian from here?"

Volpe's expression bloated with bewilderment. He stood to one side like an English Jeeves in a seventies revival, and bowed a little. Nudging Blunt, Pancho Narvaez entered the Freemen's lair.

To tranquilize his fear he thought of the exquisite relief that would be afforded him by the prick of the air-spray on the pores of his left arm, of the warmth of eternal life that would course through his veins and settle in everlasting deposits in his glands and organs, rejuvenating him and ascertaining that, short of being torn apart by a Bureau shredder, he would be hale and hearty a couple of centuries hence when *gringo* dudes like Volpe and Smolkin and this Blunt *bastudo* were all dead and gone. It didn't matter if Blunt had surrendered to him just to get a free ride down the mountain; it still looked like his capture and he could probably play it up a little to the blond.

The jet-el took them to the eighth floor, a double-deep dining area where, far back in the past, troupes of gorgeous girls had danced with bowls of fruit on their heads when the Voladores was a hotel and catered for the vulgar tastes of *turistas*. Now it was used, largely, as a store for the miles of virgin tape that Smolkin insisted on keeping on hand, all spooled and polyethylene-wrappered and cartoned. In the center of the area was a rusted fountain and a dry pond about the size of a sombrero. A mezzanine gallery ran around the room, like a horseshoe, and elegant staircases curved up to it from both wings.

Armed with a Firebow Mercury, Slattery waited there. Smolkin skulked in a niche in the cartons under the gallery. There was a folding table, nice and shiny and sanitized. On it was a hypo and an ampule of Immortality Serum. Boots clacked a little on the old-fashioned flooring, and Volpe's voice sounded almost animate in echo.

"Blunt wants to communicate personally with Florian. Do we permit it?"

Slattery had no opinion.

From his niche, Smolkin said, "Hey, Mr. Blunt, I like your pieces. I like *Whale Song* and *Robes for all Seasons*, and . . ."

"Shut your mouth, Harv," Volpe said.

Blunt said, "Unless I'm mistaken you are Harvard Smolkin?"

"That's me, sir."

"And you," Alex said to Volpe and Slattery, "are presumably Florian's ambassadors. What do you know about the situation as it is now?"

Volpe was a little nonplussed. He was intelligent enough to realize that his guns were being spiked by this bold, almost arrogant renegade. Blunt was a bard, a high-status Laureate—or had been before his lam—and Volpe was highly suspicious of that class. He wavered, transmitting uncertainty to Slattery. The sonar-knob of the Firebow Mercury dropped an inch.

Volpe said, "I have no orders about that."

Blunt said, "But you can video Florian from here?"

Smolkin said, "I have a satellite connection."

Blunt said, "Open?"

Smolkin said, "Sure thing."

Blunt said, "Very well, gentlemen. I will impart my information to Florian immediately."

"Impart to us," Slattery managed.

"To Florian, and only to Florian. In private, too," Blunt said.

Narvaez said, "And while he's doing it you can maybe geeve me my reward, huh?"

Volpe's chin had receded a little more, drawing his

small face in on itself, making two sacs of hard flesh appear at the bottom corners of his mouth. He was used to making rapid, responsible decisions about whether to shoot a man's ear off, or go for his kneecap or his codlings, whether to keep up electrostatic persuasion for forty minutes or forty-five, but he was thrown by political wheeler-dealering and would not, perhaps, have reached a decision at all, except to blast Blunt and fabricate the circumstances, if Blunt and Smolkin between them hadn't quietly taken the matter out of his hands.

"I'll show you the way," Smolkin said.

"Thank you," Blunt said.

As the couple walked off down the length of the room, Volpe felt his strength ebb. Slattery too was weakened. Blunt had no fear of them. It was as if he had dealt all his life with originals of that order. Frightened, Slattery raised the Firebow Mercury and allowed it to draw its bead on Blunt's retreating shoulder blades. His dark Irish eyes smiled again as his foreknuckle dusted the button.

"No," Volpe suddenly snapped.

Slattery did not break the pose until the doors at the room's end closed behind the victims. He might have stood like that, rigid and patient, until the targets returned—but for the Mexican.

Sidling up to the white folding table, already unzipping his shirt, Pancho Narvaez said eagerly, "It ees time for my reward, *amigos*. I have earned it, no?"

Slattery did not even glance at his companion. The order was received instinctively, the order that offered solace, consolation, of a sort.

Holstering the Firebow under his right armpit, Slattery said, "Step this way, greaser," broke the ampule, and siphoned the hypo full.

Pancho closed his eyes in ecstasy when the eternal warmth flowed into his veins.

Nine minutes and eleven seconds later Pancho died in chattering agony as a dilute solution of hyaluronidazine finally dismembered his tissue cells and his liver, as it happened, decayed beyond function.

Thoughtfully Narvaez had twitched, writhed, and spasmed his way around the room and eventually snuffed it close to the exit door.

Volpe and Slattery were as preeningly gratified as if they had planned this convenient bonus. It saved them trouble and strain. They lifted Narvaez like a slaughtered hog, lugged him down to ground level, and slung him out into the street where Bureau officers, or buzzards, would soon scavenge the rotting carcass away.

H. A. Smolkin and Alexander Blunt stood in the jet-el and watched the door close.

Blunt said, "Listen, Mr. Smolkin, I bring a message from Morello."

"Uh-oh!" H. A. exclaimed.

"How long will it take you to make three miniatures of the Lambard tape?"

"Maybe four hours of simultaneous transfer."

"You have the materials?"

"Sure."

"Then do it."

"With that pair of . . . ?"

"I'll get them out of here."

"*You* will?"

"It's Morello's idea, his plan," Alex said. "I'm only following his instructions."

"What's he up to? I don't wanna be inv . . ."

The jet-el purred to a standstill. The door opened.

The two conspirators stared bleakly into the corridor.

"Is this place bugged?" asked Blunt.

"Not that I know of," said Smolkin. "There were some hypno-plants one time but I had them dug out—with permission. They interfered with low-frequency computerized transmissions."

The jet-el's door remained obediently open, Alex's left hand across the invisible beam. He doubted if Volpe or Slattery would be checking on them to that degree. He spoke quickly, coolly.

"You are involved, Mr. Smolkin," said Blunt.

"All I'm doing is . . . Hey?" An unpleasant thought darted into H.A.'s mind. "Hey, are you . . . ?"

"Morello told me," Alex said. "He had little or no alternative. I know where the tape is. It's here. That's the point, Mr. Smolkin. You make three copies, then you program the original."

"You mean, for *broadcast?*"

"I don't mean for shredding," Alex said. "Program it for peak."

"Peak is supper time," Smolkin said. "Seven till ten."

"Right," Alex said. "Put the three copies where the original tape was stored. Morello knows that, doesn't he?" Smolkin nodded.

"Program the original tape for peak time tonight, and tune your distributors into the Universal wave band."

"I daren't."

"Yes, you must do it."

"They'll kill me for that."

"With any luck at all," Alex said, reassuringly, "Volpe and Slattery won't be back."

"It makes no matter," H.A. said, in terror. *"Somebody'll* kill me."

"But you won't be here."

"I *live* here, goddamn it," H.A. shouted. "Don't you dig that: this is where I live. I can't leave now. God, I've only just started to retrieve and restore the oldies, and . . ."

"It's too late, Harv," Blunt said, sympathetically. "You and me, we're caught up in something much larger than the past—any kind of past."

"Nothing is more important than the past," Smolkin declared with great vehemence. "I got a lifetime's work invested here. I won't do it."

"Volpe and Slattery have orders to kill you," Alex said. "Balls!"

"It's true. They'll kill you and me and Morello, and anybody else they can. That's why Florian sent them here. Once they have the tape, then we'll all be for the chop."

"You're conning me. Morello's conning me," Harv Smolkin howled softly.

"Do you want to hold onto history, or help make it?" said Alex, hoping that a touch of goo from "After Hours" might work with this guy. Eugene had warned him that it would not be easy.

"I don't give a fuck about being part of history," said Smolkin.

"Keep your voice down."

"I don't give a . . ." Harv whispered.

"All right," interrupted Alex. "But that pair of Gila monsters downstairs don't give a fuck about you, Harvard. They're human computers, programmed to kill—not for the Bureau, or the Freemen, but for Florian; your boss, my boss. He wants us eliminated. He's got the bomb in the building."

"What bomb? What building? This building?"

163

"I mean Volpe and Slattery," Alex explained.

Smolkin shook his head vigorously. "I won't do it. While there's life there's hope, you know. I mean, even if Florian closes this place, I have excellent status and a clean . . ."

"Do it, or I'll peach to Florian tonight."

"You can't. You wouldn't," said Smolkin, aghast.

"I've been in your shoes, Harv," Alex went on. "Eight, ten weeks ago I was a company man to the roots of my hair, only I came to realize that it wasn't loyalty but possession that Florian wanted."

"I'm only a humble archivist," pleaded Smolkin. "I don't understand any of this. Preservation and reclamation of the treasures of the past, that's my gig, sir, and all the rest of this schmoo is way over my head, I assure you."

"The innocent and the guilty alike: it makes no odds to Florian, Harv," Alex said.

"Make a trip-cop of the Lambard tape? Jesus, that's serious enough! But program it! Holy Cow! I may not understand much of this, but I *know* what that tape can do."

"All right, Harv," Alex said. "I'm going to talk to Florian. You listen."

"He'll know I'm tuned. Those two-way satellite eidophor projectors are sensitive as hell. I mean, Florian will know I'm eavesdropping."

"Not if you stand on the extension line of the screen," Alex said. "I've enough technical experience to know that. You can blot out the pickup if you stay absolutely motionless on the horizontal plane. That's where sync technicians stand when they need pointer shots on a prerun."

"Okay! All right! You win!" H.A. groaned, without the trace of a tune in his quavering voice. "I'll listen. I don't say I'll do what you ask, though."

"What Morello asks," Alex corrected.

". . . but I'll listen."

"Good. Fine." Alex took H. A. Smolkin by the elbow. "Where's the projection room?"

"This way."

Smolkin led the New Yorker from the jet-el, which closed its door with what sounded like a faint sigh of relief.

"Lissen, I mean, what do they want to ace me for?" Harv said. "I've done nothing, not anything, against anybody."

"Who's your minder?"

"Miss Spears."

"Where is she?"

"I don't know: around."

"Don't trust her."

"But . . ."

"You heard me," Alex said, harshly. "Don't trust her an inch. Whatever you do, make sure she doesn't have access to or video scan on your activities over the next eight hours. When the copies are made, hide them at once."

"I'm not doing it."

"Program the Lambard tape original."

"I'm not doing it."

"Fix the program coordinates as usual."

"I'm not doing it."

"One hour before the Lambard tape is due for transmission, recompute onto the Universal wave band, and boost the audio-visual."

"I'm not doing it."

"Set the A-V on a rising graph, and lock."

"I tell you, I'm not doing it, sir."

"Lock the whole system by computer code."

"No, lissen, I'm not . . ."

"Grab the three copies and blow."

"Blow?"

"Get the hell out of here."

"Outside? You mean, *Mexico?*"

"We'll pick you up."

"No."

"We'll pick you up at eight o'clock, CA time, prompt, tonight."

"Pick me up in what? A basket?"

"Do you understand, Harvard?"

"I'm not doing it," H. A. Smolkin said. "Here, in here."

Alex sat in the center of the front row. He could have touched the screen with his toes if he sunk into a matinee slouch, but he did not. He sat upright, relaxed and dignified, in spite of the eccentricity of his garb. He thought of lighting a smoke but he decided that it would be better to give Florian no hint that he had slid off the slope that the Freemen had greased for him. Eugene had not known, of course, that the agents would be of this caliber. Oddly, Alex was less scared of the pair than he should have been. Couple of months back they would have scared him witless. But they lay close enough to some of the roles he

165

had lived through in the course of his travels for him to equate his strength with theirs. If he didn't share their dynamic viciousness, he was more intelligent. Status had given him that. Words would not deflect a mercury ball, but at least words could stay the knuckle on the button.

He nodded to Smolkin who stepped in front of the screen for an instant and operated the bleeper which would summon Florian to the New York video transceiver. The screen came alive. The audio caught some background static from space, or maybe from the proximity of the urban belt. Wistfully Alex thought he recognized the songs of the whales in the Sutler Dock Aquatarium—an illusion. For one split-second, however, he did pick up an audible, unintelligible fragment of conversation, in a language whose very patterning was alien to him and did not belong to any of the five civilized communication currencies.

From his stance in exact line with the screen's horizontal plane, H.A. Smolkin frowned in bewilderment, too. Alex shook his head. Possibly Florian was already on beam, holding off on visual establishment in the hope of picking up just such a slip between the summoners. Alex realized abruptly that his perspective had so altered that he now regarded Florian as an enemy, wily and sly and lethal. He had not been aware of reaching a decision to trust Dowd Hartmann and Gene Morello to this extent.

The alien speech, much fainter, clipped out a dozen oral units, then struck off just as Florian's huge visage coalesced rapidly on the screen.

"Was that you?" Florian asked, frowning. "That . . . that voice?"

"No, I thought it was your end," Alex said.

"Are you tapped?"

"I don't know, do I?" said Alex. "It's all your equipment."

"Where's Smolkin?"

"Somewhere below."

"Are you alone, Alexander?"

"Yes."

"Have you encountered my . . . er, ambassadors?"

"Yes."

"Ah!" said Florian, fishing for an explanation!

"You don't seem unduly surprised to see me here, sir."

"No, no, I rather thought you might strike out after Morello. Tell me, my boy, is he alive or dead?"

166

"Alive."

"Have you . . . er, seen him then?"

"Yes."

"And?"

"I'm sorry about Miss Abbott," said Alex. "You see why I had no choice but to run, sir. It wasn't intended as disrespectful to you, or anything, but the truth is that I *think* Morello had me tampered with, psycho-cerebrally."

"So that's how it was done."

"Morello won't admit it, of course, but I wheedled something out of Dowd Hartmann."

Florian looked completely surprised. "Hartmann? *The* Dowd Hartmann?"

"With due respect, sir, I think you're role-playing a little there. You've known all along that Hartmann was in the hinterland."

"Did he tell you that?"

"He did, and I believe that part of his story."

"Did they—Morello and Hartmann—send you to talk with me?"

"No."

"Didn't they try to prevent you?"

"Naturally."

"What is it, Alexander? You can tell *me,* surely."

"I don't like it out here, Florian. I want amnesty to return to New York and resume my work."

"But the Bureau will never wash out a Life-Theft."

"I have the feeling that you covered for me: did you?" Florian simpered pinkly. "Well, actually—yes."

"If I can make my way back to New York, will you take me into the company again?"

"It . . . well, it rather depends, my boy."

"On what, sir?"

"The Club isn't happy about the state of things in Mexico. That's why my two ambassadors are there."

"To kill people?"

Florian appeared shocked. He flushed, and his eyes went around, widening until it seemed that he was being asphyxiated by consternation.

"My ambassadors don't kill people, Alexander. Life-theft is a highly un-Ethical act."

"Florian," Alexander interrupted, "I am not so naive as I was. I understand that the situation is critical. It must be or you would have been more cautious, and much

167

more neat in implementing your strategy. The problem is that Morello has told me many things, some of which I accept as the truth; others are patently lies. I'm having a personal Ethical problem in sorting out the wheat from the chaff."

"You have always trusted me until now, my boy."

"I still trust you, Florian. But I appreciate that there *are* major issues involved, and I remember my high school indoctrinations sufficiently well to realize that I am much less important than the security of the All-City States."

Florian nodded. "I see."

"However, I will take your word against Morello's. He has promised me a high status in some nebulous empire which he hopes to build on the strength of a taped exposé—by Lambard, no less—of the activities of the Freemen's Club. I accept that I was quite wrong about Lambard. I thought he was a sane man: now, I have my doubts. Morello is not for me, either, though I confess that I see some quality in his reasoning."

"What are you trying to say, Alexander? Please be more cryptic."

"I believe I know where the Lambard tape is."

Florian lost control of himself sufficiently to clear his throat, covering his mouth and jowls with his hand, politely. The kinetics were revealing. His feverish anxiety to lay hands on the Lambard tape would be his sure undoing. Morello had read that right.

Florian said, "Oh, really! Ah . . . where?"

"They—Hartmann and Morello—have gone now to an ancient temple in a placed called Tontala. It isn't far from here, somewhere en route to Jalapa, I think."

"How do you know this?"

"I navigated for Hartmann, and memorized some of the maps."

"But why Tontala, and what's the tape doing there?"

"Look, Florian, I can vouch for the accuracy of what I overheard, but much of it makes no real sense to me."

"Answer as best you can, Alexander."

"There's some kind of power source in or near Tontala," said Alexander. "Morello has been working on it. That may be why he has been incommunicado."

"Possibly: possibly," said Florian. "Why he feigned suicide, yes, yes."

"He lured me down here," Alexander lied, "with a little aid from you, I think."

"Admitted: admitted," said Florian, magnanimously.

"He lured me down here with the hope of utilizing my expertise in transmission systems. At least, Morello thought I knew more about them than he does. In fact, I don't. Be that as it may, he figured that he could use me and that I would be keen to join him."

"Succinctly, *please*, Alexander."

"Very well, Florian. The tape has been hidden in this temple, for many years, while Morello worked out how to broadcast it."

"Broadcast; you mean . . . ?"

"He adapted the Riss-Interlink," Alex went on. "The topographic situation of Tontala vectors perfectly across a quadrant of Central America. I think—though I can't be sure—that you can't jam or block the transmission."

"That doesn't sound . . . feasible."

"Morello was guarded about what's on that tape, Florian. Will you tell me, please, why all the fuss?"

Florian was nibbling his lower lip. "It's important, my boy, but better kept from you. You've done well. I'm awfully pleased with you. I thought all along that you had been tampered with. I'm glad to see that you did not slip so far into lunacy as to be irrecoverable—also that you still trust me in spite of the lies that must have been told about me."

"I escaped, by the way," said Alex. "They weren't guarding me very carefully. I sneaked out last night and found the encampment of a Mexican called Narvaez about whom Morello had told me a little. Strangely, he brought me here."

"Ah, yes, Narvaez." Florian was obviously thinking of something more important than a *bandido,* a mere cog in the wheel of progress. "Now listen, Alexander."

"Yes, Florian."

"Are you willing to guide my men to Morello?"

"Your ambassadors?"

"Mr. Volpe and Mr. Slattery, yes."

"Guide them to Tontala? But is that necessary? I'd prefer not to be further involved, actually."

"You must trap Morello. You must acquire the tape for me."

169

"But Mr. Volpe and Mr. Slattery are . . . are surely experts at this kind of thing?"

"Morello may still trust you enough to let you into the sanctum where the tape is kept. When does he plan to broadcast?"

"Very soon, I imagine," said Alex. "Tomorrow or the next day."

"You will take my ambassadors to Tontala," Florian said. "You will redeem the tape, Alexander, and I will arrange for you to return to New York without a stain on your character."

"But what of the others—this Narvaez, and Smolkin: Morello and Hartmann?"

"I will attend to them."

"How?"

"Have you changed that much, Alexander?"

"You intend to remove them, Florian, don't you?"

"Yes."

"What guarantee have I that you won't also remove me?"

"You will have the tape. Besides, you are mine, *my* man. I've always had a very soft spot for you, my boy. Even Freemen are allowed irrational sentiments from time to time. You have my *word* that you will come to no harm."

Alex hesitated.

By the screen poor Harv Smolkin's face had turned a ghastly shade of gray.

Alex said, "I suppose all this furor will be ascribed to the work of the ROT faction in Mexico?"

"Probably."

"And there is no ROT faction?"

"Not as such, my boy: no."

Alex said, "I don't care much about the others, Florian. They are nothing to me. I only want back to my liner, my work. It's too coarse and uncomfortable in the hinterland for my taste. If you promise me on your Freeman's oath that I won't be harmed, then I'll do as you ask."

"I promise you, Alexander," said Florian, solemnly.

"Then I will bring you the tape."

Before Florian could prevent it, Alex stepped from the center row and touched the operating switch. Sound and image wavered amid some sizzling static and Harvard

Smolkin, hand to his mouth, ran out of the little theater into the corridor where he threw up all over the floor.

A moment later Alex closed the doors of the viewing room.

"Well, Mr. Smolkin?"

"I'll do it," Harv said, blubbering. "I knew it was too good to last."

"What was too good to last?"

"Everything," the archivist replied.

: 5 :

EUGENE MORELLO knew now that even if he so wished he could not sacrifice Alexander Blunt to the cause of progress. It was written out another way. Blunt wasn't the pawn, the scapecoat. Blunt was destined to be the Phoenix of Veracruz, to survive whatever the Freemen flung at him in retribution for broadcasting the tape. Morello was grieved that it should be Blunt and not himself. But he had absorbed enough from Papan's soliloquies on the duality of past and future to understand that the one was never over and the other never begun. He regretted that he would not survive long enough to impart some of this wisdom to Blunt, the wetback revolutionary.

As he waited for the first battle of the new war to begin, Morello remembered one of his own student poems, a fugitive piece that had never seen print nor screen: *If I had a brother, I would create the world.* Heartfelt, if not original. Throughout his comparatively short life, he had nurtured the arrogance of the creator, refused to allow his talent to become a weapon of self-destruction. But now, this past year or more, all his voices were stilled. He heard nothing in his head but echoes of age-old battle hymns, songs his father had sung him to sleep with when he was a refugee *Wunderkind* hiding from street guerrillas in a cigar store at the back of the family town house on the fringe of the city. A long way back, Gene: reaching, touching, saddened yet consoled by the memory. There had been many innovators since then, prophets to the messiah. At least he had been privileged to be the last of them. If Blunt was any kind of man at all, the least he could do, in some settled future time, would be to compose a eulogy in praise of Gene Morello. Better off than poor old Dowd, who had only had a comix strip as an obit.

The light was waning a little. It must be moving toward five in the afternoon—the hour of the torero. The snow on the Sierras was blue-white, rinsed with coming dusk. The Mastodon was hidden away in the trees north of Tontala. The old woman and the girl had retired to the sanctuary of the temple court, down a stairwell that snuck into the earth and, thanks to another war, seventy years ago, had never been fully excavated. Dowd was stationed on the steps of the Pyramid of the Sun, well hidden. Their one prop-mortar, assembled and wedged firm with stones, was trained on the rim of the ball court over which Alex would guide Florian's pirates. Just how many, Morello did not know. He did not anticipate more than four: the rogue Freeman's maneuvers were still secret enough to inhibit full-scale attack.

They would use some kind of vehicle. If Alexander had lied effectively, they would most likely arrive before nightfall. Every hour that passed would make the risk of broadcast more dangerous, Florian's plot more precarious.

There had been times of late when Morello had almost forgotten what he was fighting for, times when distant static in the vaults of reason had overwhelmed his sense of purpose and confused his direction. Maybe that was how it had always been with warriors and revolutionaries. Which way to turn the wheel, lads, that is the question. But motion of any sort would be a triumph.

It was wrong of him to envy Blunt possession of Flower Feather. Poor Alexander would be as shy a bull as ever trod the clover. Eternal purposes, however grandiose, were not without comic undertones.

Morello cuddled the Turkus under his right armpit, his cheek pressed against the stock. He had not programmed the digital calculator embedded in the base of the short, stout muzzle, preferring to retain manual control of the weapon. He had filled the chambers with alternate shells, to give a medley of blast and scorch. The first shell, on explosion, would create a wall of shock waves against which the second shell would impact and release a spectacular sheet of flame. Interaction fire had been a much-loved innovation of the Urban Wars and the

Turkus's pyrotechnical displays had delighted pin-headed guerrillas enormously. In this kind of combat, a Turkus was still a most effective weapon, especially when backed by Dowd's prop-mortar, accurate to the inch at ranges of up to a mile. The P.M.'s finger-length missiles were loaded with conventional nitro compound stabilized by a jelly crust that would melt only when maximum temperature/ velocity was reached. A deadly number.

What if Florian's troopers also had such weapons, or even more sophisticated armaments? How long would he last? How painful would his death be? Eugene tried to contemplate death not as the theft of life but as a change of state, a release from the clinging, selfish fetus that was the binder of every man's soul.

Flower Feather had comforted him with traditional tales. According to the Totonac girl the dead traveled to the House of the Sun to be transformed into rich-plumaged birds and sip nectar in the sweet country where the soft winds dwelled. Perhaps he would be earmarked instead for the warriors' Valhalla, domain of the rain god, Tlalochan— or be summoned to the mysterious, cool blue valley of Tamoanchan, the House of Birth, where there were fountains, glades, meadows, an abundance of fruit, and many dwarfs, jesters, and buffoons to sing and dance and make merry.

Yeah, Morello thought, stoically, that's the dive for me.

The stealthy sound of the Slovak Landcrab's approach dispersed his daydreams. He should have remembered that Narvaez had once told him there were four or five of the machines preserved in the central region in case the Bureau territory was ever imperiled.

The throbbing of its engine fluctuated as the Slovak wound around the track on the shoulder of the plateau.

Dowd Hartmann stuck his head up from behind Pyramid statuary and yelled, "Two-man Slovak, reckon."

Morello waved his hand in acknowledgment.

A two-man Slovak was not large enough to be indestructible, not like the big jobs in the range, entities of tungstenpell and thread steel which could obliterate whole battalions of trained urban guerrillas in seconds. But the two-man version, probably requisitioned from the Bureau bunker in Veracruz, was hardly more than a swift means of transportation. Only a nut would use it as a base in a showdown fight.

Using sluiced diesel oil pumped by a forty-second jet of compressed alcohol, the Landcrab's power source was about the size of a bandbox, sunk in the guts of the beast and consequently difficult to sabotage. As a youth, Dowd had fought against Slovak prototypes. He figured that they were vulnerable only from below, where the air siphon screens were unprotected. A Landcrab driver's field of vision was total, through a toughened Perspex dome and four prismatic gimbals. The traction of eighty-plate rotators made even miniatures difficult to overturn. Sure, they could blast the brute into oblivion—they had the fire-power for that—but then Alex, who was presumably inside, would be fried too.

For a moment Morello was intrigued by the prospect of throwing the onus of responsibility for Blunt's welfare back on the nebulous powers of the fate that had ordained him. After all, *he* wasn't supposed to negotiate as a free agent. The knowledge that Papan had imparted of the climax of events guaranteed that outcome. Only the intervening buildup, the bridge to certain resolution, remained obscure. Supposing, Morello thought, I just blast the bastard to bits—what then? How would Blunt escape? How would I die? Need I die at all? Could the mirror phophecy be wrong? He had settled the question of his faith in Papan many months ago. He knew that he must act rationally, save Blunt at whatever cost. That was the order of things and he couldn't buck it.

"I can see it," Dowd shouted, not showing himself. "It's an old-style two-man smoothie. Christ, I ain't clapped eyes on one in decades. Beautiful, baby."

Morello called, "Compute its range, and pattern the mortar's sonar scanner. The engine's loud enough so she won't blip out even when the shooting starts."

"Got yuh!"

"How long, Dowd?"

"Now, son: thar she blows."

The Landcrab waddled over the cornice of tussocky grass that fringed the shallow cliff at the ball court's southern end. It ground a few half-buried shards of the graven columns to powder and, weaving in an evasive tactic that wouldn't fool the mortar's scanner, swung itself around prow to ass and came on backward into the middle of the walled area.

Manacled by wrists and ankles to drag-capstans on the

175

Landcrab's butt, Alex Blunt braced himself, then sagged, his galled muscles overtaxed by the rough ride up from the jungle. Between his legs the face of a simian trooper could vaguely be discerned inside the glossy dome.

Thwarted now, Hartmann and Morello lay low.

The Slovak's loudhailer boomed, "We know you are here, Morello. We advise you to surrender peacefully."

Eugene kept his head down.

"Show yourself, Morello. Return the Freemen's property and no harm will come to you, we promise."

Blunt had squirmed upright. He looked now as if he was about to leap from the Landcrab's hull, except that he was still chained to it. He peered into the darkening shadows of the ruins. For a moment it crossed Morello's mind that Alex was playacting, that he had been party to Florian's duplicity all along, a double-dealer. On consideration, though, it did not seem likely. Whatever else the company had taught Blunt, it had drilled him well in a kind of honesty.

Neither of the groups dared move. If the agents quit the Landcrab they would be vulnerable. They could not, however, search the site thoroughly with their devices. Slovaks were armed with a basic laser, plus other portable weaponry. Morello supposed that the agents might begin blasting holes in the stonework in the hope of flushing out their quarry. The Pyramid was the most obvious target. The laser had no visible muzzle to show him its direction of fire. Besides, it was too dark now to make out details of the Landcrab. Even the dome had gone dim, the interior bathed in infrared light.

Though he had never fought in armed combat before, Morello was intelligent enough to predict the agents' moves. They had forestalled surprise attack by using Blunt as a shield. Next they must ascertain that the enemy was, in fact, somewhere in the Tontala area. To do that, before dark, one man at least must leave the security of the 'crab.'

The Slovak prowled another thirty yards past the center of the ball court. It halted again within fifty yards of the altar.

So far Alex had said nothing.

Morello felt a quickening in his pulses, a strange kind of exultation in his brain. He was full of war-songs, his mind vivid with the battle hymns of his father's genera-

176

tion. The Landcrab, not its tenants, seemed to have become both source and focus of this glorious feeling of life. He sizzled with it. He had to struggle against the urge to rise up and charge the Slovak, blasting away with the Turkus.

Looking around, he noticed Dowd Hartmann creeping through the fringe grasses, sheltered by the gable of the wall. The old man reached him.

Putting his mouth close to Morello's ear, Dowd murmured, "We can't afford to wait until dark, son."

"Can they?"

"I dunno. They may have powerful lamps."

"Jesus," Morello said. "I wish I could be sure that Alexander got the message through to Smolkin. And where's Narvaez?"

"Forget Narvaez," Dowd advised. "I've trained the prop-mortar on that range, ten feet back from the prow of the Slovak. Let *them* make the move. One of them must get out."

"They might try flushing us out, you know."

"And risk destroying the tape?"

"I never thought of that," Morello whispered.

"Know what they used to call this kind of situation? A Mexican standoff. Appropriate, huh?" Dowd said. "It'll be full dark in a half hour. They can't be *sure* that we haven't got fifty guys up here. They only have Alex's word for it. They don't even know yet that it's a trap."

"Unless they broke him?"

"They didn't break him. He's a hostage, that's all," Dowd said. "Can you get yourself and the Turkus down to the corner, diagonally opposite that Slovak's ass?"

"Yeah, I think so."

"They'll leave one—maybe two—in the 'crab' and send a solo out to draw fire. That's when we'll take them. Use the guy outside as a target. Spread a fireveil. Go through it. They may not know that you can break through a fireveil easy. It forms a thin kind of membrane in the air for four, five seconds after explosion. Use the Turkus properly and you can limpet yourself to the hull of the 'crab' and blast off the capstans Alex's attached to."

Morello inched his head up and looked down at the Slovak. Nothing had happened. It stood motionless, gray as a dead armadillo. He could see how Dowd's plan might work. The problem was that there would be one, maybe two agents still left in the 'crab.' They wouldn't sit still.

177

They might try to grind him onto the wall the way a bullock will chaff off a fly on its hide.

Success demanded speed, dexterity, and courage. He was confident of his courage, but the rest? He could not predict. Maybe this was how fate would have its nickel's worth. Shit! What did it matter? Maybe it wouldn't happen today at all. The only sure thing was that he had devised a means of bringing war back into the world. To the best of his knowledge, which was pretty extensive one way and another, no man had raised arms against another in fair combat since the second decade of the Freemen's Club. Assassinations, murders, killings discreetly executed by Bureau agents—but not old-style blood 'n' guts fighting.

"What other portable weapons have you, Dowd?"

"Just my old Blackhawk Magnum," Dowd said. "It's slow and inaccurate, but it'll do. I'll get me up on the far wall. Leave the agents to me. You get Blunt safe off'n that 'crab.'"

Morello said, "Is there another way, Dowd?"

"Nope."

Morello patted the old man's shoulder and signaled him to retreat. A Turkus and an antique Blackhawk against Bureau arms seemed like long odds. That, too, excited him. He glanced around, watching the old man scuttle away in a wide detour. It would take Dowd five, six minutes to get around the site to the far wall. Morello prayed, to Hebrew gods, that Florian's agents wouldn't make their move before Hartmann was in position.

He counted the minutes on his luminous wristband.

Inside the Landcrab the agents would be having similar problems deciding strategy. They would be vectoring the site with their instruments, of course, but he doubted if a two-man machine would have anything as sophisticated as a biohomer on board. They would have to make do with visuals. He had no intention of giving them so much as a glimpse of movement before Dowd was set.

Eight minutes passed. Alex had seated himself on the Perspex dome, shackled wrists draped over his knees. He looked bored.

The light was dying fast, the long shadows of the colossi thickening into shadows flung like blankets from the hills, walls, and clustering trees to the west. Morello thought: Christ, they're going to sit us out. Maybe they're waiting for reinforcements. Maybe a squadron of Bureau agents has been marshaled, is even now sneaking around the back of the Pyramid to run us down under cover of the Slovak's laser.

He wiped his hands on his beard, slicking off sweat. He could not see Dowd. He had to trust that the old man made it. If the 'crab' shifted its location again, their plan would go *phut*. He would have to improvise an attack. If only they hadn't chained Blunt to the goddamn 'crab' like that.

What time? Almost six. In a couple of hours, the late Robert Lambard would broadcast to the nation and the real war, the Freemen's war, would be underway at last. Florian would be wiped out for starters. Maybe delay was all to the good. There had to be somebody left—Blunt?—somebody to carry on the fight.

Morello prayed again, repeating a chant that Flower Feather had taught him, which the girl had had from Papan. It was almost meaningless, only the cadences seemed to fit this scene: *And they say that in the inner heaven, the warrior is welcomed, in eagle-feathers and in blood, welcomed of the astral sun-gods who rise above the stars, masters of our flesh, lords of our flesh, navigators of souls, clothed in charcoal, dwellers in the obsidian disc, seekers of the true men in the twilight of destiny; summoning redeemers who come gladly to the knives, clothed in eagle feathers, clothed in blood, who giveth food to the earth in the shape of new bones. Take sacrifice from me. I am the heaven-studded warrior, the turner of the wheel.*

The dome of the Slovak Landcrab slid back. A blond young man in an emerald slipsuit slithered out. Alex whipped around, looked at him, and said something. The blond did not answer.

Morello tightened his grip on the Turkus and tracked back and down the hidden angle of the temple steps, knees bent, holding the gun up to keep it from making any tattletale sounds on the stones.

When he reached the bottom corner, he cradled the Turkus on his arm and, lying on his right shoulder, peered around the base.

The agent in the slipsuit had come away from the 'crab.' He moved toward the dais, walking cautiously, lightly past Alex. Bad news. If the Turkus fire coned backward Blunt would collect some of the blast. The agent carried what looked like a Firebow in his right hand. That was all; no torch, not even a radiant belt.

Morello realized that he had to reach a decision. Responsibility increased his excitement. He felt like he had the first time he had taken a woman, three years ago, only more so, nervous interactions in body and brain raised to the tenth power over that simple act of bodily knowledge. Release would come when he ran, when he fired, when he opened himself to death in exchange for death. Gambled: risked: dared. That was the pleasure of conflict, exquisitely corporeal and basic to man.

Morello counted the agent's steps—ten, twelve, fourteen, fifteen—a yard at a time, away from Alex, away from the protection of the Landcrab. Dowd would have a bead on the agent now for sure, from the ridge of the banked wall or one of the dozen slots in its upper structure where the winds used to come to watch the sport.

Make it twenty, Gene.

Settle on that.

Eighteen: nineteen: almost at the base of the altar dais, the trooper hesitated.

Twenty.

Morello rose, hoisted the Turkus to his hip, and fired. The first shell smashed into the blond's chest. The second shell melted into the shock waves. A slow flood of flame, scarlet as hibiscus, bloomed from around the incendiary core that, an instant before, had been Florian's private agent.

Morello ran.

As if blown by a gale, the fire fanned back toward the 'crab.' The silent beam of the Slovak's laser sliced through the Turkus's flame. A statue of flimsy ash, the blond trooper's human shape peeled off into flecks and speckles of black carbon. The laser raked the area, drilling uselessly into walls and searing the grass in sooty wedges.

Screened by the curtain of flame, Morello ran on.

If the laser swung to this arc, he would be reduced to ash, too.

He thought he could hear Blunt screaming.

He did not fire the Turkus again, remaining undetected for as long as possible. The breath of the firewall singed his hair and mustache. He took some of it down into his lungs where it burned like alcohol and made him gasp. He came out of the mist at the edge of the firewall. He looked into the ruby eye of the laser. He twitched his hips, ducked and zigzagged frantically to his left, doubling at once to his right again.

The laser beam ate up distant vegetation far beyond the altar dais, consuming leaves and branches. But it was weak at that set-range. Morello realized that it had no commander. Eyes blurred by heat and sweat, he could only discern the big, silvery shape of the 'crab' close_by. He leapt and flung himself down, rolled hard against the tungstenpell flanges that protected the rotators.

Dowd was yelling. Blunt was yelling.

Reaching up, Morello caught the nearest capstan and hauled himself onto the Landcrab. The smooth metal gave no friction. The strength required to hoist his body weight up the curved flank was massive. With every spasm of effort, however, he seemed to find fresh reserves of stamina, to tap primitive sources of joy that had been buried under the Freemen's regime.

Dowd was plugging away from the wall top. The Blackhawk sounded slow and ineffectual, like catapult pebbles bouncing harmlessly on a shingle roof.

Blunt yelled, "One more: one more inside."

"Stand still, Alex," Morello told him.

Aiming the Turkus short range, he blasted away the chain links at the capstan bollard. The sound of the shot was deafening as the shell tore and splintered the steel and spat off the Slovak's hull with a screech that scored but did not penetrate the tungstenpell. Morello ejected the fireshell manually. He fired another explosive, which disintegrated the second bollard and finally freed Blunt from the Landcrab.

Even as the chain fell away, the 'crab' stirred and reversed, swerving, stern sliding around at the ball-court wall. Blunt toppled backward and vanished. Morello flung the Turkus from left hand to right and just managed to grab the rim of the half-open dome. His legs flailed out from the hull as another abrupt change of direction almost shook him loose. Desperately he stuffed the gun's blunt muzzle into the aperture in the dome and activated it. Explosions and gigantic drafts of flame jetted up from within the Slovak. Immediately its progress became erratic.

Morello looked around, then down, perching his knees on the flange of the rotators. He could not believe that the battle was over. He could not believe that anyone within

181

the craft could still be alive. But the design of the Bureau Slovak precluded such attack. A bulkhead cut off the driver's chamber from the armaments section.

Morello was still hanging grimly to the edge of the dome when the elliptical section of toughened Perspex blasted into him, stunning him and knocking him clear of the vehicle. He fell heavily, left hand crushed, blood running from a scattering of tiny lacerations across his forehead. The driver had ejected the Landcrab's dome. As the 'crab' went weaving on down the ball court to the south, the agent—Slattery—sprang clear, dropping as lithely as a monkey on his attacker's blind side.

Dazed, shaken, disoriented, Morello could touch nothing with his left hand. Pain clouded his thinking. He rolled over, crouched, and let his head hang. Blood dripped onto the grass.

The laser was flaying the stonework, flaring up into the sky, seeking some solid object upon which to work its destructive chemistry, finding only random targets as the abandoned Slovak dithered on toward the rim of the plateau. The interior was burning hotly. Though he was fascinated by the sight, Morello could not take focus on it.

Somewhere behind him Florian's trooper was on the loose.

Gathering himself by an effort of will, he rose and swung around.

Blunt and Hartmann were together, the old man dragging Alex, who stumbled drunkenly toward shelter. Behind them, defined against the red, reflected glow upon the court wall, was the agent, lifting the Firebow.

Morello activated the Turkus.

Explosions and flames poured out of it, forming a canopy of fire in the air—off target.

Morello did not hear the sound of the mercury ball. It struck him on the breastbone and plowed out his lungs and heart, opening a tunnel for itself at the point of impact and hauling away its bloody cargo through a massive excavation in Morello's spine.

Morello was dead before he hit the ground.

Dowd Hartmann plucked the trigger of the quaint handgun and whooped with glee as he saw the little man spin around with the force of the bullet and the Mercury Firebow leap out of his left hand. He hoped that he had

182

killed the agent outright but, to his disappointment, saw the guy flop over and, even as he hit the grass, roll and dart away into a long plume of shadow.

Hartmann fired again. Instinct told him that the agent had escaped. His anxiety, however, was overridden by fears for Morello and by his relief at still being alive. The flickering, directionless tongue of the laser had scared him badly.

Blunt groaned on the grass at his feet. Dowd knelt, fingers feeling for the vertebrae of the neck and the revival point that he had been taught as a lad. He found it, applied pressure, and had the satisfaction of watching Alex jerk bolt upright.

Alex gave out a grating shout, like a man waking from nightmare.

"You're okay, son: you're fine," Dowd assured him.

Alex was staring down at the ball court to the south. Dowd glanced around.

The Landcrab was poised on the lip of grass. Even as the men watched, it slanted upward, the long, fading ruby-red of the laser beam striking aimlessly into the twilit sky, then whipping away as the craft's rotors bit on air. Lazily, the 'crab' upended, plunged rapidly stern over prow into the volcanic glow of its own self-generated destruction. A rain of earth and hot debris showered the men. The shadows of oily black clouds swam over them. For a flickering instant, Dowd Hartmann thought he saw the monkey shape of the surviving trooper silhouetted against the fireball. But he could not be sure. No shell or ball sang at him. Reflexively, he flung himself on Alex and plastered him to the grass.

The explosion of the Slovak Landcrab marked the final punctuation of the combat. Minutes later, the rain of debris had ceased. Even the stink of burning, drifting on the cool night wind, was already dispersing.

Holding the Blackhawk ready, Dowd crawled across the ball court to Morello's mangled corpse. He knew before he got there that the old woman's prophecy had borne fruit.

They had their triumph, and had lost Eugene.

The future lay with Alexander Blunt.

They gathered around *him* now, Dowd, Papan, and Flower Feather. He wished that he could stop his hands

183

from trembling. It was muscular tension, not fear, that made them shake. Morello lay dead at his feet, like an enemy that he had slain, not a comrade fallen bravely in war. Why did he feel no sorrow, no rage or grief? Morello seemed to have shrunk now, though his big ursine head was intact, except for the gridwork of minute wounds that leaked into his mustache and stained it red. His chest was a quagmire of bloody tissue.

"Can we do anything for him?" Alex asked.

"No, son," Dowd said. "He's dead for sure."

"Papan?"

The old woman shook her head.

She was singing, almost inaudibly.

Alex ignored her.

He said curtly, "The Lambard tape's computed. It'll begin to broadcast at eight, CA time."

"Then we've a couple of hours only to get the hell out of here. The Freemen will flatten this whole province."

"Bring up the Mastodon," Alex said.

Dowd said, "What happened in the Voladores?"

"After promising me immunity in exchange for the tape, Florian spoke to the agents. Obviously he instructed them not to give me too much rope. Volpe's dead. You saw that. Did you hit the other one; Slattery?"

"Yep."

"Maybe he's dead, too," Alex said. "Anyhow, let's get out of here."

"We'll bury Gene first," Dowd said.

"No."

"But . . ."

"Fetch the Mastodon, old man."

"But, son?"

"We have less than two hours to hit Veracruz."

"We don't have to go near Veracruz: we can hide out in the . . ."

"I promised Smolkin."

"Forget Smolkin," Dowd said. "He's a zero. He ain't worth the saving."

When Alex looked at him, the old man knew why Blunt had been chosen.

Alex said, "*I* don't break promises, old man."

"I'll git the Mastodon," Dowd said, turning away.

"Don't take the women," Alex said. "Leave them here hidden. This is man's work, and dangerous. Besides, I

184

need something to come back to. We'll pick them up later."

Stooping, he lifted Morello's Turkus from the grass.

"You, girl: how does this thing work?" he demanded.

Meekly the Totonac princess showed him, while the old Aztec prophetess looked on, apparently unmoved.

They had chosen well, the masters, as was their way.

–: PART FOUR :–

The Past Masters

BORN IS THE STORM GOD
IN THE HOUSE OF ASCENT
IN THE PLACE WHERE THE FLOWERS ARE
IN THE PLACE OF THE BREATH OF THE SUN.
ONE FLOWER, THE STORM GOD IS BORN
IN THE PLACE OF JOY AND TRUTH
WHERE THE CHILDREN OF MEN ARE MADE

Traditional Song

: 1 :

THE CIRCULAR OAK TABLE was forty feet in diameter and almost filled the room of the fourth floor of the Freemen's Club in Campbell Plaza, New York. Around its circumference were forty chairs, thirty-eight of which were occupied. Of the two unoccupied chairs, one was upright behind Faulkner's knees and the other, with its engraved coral-plastic plate bearing Florian's name, was tilted to rest its carved back against the table. The other chairs held thirty-eight Freemen, dressed in a variety of sober uniforms. Faulkner wore the military rig of a general. Only Florian was in civilian garb, a Harvard suit with full mourning trimmings.

Faulkner had been appointed chairman by popular vote. He had held the floor for twenty minutes now, delivering his oration in a dry, grave voice. The others listened in silence.

Faulkner said, "It is a mark in your favor, Florian, that, having played a dangerous game and lost, you had honor enough to make full confession here before us at this extraordinary meeting. Are you sure that your private agents have been defeated?"

Florian, who could not bring himself to speak, nodded.

Faulkner said, "Are you sure that the transmitter in the Bureau Slovak gave you the whole story?"

Again Florian nodded.

Faulkner said, "Are you convinced in your own mind, Florian, that the Lambard tape is now in the possession of our enemies?"

189

"I am."

"And what, Florian, do you think they will do with it?"

"Broadcast it."

"From the Voladores Studios, do you mean?"

"I do."

Silence sat heavily on the Freemen.

"How long have you known this?" asked Faulkner.

"One hour," said Florian.

"It is now seven-forty in the Central American zone," said Faulkner. "We must assume that the rebels are sufficiently well rehearsed to broadcast in prime time."

"Eight," said Florian. "They'll program for eight."

His pink complexion had turned steadily redder during the confessional. He could no longer look his fellow Freemen straight in the eye. Head bowed, his gaze was fixed on an ornate knot in the polished surface of the table.

Faulkner said, "Do you admit to anti-Ethical Behavior, Florian? Do you freely confess to seeking private power by ungentlemanly means, succumbing to greed for self-glorification to the detriment of your brethren in this Club and the hazard of the stability of our society as a whole?"

Florian sobbed. "I . . . do."

"We will leave you now, Florian," Faulkner said. "We will retire to the recreational area, there to discuss our strategy. You will not join us. You are refused the rights of a Freeman of this Club, debarred from all participation in fraternal decisions. Consider yourself stripped of democratic honors, and cast out."

"But I came to you," Florian said. "I came to you, my friends. I didn't try to hide it, did I? As soon as I realized that my . . . my mischievousness had . . . had gotten out of hand and that our Club was threatened, I had absolutely no hesitation in coming to you and baring my breast."

"Too late, Florian," said Faulkner. "By your last action you proved that you had not sacrificed all your honor on the altar of ambition. But the situation, the threat to security, stemmed exclusively from your machinations, a long-calculated program of treachery. You knew that the world would not be large enough to hide you from our justice. That is why you confessed, is it not?"

"Faulkner, friends, I . . ."

"Time is pressing," Faulkner said. "Gentlemen, shall we retire?"

"I appeal for . . . for clemency."

Faulkner had already begun to move away from the Freemen pushing away their chairs.

"Gentlemen," he rapped, "if there is a voice for clemency, let it be raised now."

The Freemen froze like statues, sliding surreptitious glances around the table. There were no voices raised in Florian's defense. He did not expect it.

Florian sagged his belly against the table as the Freemen filed out of the conference room and along a short corridor into the recreational area. Within a minute Florian was alone in the room: only Faulkner lingered by the door, waiting long enough to usher in a white-coated waiter with a silver salver upon which, in a fluted goblet, the Burgundy was brought.

The waiter walked briskly round the table and set the goblet down by Florian's right hand. He tucked the salver under his arm, walked on around the table and out of the room again.

Faulkner said, "At least, Florian, you had sense enough to confess."

"It . . . it did me no good."

"You will be interred with all honors," Faulkner said. "You will have that."

Florian laughed, sneeringly. "Yes, Faulkner, you may feign tranquility, but, I tell you, your days are numbered. It's too late now, is it not? It's too late to prevent that broadcast. My men—Florian trained and Florian manipulated—are smarter than you. They will prevail. I'm only the first of the brethren to die. Only the first." Florian swept up the goblet, opened his mouth, and poured the sticky, ruby-red contents back over his throat. He dabbed his lips with a kerchief. "Only the first of many, Faulkner. Remember that I *chose* to die rather than live without power. I . . . chose . . . to . . ."

Florian pressed his plump hands to his breast and slumped forward over the table. He twitched once, elbows sliding across the polished wood so that his weight lifted him grotesquely onto his toes. He looked then, Faulkner thought, like a child reaching for a cookie, straining to satisfy greed.

Florian's rotund head cocked, his cheek spread upon the oak like a milk pudding. Though his eyes were wide open, it was quite clear that he was dead.

Hastily, Freeman Faulkner closed the door.

They were waiting, the thirty-eight remaining Freemen, for the leadership that Faulkner seemed willing to provide. Even within a democratic brotherhood like the Freemen's Club, there had to be a coterie of men stronger than the ruck, natural-born leaders who, in time of crisis, would emerge to guide the course of events in the interests of all.

The Flying Wing was not a secret organization. All the Freemen knew of its existence, though some peripheral members—those furthest from the administration of Montagu Centers—were hazy as to its precise function. It had never been used before, not in fifty years. Among the members present that December afternoon were several who would have engaged in prolonged discussion as to their Ethical right to operate a primitive fail-safe device that had been set up when times were less settled than they were now.

Faulkner scotched all such prevarication.

He switched on the wall-graph which hid behind innocent plastic panels engraved with vistas of New York. The graphs clearly showed the flight paths of the Shiva missiles, like some multilegged red spider covering the continent, its tiny body crouched on Larkin in the middle of the Kansas plains. A former plague area, Larkin had been declared a limited zone for 200 miles all around. In reality, though, Larkin was the Freemen's flail, the long arm by which they could reach out and thrash any infant rebellions that might threaten the security of the All-City State.

Strictly speaking, Faulkner was only one of ten All-City Freemen responsible for the maintenance of Larkin's Flying Wing. But it was coded that any single city officer across the board could, if he considered it imperative, activate the strike force. He would have to answer to his All-City colleagues later, had better have valid reasons for making the ultimate move. But Faulkner of New York was not afraid of responsibility. He did not flinch from applying the forces at his command.

To the assembled Freemen he said, "Gentlemen, in fifteen minutes or so, we believe that an anti-Ethical agent will begin broadcasting information detrimental to the comfort of the peoples of America. I ask your permission to operate the Flying Wing. I would point out that this has never been done before. I would also point out that you, as Freemen of New York, do not carry total responsibility for the decision. You are obliged only to second, or to veto, my motion that the Wing is so activated."

"I will second," Furneaux said.

"Dissenters?" asked Faulkner.

There were no dissenters, though some of the Freemen seemed sheepishly inclined to debate the issue.

Featley, the city's landscaper and a devoted aesthete, said, "Are Shiva missiles nuclear?"

"No, the one we will use has a conventional warhead," Faulkner said. "I must press you for a decision, gentlemen. I propose to activate a single Shiva rocket. It will be vectored on the Voladores Studio in Veracruz. It will destroy the Studio and a little of the town around the building, but damage will not be extensive."

"The Bureau offices are . . ." Freeman Flannigan began.

"I have already evacuated the Bureau, and the Booster Station," said Faulkner, "as a precaution."

"Can all this be done in time?" asked Freeman Fusaro, who was too young to have assimilated the details of the Flying Wing.

"Larkin to Veracruz will take eight minutes," Faulkner said. "Computation and vectoring can be done in three. It is now ten minutes to eight o'clock, CA-ST. I have already signaled the Flying Wing to set coordinates and prime the Shiva. I took that liberty, too, gentlemen."

The Freemen were confused. Faulkner led them inexorably on, urgently pressing for their sanction.

"Are we, the Freemen of New York, agreed?" he called.

"Dissenters?" shouted Furneaux. "Speak now."

Nobody spoke.

Faulkner lifted an innocent-looking manual audio set from a slot under the wall-graph. He punched buttons. The pictogram of America was replaced by the face of a Bureau officer, sedate in a button-down tropical denim bush jacket and a cheesecutter cap.

"Freeman Faulkner," he said, addressing the whole assembly in a conversational tone, "we are ready here in Flying Wing."

"The target is as given. The time is now," Faulkner said. "Activate Shiva Four."

"Yes, sir," the officer said. "Thank you, Freeman Faulkner. It is not too late to recant."

"I do not wish to recant," Faulkner said.

The officer's face slid away. In its place appeared a video of dramatic cupolas sliding back from a bank of Shiva missiles, each nose cone painted in a different color to indicate the type of warhead. Even as the Freemen watched, fascinated, the jade-green snout of the primed Shiva rose and steadied at an angle of forty-one degrees.

There were no further orders, checks, countdowns, or commands.

One minute and fifty-one seconds after Faulkner had declined to recant, the Shiva took off. In eight minutes—no more, no less—it would crunch through the roof of the Voladores Studio in Veracruz. Four seconds later its warhead would explode, destroying the building and everyone and everything inside.

Faulkner turned his back on the video-graph.

Though the Freemen faced him, their eyes remained glued to the screen, to the stain of white fire that marked the rocket's departure.

Faulkner said, "I ask also for permission to send in one troop of Bureau officers. They can be scrambled from Houston and jet-gyroed to the scene in fifteen minutes."

"Will one troop be enough?" asked Freeman Farrar, who always liked to make his voice heard.

"One troop is all we maintain in the close proximity of Veracruz," Faulkner answered. "It's probably not necessary. We'll land them in the foothills."

"Put them in," Farrar said, amicably. "By all means, Faulkner: put them in."

"Dissenters?"

No argument.

Faulkner lifted the manual audio again and contacted the Bureau in Houston. He was satisfied that the swift and terrible retribution of the Freemen would eliminate the virus of rebellion once and for all.

Three Florian wordsmiths and a handful of miserable Mexicans could not withstand the fist of the Freemen, champions of the status quo and defenders of the passive state. Faulkner did not regard his strategy as a first step toward progress: on the contrary, by using force at all, he thought that he had retrogressed into a more primitive time.

It was three minutes and nine seconds to eight o'clock, CA-ST. Right now the Shiva rocket would be curving over Texas and settling to its long, lethal descent down into Veracruz.

Instinct, and the fact that Florian had not materialized that afternoon, suggested to Harvard Smolkin that the world as he knew it was rapidly coming to an end. He had done exactly as Morello had ordered. He wondered if Appenzell had felt like this before he made his big rally broadcast back in 09, knowing that the minute he opened his mouth he would be pulverized with cannons and reduced to a wisp of charred stuff so fine that his supporters wouldn't be able to find enough of him to fill a thimble, let alone an urn. He wondered, too, if Orson Welles, way, way back in the early twentieth century, had shivered with a palsy of apprehension before he put out the radio drama that sent half America crazy. In those days, the innocent ear was still alive. Would it work now, though, H.A. wondered, or was the importance of the Lambard tape just a Morello pipe dream?

Harv had listened and watched and didn't believe much of it. It seemed to him that Lambard, having conned his disciples into believing him, was now engaged in seeing just how far he could push credulity.

It was all too much for H. A. Smolkin. If the ship was sinking he would go down with it. He had done what they asked of him. He had copied the Lambard Marchat Show from the first whistle to the last snort. He had programmed his tapes with booster adjustments to power the four-hour show all across the continent of All-City America, where it would reach down into the dum-dums' minds and, maybe, curdle a little curiosity about the way they were governed. But Lambard's arguments were all based on the freedom syndrome—and who the hell really wanted to be free? You could live for a couple of centuries, in good health and without fear, *sans* discomfort even, if you kept a low profile and toed the Bureau line. And, God, the Bureau line wasn't that rigid. All that was really asked of a man was that he did his job and didn't make waves: a reasonable request.

H. A. Smolkin looked at the digital clock. He had rather

expected his minder to barge in on him. He was disappointed that she had not done so. He would've liked to share his last hours with her, no matter if she looked like Leigh Paulson as *The Lady Frankenstein*. Beauty was all in the eye of the beholder, anyhow. As a last romantic gesture, he was willing to overlook any faults that Miss Spears might have had in that department.

But the minder didn't come; Bosun Jones didn't come. None of the others came. H.A. did as he had been told to do, just like a bit-part player of long experience following a script. He hid the three copies of the Lambard tape for collection later. He even took the liberty of doing some locational checking—this was around seven o'clock—and discovered, not surprisingly, that his staff had abandoned him.

Volpe and Slattery did not return. The revolutionary, Morello, had probably gobbled them up.

Somewhere, someplace, the Freemen were ganging up on Mexico. Harv could sense it. He knew the upshot of the last reel, what the fate of the bad guys would be, sure as shootin'. And Harv Smolkin decided that if the time had come for him to bid *adieu* to the world as he knew it, then he would do so in style, *his* style.

He built himself a Bumstead Special with foodstuffs raided from the three snackeries that Miss Spears had dutifully filled before she snuck off to safety. He laced the tiers of the Bumstead with mustard pickle, horseradish sauce, red cabbage, and just a whiff of Tabasco, and carried it, together with a carton of hot coffee, into the private antechamber by the bedroom where he kept his extra-special stock of miniature classics. He loaded his table-size set with cartridges, all his favorites, as if, like some pharaoh, he would require entertainment during his lengthy journey into the realm of the dead.

Above him on the wall a checking screen unraveled an oscilloscopic wave band and the evening program presented itself visually for his scrutiny. At that moment, a half hour past the witching hour of seven, the peons were being treated to a four-minute Bureau clip on the *Parable of the Four Oxen*, an insertion that the peons had suffered (or maybe enjoyed, for all Harv knew) eighteen times that season. At least it broke the monotony of the documentary on the making of Camembert, a fresh look at milk products, with a spoken commentary by Phyllis Schmidt from the House of Florian.

Harv foot-operated his video, turned his back completely on the checking screen, and let the soundtrack of *Sullivan's Travels* wash over him. He filled in Joel McCrea's dialogue in his head as the movie unwound, grinning round mouthfuls of the Bumstead Special and chuckling into his coffee carton.

It might have been any old night, not the beginning of a new era, the Golden Age, which H. A. Smolkin, marinated in the romance of the past, could not see through the celluloid.

The little man settled into his chair and propped his feet on the edge of the table, to one side of the set.

At eight o'clock precisely, with all the Voladores's automated systems locked, Robert Lambard's Last Marchat was shoveled out to pour into every set in every home in every city, town, or hamlet in the great land of America.

Harv Smolkin did not even turn around.

On the checking screen, Lambard's none-too-handsome and very intense visage streaked like a moon out of the infinite depths of space. The familiar melody of a standard Marchat writhed soundlessly along the green serpent of H.A.'s audio-scannerscope.

If Harvard Smolkin had been watching he would have seen Bob Lambard's carefully selected montage of stills, a gallery of portraits of Freemen, past and present, ripped in with vids of the *Double Kay,* the Club, the College, a B. of E. cab, a Montagu Station, a couple of rare actions of the A.C.P.I. lighter ship cruising out of Nantucket and of the interior of a Breeder Cell (this last, alone, was enough to raise hair on the nape of every Freeman on the surface of God's green earth), then back, out of black space, to a grainy shot of Mister Marchat himself sitting alone in his own home. Robert Lambard, long dead and gone, opened his mouth to spill the beans.

But Harvard Smolkin had just met up with Veronica once more and paid the prophet of doom no mind at all.

He was still sitting there with the last of the crusty sandwich on a tissue in his lap, when the Shiva broke through the roof and, as Harv tutted in annoyance, exploded. He died as close to happy as any man had a right to expect, at the helm of his Peekaboo ship: amen.

The Lambard tapes, an original and three copies, went up with the archivist in a hurricane of debris and smoke.

"What the hell is it?" Dowd Hartmann asked.

"Couple of minutes to eight," Alex Blunt answered.

"Where is Smolkin?"

"I don't know. He'll be here. Maybe he's checking that the tape's programmed properly."

"I don't like this, son."

"We'll give him 'til five past."

"Let's go right now."

"What's bugging you, Dowd?"

"It's too goddamn quiet."

"Would you prefer troopers with guns?"

"Look at the Bureau bunker," Dowd said. "Those are steel shutters on the windows."

"So?"

"I don't like it, son," said Dowd again.

"Just keep the engine running, old man."

Dowd said, "I feel like some kind of a target sitting here in this beast in the middle of Bureau territory."

"If we can handle a Landcrab, we can handle anything this hick outpost is liable to attack us with," Alex said. "Besides, Smolkin will have the three copies of the tape, and that's what I really want to get my hands on. With a blueprint of the Freemen's activities, a plan for their destruction, I can do almost anything that Morello would have done."

"It ain't that simple," Dowd said.

"Patience, exile, and cunning," Alex said. "That's a quote from somewhere, I think."

"Is it always this quiet in Veracruz?" Dowd mused.

"How would I know?"

"What's that you have there?"

"The Mercury Firebow we picked up," Alex said.

"Be careful with that thing."

"We need all the weapons we can get."

"What time is it?"

"Eight precisely."

Dowd Hartmann said, "So old Bob's on the air again." He looked from the open window of the Mastodon across the plaza to the doorway of the Voladores Studio, then cocked his head and scanned the roof as if in hope of see-

198

ing pollenlike grains of a televisual image go fanning out into the dark sky. "I liked Bob Lambard."

Alex said, "We'll give Smolkin a couple of minutes, then I'll go in for him."

"That ain't wise, son. It could be a trap."

"Could be," Alex agreed. "But how can we find out, unless . . ."

"Listen."

"What?"

"Listen, that noise. Listen."

"What noise?"

"Jesus," Dowd said, slamming his fist onto the Mastodon's control and activating the engine at once. *"Jesus H. Christ."*

"Dowd, what is . . . ?"

Hartmann did not reply. He was hunched over the truck's wheel, fisting it, swinging the clumsy vehicle over the broken cobbles of the delta of avenue and plaza. The fender crunched against a broken horse-trough. At first the roar of the engine was too loud to permit the soft, approaching whine of the Shiva to reach Alex. Hartmann snapped on the full battery of lamps, beams cleaving the darkness of the plaza. He tramped down, tooling the Mastodon through automated gears to maximum speed, praying to the gods that the old-fashioned mechanics would not stall.

In four or five seconds the whine of the rocket became a scream; it was visible, fleetingly, in the sky above the Studio.

"What is it?" Alex bawled.

"They're bombing the town," Dowd cried.

"What time is it?" Alex shouted.

"Too late," Dowd answered. "Too fuckin' late, son."

The back end of the Mastodon rose, tipping the weight of the vehicle onto its front wheels, skidding it around violently.

The explosion was ear-splitting. In the prisms Alex saw the reflection of the Voladores lit from within. For an instant it looked like a gigantic Booster Day Cake, cream and raspberry syrup spilling thickly from inside its flaking shell. Then the shell broke up completely in a blinding flash.

Dowd covered his eyes with his left arm, locking down on the wheel with his right. The Mastodon went on skidding, shoved across the cobbles, like a puck on ice, in a long, sluggish spin. Only an adobe wall halted it, slamming the side fender into the bodywork, shaking the men in the cab so badly that they were dazed and inattentive. Dowd briefly lost control of the truck as it seemed to assume a life of its own and, like a dinosaur, to clank ponderously off into the darkness in search of survival from the holocaust on its heels.

A timpani of stones sounded on the steel. Only the innate strength of the bodywork prevented shrapnel piercing the armor and reaching the men. There was no need for the headlights now. The sky blazed with ruddy light, too bright yet even to flicker, a sheen lying over all the buildings, ruined and intact, lumpily lighting up rocks, jagged shards of concrete, mock marble, twisted girders and metal struts which bombarded the roofs of the dwellings in that area. Peons were running out into the street, open doorways like faded postcards in the darkness. Screaming and chattering, a ghostly flock of Mexican troglodytes fluttered across the Mastodon's bows.

Dowd had some control again, yanking and sawing at the wheel. A sickening, muffled thud told Alex that the fender had scythed down one of the peons. But he did not feel compelled to halt, to return. It was like hitting a moth or a bat, no more.

Another prolonged rumbling shook the cobbles, though they were now a couple of miles from the Studio. A buried and forgotten water main thrust up through the asphalt, splattering the windscreen and momentarily blinding Dowd before the wiper blades could sweep it away. The fender caromed off a lamp-standard which, all rusted away inside, broke like a matchstick. Dowd did not lift his foot, mounting the speed up. The stench of kerosene made Alex gag. He was deathly afraid that the Mastodon would detonate itself by internal combustion. Then, quite abruptly, the big truck was free of the destruction and the uninhabited streets of the suburbs gathered into a clear ribbon of road, a Landways' turnpike, and there were no more peons for a while.

Alex thumbed down the side vent of the Mastodon. He leaned out and looked back at the glow that lit up the sky. It wasn't a tall building now, though, more like a mammoth haystack burning down close to the ground, but with such intensity that its light could be seen far out in space.

Dowd drew in a deep breath and cut back on the speed a little. He glanced at Alex, grinning.

"Shit and corruption!" he said. "Shit and corruption! They *did* it. They fell for it like blamed fools."

"Fell for what, Dowd?"

"They started a war."

"I don't understand. They blasted the Studio, and destroyed the Lambard tapes—didn't they?"

"Sure they did," Dowd said. "But the Lambard tapes would never have roused the sleepers of America. The Lambard tapes, though they did contain useful hints for boy revolutionaries, weren't *that* spectacular."

"You mean the Freemen were scared of nothing?"

"A little fire and a lot of smoke," Dowd said.

"But the location of the Montagu manufactory, the Breeder Cells, all that stuff . . . ?"

"Guesses: speculations," said Dowd. "Maybe some of them were accurate. But Bob didn't have all that much inside information. He was trained in building something out of nothing; that's what he did for his last show. He deluded the whole gang, scared the pants off them. When *they* saw the tape, they read more facts into it than it contained."

"Conjecture can be damaging, too."

"Not damaging enough," Dowd said. "Morello used it. He planned the whole long, involved campaign just to force the Freemen, the Bureau, the Establishment to retaliate. Action breeds reaction, son. That's how you create motion, the pendulum effect that Gene wanted."

"You mean, the fact that the Freemen ordered a missile to be fired and destroyed their own Studio, out here in the hinterland, is enough to . . . to start the ball rolling again?"

"You can wipe out a tape, but you can't wipe out an act of aggression," Dowd said. "You think those farmers back there are going to forget the night their TV Redistribution Center went up in smoke?"

"But what can I do about it?"

"Keep it going, son, that's all."

"Without men, without weapons?"

"One man, one weapon is enough."

"What about the girl and the old woman?"

"You can find that out for yourself," Dowd said. "I have only one piece of advice, Alex. Don't rush your fences. Take your time."

"Without boosters, I may not have much time."

"Long enough," Dowd said.

"Stop being so goddamn enigmatic, Dowd."

"Next time out, the Freemen will be quicker to arm, faster to strike. The time after that they will slip into a warlike stance at the drop of a hat."

"My hat, you mean?"

"Yep, your hat, Alex. Escalation—that's the way the scenario reads."

Alex said nothing for several miles. They were out of the immediate vicinity of Veracruz, covering distance swiftly up the tarmac, soon to veer off into the hills and crawl on up to the plateau of Totonac. Already there were huts and shacks and haciendas under cultivation, their occupants, deprived of the video and puzzled by this loss, standing bewildered by the doorways, gaping at the strange vehicle as it plowed on past.

Dowd slowed and swung off the turnpike. At once vegetation closed in. He switched on the lights again.

Above the black slopes of the mountain the sky was calm and star-sprinkled.

"I assume Smolkin didn't get out?" Alex said.

Dowd grunted. He was a hawk under the skin. He loved the concept of war. He had been born to it. The poetry in him had martial cadences, like Morello's. They were not cut from the same cloth as he was, Alex decided. Yet he was the survivor. Dowd might be around for a while, particularly if they could lay hands on some Montagu Serum, but it was onto the shoulders of a wordsmith, a bard, that the mantle seemed to have fallen, or had, perhaps, been placed.

Alex felt himself stiffen with the pride of responsibility. The Turkus lay across his knees. The Firebow was tucked into the chart-pocket just in front of him, its gracefully curved stock glinting in the glow of the compass light from the binnacle.

Sound and fury were to be his lot, then, that's what Dowd meant. But was he different? He had been Florian trained. He could think like the Freemen. He would use their psychic roles against them, work in exile, patiently and with cunning. Essentially, Morello had been crude in style and Dowd Hartmann, much as he loved the old man, was no more subtle than his own comix alter ego.

For all his pride, Alex Blunt did not yet feel complete.

Some element was missing. Perhaps time and experience, and contact with the old Mexican and the girl, would supply it. What Dowd said was right in one respect. He would be in no hurry. He must think it all out. After all, he wasn't taking on one guy: he was taking on the rulers of the world.

"I suggest we pick up the women and head for the mountains inland," Alex said, crisply. "We'll hole out for a month or two. The Freemen may send agents to search for us but I'm not sure that Flower Feather and Papan know of safe places to hide."

"Sounds sensible," Dowd said.

"That's what we'll do," Alex decided. "We'll let things cool off a little, and plan how to hit them again."

"Sure," Dowd Hartmann said.

"How far to Totonac?"

"Eight, nine miles."

"Then we're home free."

"Maybe," Dowd Hartmann said.

: 2 :

FLOWER FEATHER stirred beside the old woman. Papan was not asleep, merely motionless, lying on her back with her hands folded on her breast as if practicing to be a corpse again. Papan's time was short. The call that would soon be made on her would consume the dregs of her physic energy. Eugene Morello had reminded her of many of the brash young men whom she had befriended in past lives, and Blunt brought to mind a late-blooming spinster in the court of her first father, Montezuma. Papan was not at the beck and call of such little men as these, yet she was instructed to serve them, succor them with a syrup of wisdom she had acquired on her travels through and between lives. When human weakness possessed her, as it occasionally did, she pitied them their loneliness and incomprehensible remorse at the loss of their ultimate goal, that homesickness that was the malaise of all travelers on the tiny green planet Earth. She had confessed to the girl that she would be glad of regeneration and the strength that would come with youth.

Flower Feather could not be sure if the old woman heard the sound or not. Certainly it was faint, but not so faint that the girl's sharp young ears could not detect it and, though she had never seen a gyro-jet, interpret it as a new threat to the progression that Papan had outlined and the charge she had been given of the New Yorker. She was glad to accept that charge. She preferred Alex to Eugene, though her preference had nothing to do with it. She would have done for Eugene what she would now do for Alex just as thoroughly and with as much kindness. She was ripe in all ways for the seeds of destiny. But, unlike the old woman, her spiritual mother, she had no precognitive vision of what obstacles would be put in her path in the road to Tamoanchan.

Flower Feather sat up from the gaudy blanket. The very stones of the temple itself now seemed to be throbbing with the sound. And still Papan lay like one already dead.

At length the girl touched the old woman's shoulder.

"Mother, what is the noise? What does it mean? Do you hear it?"

"I hear it, child," said Papan, through dry lips.

"Is it Alex?"

"No, it is the enemy again."

In the clear night air the roar of the gyro-jets was monstrous, disturbing the peace of the plateau and the jungle for many miles around.

Papan said, "Only man would go to war with such a rattle."

"War, mother?"

"There is no need for you to be afraid."

"I am not afraid."

The old woman raised herself. She seemed stiff and weary and her face was haggard. She pulled the blanket around her shoulders and, lifting the wallet from the flagstones, got unsteadily to her feet.

"Will I help you, mother?" Flower Feather asked.

"I need no help, child. You stay here."

"And you?"

"I must . . . make water, child," the old woman said, giggling in a cracked voice. "Aye, I must make water on the dais of the Stormbringer. It is a simple enough thing to do, but very tiring."

Flower Feather had risen to her feet. Something in the old woman's manner disturbed her. She felt sadness in her heart. Papan took the obsidian mirror from her wallet and tossed the rest of the package aside. She held the oblong strip of polished stone before her face and by the guttering light of the kerosene lantern breathed on it and polished it against her breast.

The sky above Tontala was flayed by the roar of the gyro-jet engines as four huge craft pivoted in a graceless

205

path over the stoop of the mountain and hung in file over the ruins.

Papan hurried now, descending the steps briskly and crossing the grass, all rippled and harassed by the hot downstreams from the aerocraft. As she reached the dais, the gyros were disgorging their short-fall chutes like brown banana leaves, holding rigidly in their computed stations, ready to drop the troopers neatly onto the ball court.

Papan did not even deign to glance at the gyros. She had seen much more frightening sights, more warlike raiders descend on this very spot, making enough clatter to persuade the dead to stay buried. Four ugly birds did not interest her: nor the sixty youths who would chute down the tubes like feces, to fertilize the ball court once more with bones.

The old woman reached the flat summit of the dais. Her movements were strangely limber now, without the deliberateness that might be expected from a ceremonial priestess. Slipping off the blanket, Papan bared her body to the night air. Her thighs and shanks were shrunken, her breasts withered. Her throat was wrinkled like that of a turkey buzzard and her face barbed by the bones beneath the taut-stretched coppery flesh. Her eyes though were bright and eager as she raised her arms. Clasping the upright pillar of obsidian in both fists, she began to circle slowly, padding on naked soles, around the compass points. The pace increased, without tempo or guiding rhythm, building steadily up until the drumming of the old woman's heels on the stones, if it could have been heard above the machines, would have been as rapid and precise and regular as a ritual dance.

The riding lights of the gyro-jets winked down at her; then the stalk-beams of the landing lamps flooded the Tontala area with brilliant white.

Crewmen craned from the cabins, gaping down at the apparition of the naked old woman jigging furiously on the platform. Maybe they laughed and joshed among themselves, for the Flying Wing command had been cut off too long from urbanites to be quite gentlemen, and the secret barracks in Houston was not like New York.

The gobbling jets throttled, settled, and cooled a little as the first of the file of troopers in each of the four long gyros stepped to the mouth of the chute tube and, hooking to the cable and dragging down the mask that would absorb the friction of his descent, waited for the siren snort that would send them down to their very first taste of war.

Papan stopped abruptly, without swaying, bony knees pressed together, her whole body raised up to the oblong mirror-stone in her fists. Her jaws were wide open. The cry came up out of her, shrill, piercing, and prolonged, even as she fell backward.

The sirens sounded in all four gyro-jets at once. Four eager troopers committed themselves to the ten-second ride through wrappered space.

Over the Sierras the big wind boomed.

As Dowd Hartmann tried to turn the wheel, Alex caught him by the forearm and, thrusting with all his weight, held the Mastodon in balance, snout plowing on up the crumble of the plateau into the streaming mess of leaves, twigs, and dust that fanned outward over the valley. The four gyros were still tethered in the air, connected to the earth like parasitical insects by the long, pale-brown tubes. The Mastodon lifted up and earth, mingled now with rain, showered over the windscreen.

Dowd shouted, "We gotta go back, Alex. It's not the women. They don't know about the women. They've come for us."

"Drive this fucking machine, old man," Alex screamed. He punched the key that ground down the window and, as the Mastodon whined and lurched into the teeth of the storm, leaned out the muzzle of the Turkus and activated it.

The weapon's explosions and fireveils hung an instant in the tortured air, then winnowed out like handfuls of sand, dispersing into the howling gale which tore across the plateau. Even as the shells puckered and burst, they were extinguished by torrents of rain which catapulted down from the blackened sky.

"They've come for us. The Freemen. Troopers," Dowd bawled. "Go back, Alex. Please, Christ, please, God, let's go back."

Alex did not answer. His eyes were streaming. His skin felt as if it had been honed away from his bones. The wipers chugged helplessly across the sandwich glass and the Mastodon, under full power, seemed to make no progress at all. Alex closed the side screen and sank back.

The storm shook the Mastodon and, tilting its angle, stroked rain briefly from the glass. Through the clearway, the two men watched the gyro-jets lurch and wallow in the air. The grabhooks at the mouths of the tubes hauled and parted, unzipping from the earth. The nearest of the big aerocraft suddenly stemmed away, dragged off, the chute snaking and lashing beneath it. Two troopers were flung from it, small, black-bodied shapes batted off into darkness. Stalk-lights scribbled briefly on walls and treetops, erratic and hasty, a signature of farewell; then the gyro dove down nose first and burst into the slopes below. The column of flame was snuffed out instantly by the overwhelming fury of the rain.

The second and third gyro-jets followed in the same manner, whisked off like husks, like tubers with one long tendril waving, disgorging the tiny pod-shapes that were men, flinging them out wildly, as profligate as nature. The fourth gyro, however, was commanded by a senior pilot. He had too much experience to be surprised that the weather had turned sour. Playing down the temper of the storm, he equated it with a Pacific squall, abandoned his chute and the four troopers in it, sealed the doors, and went for ground. Digging down into the turbulent, rain-heavy atmosphere with the forked jets, he felt the claw-wheels snap into the mushed earth and heeled the aerocraft over, breaking off all projections abaft and below and bedding her snug into the mud.

A cocked stalk-lamp shone like a candle behind thick glass. Rain came spinning out of it like rough-cut metal, sawing into the Mastodon, forty yards away. On reflex, the senior pilot hit the blast button and gouts of fire balled on past the truck, rocking it like fists, but wearing out aimlessly ten, twelve miles off on the fringes of the storm stream.

Alex flung the Firebow to Dowd, shouting to him to keep the Mastodon crawling forward. Logic—the feverheat logic of battle—told him that they must pin the troopers in the wounded craft and destroy it where it lay. The source of the fire was left. Dowd sagged the truck right. Diminishing a little and coming in almost dry now, the gale tore off a damaged fender and clanked the bonnet against its massive hooks as if it were a tin pot-lid.

They could hear the storm belling rapidly off into the

distance, each gust weaker than the last. Ahead of them, out of the blurred bulk of the gyro, another laser opened up. The flaring bursts were brighter and steadier now as the gyro's instruments adjusted and returned to normal functioning. It was only a matter of minutes, if the gale continued to abate at its present astonishing rate, before the laser's aim would be perfect and the Mastodon engulfed in flames.

Alex knew it and Dowd knew it. It was not the younger man now who adhered to the dead line of approach.

At which precise moment Dowd Hartmann decided to play a martyr's role, Alex could not be sure. He could not even be sure that Dowd intended to jettison him. But examination of the evidence, confused though it was, indicated that old Dowd Hartmann had gone the way of the comix-book hero at last, carrying brinkmanship to its ultimate, realistic conclusion.

Forty, thirty, twenty-five yards from the beached gyrojet, the Mastodon made headway through the dying storm. The huge wheels dug through surface mud into the solid ground, churning up divots like the hooves of a charger.

"Dowd, that's far enough."

The old man's hands moved, like a dealer's. The door sprang open. Alex reached out to slam it shut. The Mastodon swerved violently. Something struck him in the small of the back. His first thought was that the truck had been hit by the laser. Instinctively, he covered his head with his forearms. Next thing he knew, he was pitching forward through the air. All the breath was knocked from him as he struck the ground. It was like falling into a bowl of oatmeal. He slithered along it on his left shoulder, rolling, the Mastodon's wheels inches from his face. A cheesy barrage of mud blinded him. He flung himself down, hands to his eyes, wiping at the mud, rolling again, then, as he realized what was about to happen, pitching himself fulllength upon the turf.

In the final fifteen yards the Mastodon picked up speed, balling up to forty. It ran on course as the laser split the windscreen. The ground shook. The truck reeled into the gyro-jet like a fish on a red line. Alex never knew what exploded first, or what particular combustibles caused such sudden, total destruction.

The searing blast blacked him out seconds after the

Mastodon buried itself in the side of the gyro-jet, wiping out the pilot, the troopers, and Dowd Hartmann all at once.

Cool water trickled on his lips. He opened them and took a drink. At first he thought he was back in New York, wakening from a long, long sleep. He opened his eyes expecting to see Miss Abbott, full of professional concern, and beyond her the door of the living room of his liner, serene in the morning light. What he saw was the Mexican girl's white shirt, dark hair, and then, as his vision cleared, her face, sympathetic and unafraid. He sat up, groaning, and slumped against the stonework at the back of the dais. The night air was cool, too, like an unguent on his flesh. The fever was gone.

Flower Feather said, "Are you recovered?"

"What happened to . . . to Dowd?"

"He is dead. They are all dead."

"Are you sure? Did you check?"

"Yes."

"In the jungle, too," Alex said. "Did you look at the wreckage?"

"It is ugly."

He gripped her shoulder, not threateningly, but with authority. "Did you make *sure* that there were no wounded?"

"They are all dead. Some burned, some broken."

"May I have a little more of that water?"

She held the canteen, tippled water into her palm, and offered it to him. Supping the water from her cupped hand, he drank.

"Are you all right?" he asked.

"Yes."

"Listen," he said. "We'd better pick up the old woman and get out of here."

damaged fender and clanked the hood against its massive

"Jesus!" Alex shook his head. He felt a momentary sadness, a dreadful sense of loss. It did not last long. It struck him, touched him, swiftly altered him a little more, then passed, like the storm that had come up out of the mountains and broomed the plateau. He realized that he was alone. No, maybe not quite alone. He had the girl—or she had him. He didn't know what had been intended on that score. Morello, Dowd, and Papan had not had an opportunity to brief him on what he must do with the rest of his life. He supposed that now they were dead he was free again: not free to go back, only to go on, to travel out from this point into the wild hinterland, to hide, to turn into some kind of wreckage of the past like Narvaez, or bury himself in memories of the hot days of action and sustain himself on them for the next century or so, boring the ass off any peon who would listen to his tales and pretend to understand.

It did not occur to him that Florian would hunt him down. The chances were that Florian had been copped by the Freemen's Club and was on his way to a cell in some discreet establishment in the urban backwoods, or even to a rendezvous with the fishes off Nantucket.

If the Bureau sent inspectors down here to count the corpses and do some deductive reckoning, then they would be sore put to it to tally accurately who had fried and who had not. The bodies of the troopers, spilled from the chutes and wrecked gyros, would be scattered over half the Veracruz area, lunch-boxes for buzzards and vultures, soon to become mere bones dried by the Mexican sun and consumed by the vegetation. God, Morello was still out there, where they had left him.

The girl said, "We buried your friend."

Alex looked up sharply. Had she somehow invaded his thoughts? Was this another trick, a magic that he had not been told of?

"You mean Eugene?"

"Yes."

"And Papan?"

"She is above us, on the dais."

Alex got to his feet, pulling himself up by the carving of the plinth. "I'll help you bury her, then."

"No," the girl said. "She must be left."

"But . . ."

"That is her way."

Alex shrugged.

The girl said, "I will be your guide. We will leave here at once."

"Headed where?"

"I know of a valley hidden in the mountains," the girl said. "We will be safe there for a time."

"Then what?"

The girl did not answer.

Alex said, "Then what will happen?"

"I . . . I do not know."

"Didn't she tell you?"

"She only told me that I must lead you to Tamoanchan."

"How long will it take?"

The girl said, "We will cover ten miles before dawn. We will rest throughout the day. The day after we will travel westward."

Alex said, "All right. Let's see what we can find to take with us."

"I have food and water."

"I meant weapons."

"We will need no weapons in Tamoanchan."

"But getting there?" Alex said.

The girl stepped aside. Alex walked hesitantly past her to the corner of the dais. There was that light again, that Mexican radiance, which showed him the length of the plateau and the smoldering wreckage of the gyro-jet and the Mastodon. Embers burned like fierce eyes in the half-dark. The walls of the ball court were broken and one colossus uprooted by blast tilted forward to rest the bridge of its great stone nose on the turf.

The grass glistened, silvery with water. In the hills he could hear creeks and freshets falling full and fast through the trees.

Perhaps the girl was right. What did he need weapons for, at this time? He would go to this sanctuary in the mountains, to Tamoanchan. He would spend a season or two adjusting, thinking out what he should do, how to approach the problem of loneliness, the responsibilities of his unwished-for role. He felt spent, like a fuse.

The girl did not offer much compensation. Traces of the staid Bachelor remained in him, the stain of the containment of the Freemen's New York.

Flower Feather had already packed two dunnage sacks and threaded rope through them to make carrying straps. A canteen was slung across her shoulder. Her breasts made two deep smudges of shadow upon her white skirt. She seemed anxious to leave Tontala immediately.

Alex said, "Are you sure that the old woman . . . ?"

"I am certain," Flower Feather said. "We must hurry, Alex. We must leave this place in peace."

"All right," he said. "Let's go."

Strangely, as he followed the girl down the path into the trees, his loneliness left him and at last he felt free.

Another illusion: Blunt's proving was still to come.

: 3 :

SLATTERY had lain in the darkness for seven hours. The wound on his right shoulder, where the Magnum bullet had grazed his flesh, had stiffened but gave him no pain. Inside, however, there was pain, grief at the death of Volpe. He was full of the lonely, manic cunning of the lunatic now. In political terms a murder meant nothing. He did not consider his duty to Florian or his role in the dividing of the State. He wanted revenge for its own sake, as homage to his friend, brother, and partner, Volpe.

Vengeance was a true motive, an act in time and space. Anticipation carried Slattery through the long, dark hours. Hatred made him patient. He knew that the New Yorker and the grizzled old man would be sure to return to Tontala to redeem the girl. He toyed with the idea of abducting her, of doing to her some of the many inventive things that Volpe would have devised. But it did not seem a prudent plan. So he contained himself, hiding in a niche on the stones of the ball court wall.

From that stance he observed the events of the early part of the night, the battle, the storm, and its aftermath. None of it really roused him, except the destruction of the Mastodon. For a moment he was filled with panic at the thought that both his victims might have gone up in smoke. If that had happened, Slattery would have turned his attention to the killers of Volpe's killers, picked off the troops one by one. It had to be deaths for a death. Only that form of justice would satisfy him.

Slattery picked up the couple's trail at the neck of the track. He followed them by ear, a safe distance behind, off to the left of the pathway. He followed them down from

214

the plateau and up into scattered rocks and spruces. He was aware that he could not hope to trail them for long. Volpe had been the real hunter. Volpe would have groped out the terrain by instinct. He did not have the instinct that Volpe had had. His mind writhed. He wept silently, remembering his happy years in the gymnasium of the Florian Building when he shared his skills with his one friend.

The leaves of the trees dripped laggard droplets on him. The darkness was not dense to his eyes. He sniffed the wind with his wide nostrils. He made no sound even when the ground was rough and the vegetation thick. He did not know how long he could restrain his ravening urge for vengeance.

When they stop, I will kill them, Slattery promised himself.

At that moment, Slattery was as natural a force as the storm that had roared across the mountains, wiped out the troopers, and wrecked the gyro-jets.

Florian had never fully appreciated his protégé's powers and had not used them well. Slattery was a primordial force, without deceit. Under the sting of final deprivation, Slattery could have been pointed like a laser at any target in the world and, single-handed, would have wiped it out in expiation for being alive after Volpe was dead.

Pantherlike, Slattery wove on through the semi-jungle country, following the girl and the New Yorker down into the basin of the Rio Murilla and west up the river's course into the steep foothills. His right arm hung limply. When he needed strength, he got it from the skewer in its quilted sheath on his belt. He touched the talismanic ring with finger and thumb and remembered how the blood had spurted hot and red from the minder's belly back in the New York liner, and how much Volpe had admired his handiwork on that occasion.

Sentimentally, Slattery vowed that he would kill as expertly again, an honorable gesture in memory of Volpe.

At length the Mexican and the New Yorker stopped. They had covered maybe twelve miles inland from Tontala. The sky was already broadening in preparation for sunrise. They would rest up now, Slattery told himself. On his belly he serpented through the underbrush and peered down into the clearing, high on the river route under a cliff of rock. There was a low thatched-roofed shack beside

215

a patch of wild maize, a spring with a crumbled adobe horseshoe around it, a pool that glistened like an eye.

The girl led the man into the shack. He could hear their muffled voices. Slattery ducked and scuttled to the brow of an outcrop that overlooked the pool. He waited. He sensed that they would hole up here, build a fire, prepare food, sleep. He would take them here, in this nameless place.

The man called Blunt emerged from the shack carrying a tin bucket and a canteen. He approached the pool. It was light enough now to be sure that he was sleepy and inattentive.

Slattery slanted his legs under him to give him thrust. From the quilted sheath he drew the skewer, wiping the steel tool lovingly with his closed fist.

As Blunt stooped to fill the bucket at the pool, Slattery flung himself upon the crouching figure.

Flower Feather's cry brought Alex around. Even as he switched direction and glanced up, he recognized the swooping shape. He had time only to jerk the bucket to his chest before he was carried backward into the mud. The base of the bucket crushed his ribs, knocking all the breath from his lungs. The Mutton jacket was pinned under him, swaddling him tightly. Alex realized that the knife, machete, or whatever weapon the man had used, had buried itself in the soft tin of the bucket, buckling the vessel and flattening it around the blade.

Face to face, Alex identified Slattery. A raw, nerve-rotting fear sapped his volition. Slattery's left hand closed on his gullet, snapping his head back into the scummy mud, pressing inexorably until Alex felt as if his spine would crack and marrow-jelly run out through his mouth. Mud oozed over his ears, deafening him. Mud creamed over his cheeks and into his mouth. Mud poured into his nostrils.

Dread of Slattery possessed him. In the course of a single day, Alex realized that he had been reduced to the status of an animal. Prey caught at a water hole. His brain struggled with the concept, to organize a role out of the scraps of old lives and dormant desires. He would not be torn apart like a goat or sheep or roebuck. He, too, was a man, an animal filled with the predatory spirit of survival. No, it was not enough just to survive. He must struggle against the hypnotizing effect or passivity. He must make himself fight. Fight for Flower Feather, for Papan, for the whales in custody in the aquatarium, for Miss Abbott, raped by the circumstances of the times, for Morello's vanity and Dowd Hartmann's folksy cynicism, even for the clownish Narvaez, and for Harvard Smolkin, drowned in the pretty past. He must fight for *them*. Nobody else would, now. He must prove himself superior to Slattery, the drillbit of the power machine that governed America. If only he could suck in one pure breath to clear his brain and reinflate his will. Sour mud swamped him. The last thing he saw in Slattery's eyes was the cruel glitter of conquest.

But he could not allow himself to die in that humiliating manner. Ferocity, as barbarous as Slattery's and almost as irrational, flooded Alex. Pounding hips and thighs up from the mud, he wormed his knees under Slattery's groin. Releasing the bucket, he groped for his assailant's wrists. Nothing of the gentleman remained in Alexander Blunt. His philosophy had been reduced to a fundamental principle of kill or be killed.

Unexpected retaliation caught Slattery off guard. The assassin had been too engrossed in the exquisite pleasure of drowning his victim to be prepared for the flurry of blows that Alex rained upon him. He drove his knees up into Slattery's crotch so that Slattery flinched and, pulling back, slackened his grip.

Alex lifted his mud-fouled head and butted Slattery's broad nose. The weight went off him. He rolled, wiping his eyes with his wrist, and kicked again. Once more he rolled, away from the mouth of the water hole, onto one knee. As Slattery lunged, he blocked a chopping blow with his forearm, and hammered a punch into the man's bleeding face.

Slattery backed off. Extracting the skewer from the bucket with a shrill grating sound, he cradled it expertly along the palm of his left hand. As Alex hurled at him, Slattery feigned and fended off the rush, lowered the weapon and slid the point neatly under Blunt's ribs. The New Yorker screamed and obligingly wrenched away. Greasy with blood, the skewer ring slipped out of Slattery's grasp. He followed his advantage, though, swinging two short, sharp blows to Blunt's neck. The skewer was embedded in Blunt's belly, not all the way in, though, and not in the heart position.

Slattery was angered by his lack of finesse. Growling, he reached for Blunt's throat. Blunt angled his shoulders.

Painted with ocher mud, like the tribal daubs of an Indian brave, the Laureate's face screwed up in pain and anguish as he plucked at the skewer, but the shaft remained embedded in his side. Slattery's thumbs pressed into his throat. Alex threw himself back against the stump of an adobe wall. Snorting, Slattery followed, seeking out the pulse that would seize under pressure and choke the blood flow from the New Yorker's brain, drowning it in its own effluent. Volpe had taught him that trick. An opportunity for further homage to his friend would come when Blunt was dead and the girl at his mercy. He would take longer with her. But Blunt must be disposed of quickly. He had not anticipated such fierce, uncharacteristic resistance.

Smothering Blunt with his torso, Slattery bore down upon his victim, his puffed, bleeding lips drawn back in a savage grin. He could feel a limpness beginning to steal into Blunt's limbs. Blunt's right hand was out of sight. The left hand flailed wildly in the air, the blows fluttering soft as a moth's wing, weakening. Between his chest and Blunt's belly Slattery was dimly aware of the burrowing of the right hand, still vainly reaching for the burning spike, to extract it and uncork blood from his belly wound. Man could not stand an alien intrusion, the rape of his flesh. It made no matter, Slattery thought. In fifteen seconds it would be over. Blunt would be dead.

Scalding agony flooded into the hole as Alex crooked his finger in the skewer ring and, dragging the tool against his gut, sluggishly pulled it, in grabs and jerks, from his stomach. He could feel blood spurting. He thought he could even smell it. Sense impressions of that instant were etched sharp in his consciousness. He was aware of every nerve and fiber, all the myriad scents and sounds of the waning night that hung over the struggle like a cobweb. He could hear the gurgle of the creek below, and the oceanic silence of the high hills. Never before had he known so much, appreciated so much, of the intricate mechanics of the natural world. If he was privileged to live just another few moments, he might even catch the sound of magma bubbling at the earth's core, or the satin hiss of the sun gliding up over the earth's horizons.

The final flick of the skewer restored an incisive edge to his pain, however, and focused the hallucinatory vision of nature's glory into the rent in his stomach wall. He would have screamed if he had been able. That luxury was not permitted him. He committed his first killing in stoical silence, neglectful of its Ethical considerations.

In the split second it took the steel to sickle upward, pierce flesh, slither across his breastbone, and, so violent was the force of Alex's blow, shatter the rib cage and burst into the chambers of Slattery's heart, Alexander Blunt was relieved of the debris of the psychic environment that had spawned him. It was as if, by that murderous gesture, he had voided the very last of his roles.

Slattery died in three or four seconds. The lethal pressure of his thumbs eased. His hands tumbled from Blunt's throat. The skewer remained buried in his chest. There was very little blood.

Snorting like a bull, Alex lay still.

At length, contemptuously, he heaved the body of the Florian agent away and thrust himself to his feet.

Flower Feather was outlined in the black arch of the shack doorway. She waited, did not come to him, waited, let him walk to her, trudge against exhaustion and pain, lumber through the half-light of the forest clearing, away from the creek, the water hole, the mud, and the body of the man he had killed.

It was not until he reached out for her that the girl opened her arms and helped him inside.

Alex clung to her. The warmth of his blood stained her shirt, stickily pasting her flesh to his. He eased himself down by the thatched wall. He would not pass out. He would not miss this moment of clarity and feeling for all the credits in the country. He was weak with loss of blood. But what the hell! Flower Feather would heal him, restore him to strength. Then they would move on, together, into the high Sierras, to the sanctuary of Tamoanchan.

Gently the girl slit his clothing. He felt her fingers pinching the wound. He rested his head against her hair. It smelled of flowers and moist earth, a morning smell.

Outside the glade was lightening, trees rising from the darkness, rocks assuming shape and shadow as dawn came.

Yes, he would travel west into the mountains, let the girl lead him over the dusty roads. He needed peace to think, a period of love and silence. After that there would be time enough to embark on his mission.

Alex sucked in breath as Flower Feather sprinkled annealing herbs on the puncture. He could feel his blood congealing.

Washington, Frisco, Seattle, Chicago, and Detroit: all the city-states held in that gracious captivity. New York, too: little old New York. Jesus! He wanted them now. He craved their possession, power to change them, people them, bring back the richness that had been lost.

Yes, maybe that was his mission, the last role.

He tried it for size. And liked it.

What had Morello called him? The Stormbringer.

Yes.

The Stormbringer and his children would come soon. He knew it in his heart.

Outside the sun rose golden over the brow of the hill.

The sun rose into a lavender sky, breaking the edge of Tontala's plateau in a hard, shimmering crystal of light so bright that no man, that morning, could gaze into it for long without going blind. Against the ascending orb, slender threads of smoke rose from the wreckage of the night's destruction. The dead clung pitifully to the earth, faces buried in the grass, fingers clawing at the grass, bellies hugging the trees into whose boughs they had been mercilessly flung. Already the air was warm, the ground drying, dust forming on the spoiled crust of the battlefield.

The rising sun was too aloof to take account of a few shallow scratches on the planet's surface. Its beauty was tranquil and indifferent, marred only by a tiny flaw on the lip of its golden aura, a fleck of silver-green, like a spore.

As the sun climbed, the fleck grew slightly larger, though not enough to cast a shadow on the sun along whose rays it traveled, smoothly, steadily, soundlessly.

An observer would have been quite unable to calculate the obsidian disc's scale or its precise distance from the continent. Even when it leveled over the colossi who guarded the ancient temples of Tontala, the disc did not seem intrusive. No trail was visible in the atmosphere behind it. Not until it hovered motionless over the Stormbringer's dais did a subtle rainbow plumage become apparent around its outer rim. Following the oval perfectly, the pale peacock turbulence was no denser than sunlit dew.

Papan gazed up at it from her body's husk. In spite of her faith, she was always relieved at the skycraft's arrival. The disgruntlement of age and the irascibility engendered by her recent role began to slough off like a serpent's skin. Sensations of purity, innocence, eagerness stole over her.

Foam-light, her soul trembled in the wrinkled chrysalis that huddled on the plinth.

A panel on the ship's underside slid open.

A figure floated to the dais: floated, drifted, stepped— Papan could never find an appropriate word to cover that instant of descent.

The figure was tall. Golden raiment fleshed out his limbs like silken cocoons. As always, his features were indistinct within the opaque bubble that fitted over his head. Breathing gills, feathery as a stork's wings, fanned from his shoulders. A slender umbilicus connected the dome to his breast, head to heart.

"You have done well, daughter," said a soft, sourceless voice.

"Is it over?" Papan asked. "All over?"

"The phase is only begun."

"Again?"

"That is the way of it, for as long as you can contemplate."

"Father, I am weary."

"It will pass. We will refresh you."

"How long?"

"You must return again shortly, daughter."

"Where?"

"Into the womb, into the world, and through it."

"Is it he?"

"It is."

"And she?"

"For a season, Papantzin, your home will be within her."

The old woman knew better than to argue. It was true that the weariness of age would pass, that she would taste again the mortal wonders of childhood, that the fatigue of an excess of experience would be transformed into the hopeful energy of youth. But she could not stifle her disappointment. She had cherished the dream that perhaps this time the past-masters would excuse her, reward her with a permanent homecoming, a flight to the mansions of the sun.

"One more turn, Papantzin, that is all we ask of you."

One more turn of the eternal wheel: her disappointment changed to joy. A gentle swooning possessed her and a smile started in her soul, the breathing, bubbling laughter that invariably preceded her brief ascent from corporeality, out of past and future, out of mankind's limited dimension.

221

"Come, daughter, come."

Reaching, Papan strained to shed the clinging remnants of the serpent's skin. Suddenly, she felt it flake away, freeing her. Her soul was cupped and lifted in the two hands of the god and her haggard body on the dais, at that moment, began the swift process of decay.

Intimacy . . .
Sexuality . . .
Savagery . . .
In Outer Space

MINDBRIDGE

BY HUGO AND NEBULA WINNER
JOE HALDEMAN

We have met the aliens. They are very
beautiful. They are like your best sexual
dream . . . and your worst nightmare,
come true.

Why do they want to kill us? What must
humanity learn about itself to survive?

"FANTASTIC . . . A MINDBLITZ . . .
BRINGS OUT ALL THE TERROR WE RE-
PRESS AT THE POSSIBILITY OF HOW
EASILY WE MIGHT BE POSSESSED BY A
STRONGER POWER."

Los Angeles Times

MIND 2-78